tampa

also by alissa nutting

Unclean Jobs for Women and Girls

tampa

alissa nutting

An Imprint of HarperCollins Publishers

This book is a work of fiction. The characters, incidents, and dialogue are drawn from the author's imagination and are not to be construed as real. Any resemblance to actual events or persons, living or dead, is entirely coincidental.

HarperCollins books may be purchased for educational, business, or sales promotional use. For information please write: Special Markets Department, HarperCollins Publishers, 10 East 53rd Street, New York, NY 10022.

FIRST EDITION

Library of Congress Cataloging-in-Publication Data has been applied for.

ISBN 978-0-06-228054-1

13 14 15 16 17   OV/RRD   10 9 8 7 6 5 4 3 2 1

tampa

chapter one

I spent the night before my first day of teaching in an excited loop of hushed masturbation on my side of the mattress, never falling asleep. To bed I'd worn, in secret, a silk chemise and sheer panties, beneath my robe of course, so that my husband, Ford, wouldn't pillage me. He always wants to ruin the landscape. I find it hilarious that people think Ford and I are the perfect couple based solely on our looks. During his best man's speech at our wedding reception, Ford's brother said, "You two are like the his-and-hers winners of the genetic lottery." His voice slurring with noticeable envy, he then added that our faces looked Photoshopped. Rather than concluding with any sort of toast, he simply laid the microphone back down on the table after this last line and returned to his seat. His date had a lazy eye we all politely pretended not to notice.

I should find Ford needlessly attractive; everyone else does. "He's *too* good-looking," one of my sorority sisters groaned the night after our first double date back in college. "I can't even look at him without feeling like I'm being punched between my legs." My real problem with Ford is actually his age. Ford, like the husbands of most women who marry for money, is far too old. Since I'm twenty-six myself, it's true that he and I are close peers. But thirty-one is roughly seventeen years past my window of sexual interest.

I suppose in some ways marrying Ford was worth it for the ring alone—it slowed the frenetic pace at which idiot men would hit on me during daily errands. And of course it was a very nice ring. Ford himself is a cop, though his family has a great deal of money. I hoped his wealth might provide me with a distraction, but this backfired—it left me with no unfulfilled urges except the sexual. Just weeks after our wedding, I could feel my screaming libido clawing at the ornately papered walls of our gated suburban home. At dinner I began to sit with my legs clenched painfully together for fear that if I opened them even the slightest bit, it might unleash a shrill wail that would shatter the crystal wineglasses. This didn't strike me as an irrational belief. The thrum of desire had indeed grown so loud inside me—its electric network toured a constant circuit between my temples, breasts, and thighs—that a moment when lust might be able to operate my labia as a ventriloquist's dummy and speak aloud seemed inevitable.

All I could think about were the boys I'd soon be teaching. Whether or not it's the cause, I blame my very first time at fourteen years old in Evan Keller's basement for imprinting me with a fixed map of arousal—my memory of the event still flows through my mind in animated Technicolor. I was slightly taller than Evan in a way that made me feel half-god to his mortal: every time we made out I had to bend down to reach his lips. Since he was smaller, he was on top, performing with the determined athleticism of a triple-crown jockey until his body was covered in sweat. Afterward I'd gone to the bathroom and then called him in; with an expression of melancholy curiosity, as though transfixed at an aquarium, he'd watched the ruins of my hymen drifting in the blue toilet bowl water like it was the last remaining survivor of a once-plentiful species. I'd felt only an elevating aliveness: it seemed like I'd just given birth to the first day of my actual life.

When Evan had a growth spurt a few months later our sexual dynamic changed—I broke up with him and embarked on a string of repulsive dates with older boys throughout high school before realizing my true attractions lagged several years behind. At university I began throwing myself into classics studies, finding brief solace from my sexual frustrations in texts depicting ancient battles of fervent bloodshed. But my junior year after meeting Ford, I switched my major to education, and now I was finally set with a job that would allow me to go back to eighth grade permanently.

No, it wouldn't do to have Ford dipping his fingers in the pie on the eve before my years of student and substitute teaching were about to pay off. That night I'd taken such pains to set myself up perfectly, inside and out, like a model home ready for viewing. My legs, underarms, and pubis had been shaved and then creamed; every lotion applied bore the scent of strawberries. I wanted my body to seem made of readily edible fruit. Instead of having the flavor of something nearly three decades aged, my goal was for the slippery organs of my sex to taste like the near-transparent pink shaving gelée applied to them, for the sandy rouge of my nipples to have the flavor of peach cream complexion scrub. In the hopes that the fragrance would absorb, I covered each of my breasts with a layer of whipped mask and let it sit for ten minutes as I shaved; it hardened like the frosting of a confection and cast my excitement beneath a crisp, thin shell. After I'd razored every inch of body hair, I marveled at the buoyant lake of foam and stubble left in the sink. It made me think of the ice cream punch served at junior high school dances.

Imagine the fun I could soon have chaperoning one! Perhaps I'd even get to waltz with one or two of the more outgoing male students under the guise of fun and frivolity—the boys who would confidently grab my hand and lead me to the center of the floor, not realizing until our bodies were pressed that they could smell the pulsing, fragrant wetness just one layer of fabric away beneath my dress. I could subtly push against them, blow their circuitry with the confusion of blithe laughter and small talk funneled into their ear by my moist lips. Of course before I'd say it, I'd look off to the side with an idle stare that suggested nothing was happening, that I hadn't noticed my pelvic bone ironing across the erect heat inside their rented tuxedo pants. It would require the boy to be an upstanding sort—the type who wouldn't be able to convey such a sentence to his mother or father, who would second-guess and recall the moment only in the dark, liquored sleep of his loneliest adult moments: post–business dinner while traveling at some Midwestern Comfort Inn, after he'd called his wife and spoken to his children on the phone and then unwrapped the plastic skin of three or four airplane bottles of bourbon, set his alarm, and allowed himself to sit upright in bed with one hand squeezing against the growing thickness of his organ and the memory haunting him—had I really said what he thought he heard? Inside the school's walls no less, amidst the thundering electronic notes of that year's favorite pop song, a song he'd listened to at his very first job in the mall as he folded display shirts and greeted mothers and children who entered the store—had I really breathed that sentence into his ear? *But I felt it,* he'd remind himself, felt my words form in warm air, one sentence whose breathy shape dissipated in seconds, prior to the arrival of understanding or memory. For the rest of his life, part of him would always be on that dance floor, unsure and hungry for clarity. So much so that as an adult in that hotel, he might likely be willing to give up a great deal in exchange for the sense of order that I'd stolen from him, or even to have someone to say to him, *It did happen.* And I would always know, and he would always be sure, but not certain, that I had drawn the ledge of my pubic bone against the head of his penis, pressed it there like a photograph beneath the plastic velum of an album page cover and whispered that phrase: *I want to smell you come in your pants.*

The early start time of Jefferson Junior High was one of its main allures: seven thirty A.M. The boys would practically be asleep, their bodies still in various stages of lingering nocturnal arousal. From my desk, I'd be able to watch their exposed hands rubbing across their pants beneath the tables, their shame and their half-inflated genitals arm-wrestling for control.

A second boon was that I was able to get an extension classroom. These were basically trailers behind the school, but they had doors that locked, and, particularly if the loud window AC unit was running, it was impossible to hear what was going on inside. At our July faculty meeting in the cafeteria, none of the teachers had wanted to volunteer to take a mobile unit—it meant a farther walk each morning, having to trek inside the school to use the bathroom, running beneath an umbrella to go unlock the door in the rain. But I'd raised my hand, playing star pupil myself, and requested one. "I'm happy to be a team player," I'd announced, flashing my teeth in a wide grin. A red flush had covered Assistant Principal Rosen's neck; I'd lowered my face so that the trajectory of my eyes was unmistakably upon his crotch, then I pressed my lips together, met his gaze, and smiled a knowing smile. *Of course the phrase "team player" made you imagine me having group sex,* my eyes tried to tell him reassuringly. *That isn't your fault.*

"Very kind of you, Celeste," he'd said, nodding, attempting to write and then dropping his pen, picking it up and nervously clearing his throat.

"It's like I said," Janet Feinlog had piped up behind me. Janet, a world history teacher, was balding prematurely; the dark home-dye job she gave her thinning locks only served to more starkly contrast the white expanses of scalp that shone through. Like most pronounced physical flaws, it did not live in isolation. The compression hose she wore for edema gave her calves and ankles the rippled texture of warped cardboard. "Classrooms should be assigned based on seniority."

"I agree," I'd said. "I'm the new kid on the block. It's only fair." Then I'd given Janet a practiced smile that she hadn't returned. Instead she'd taken a yellowed handkerchief out of her purse and coughed in it while looking at me, as though I were a nightmarish figment that would go away if she could simply expel enough phlegm from her lungs.

Having a mobile classroom meant that I could truly make it my own. I'd put up opaque curtains, brought in my favorite perfume and spritzed it onto them, as well as onto the cloth seat of my rolling desk chair. Though I didn't yet know which of my male eighth-grade English students would be my favorites, I guessed based on name and performed a small act of voodoo, reaching up my dress to the clear ink pad between my legs, wetting my fingertip, and writing their names upon the desks in the first row, hoping by some magic they'd be conjured directly to those seats, their hormones reading the invisible script their eyes couldn't see. I played with myself behind the desk until I was sore, the chair moistened, hoping the air had been painted with pheromones that would tell the right pupils everything I wasn't allowed to verbalize. Straddling the desk's edge, I allowed my outer lips to hover dangerously close to the sharp wooden corner of its surface before sliding forward and sitting down, the hot bareness between my legs pressing against its cold layer of varnish. Those corners. If I wasn't careful getting up, they would easily scratch into the flesh of my thigh.

The rectangular desk, which was a heartland expanse of flat wood long enough for me to lie down on, felt somehow symbolic, being entirely smooth yet framed within four sharp points of danger—a reminder not to go out of bounds. Each time I'd visited the classroom in the days preceding the school's start, I'd lain down upon it and pressed my spine into its wood as I stared up at the unfinished fabrication of the ceiling and opened and closed my legs; from the waist down I moved like I was making a snow angel. When I finally sat up, I intentionally scooted off the edge at an angle so the corner would knick my asshole and give me just a little pain to carry around like a consolation prize as I waited for classes to begin. Each time I'd shut down the chugging window AC unit and go to leave, it felt like I was unplugging the engine powering my fantasies. In the silence that followed, the room reconfigured itself: The imagined tang of pubescent sweat became engulfed by the laminate odor of faux-wood walls. The chalk dust floating inside a beam of sun fell stagnant, its particles petrified bugs in the amber of the light. With the air conditioner on, these flecks had been frantic with motion, racing against the vent like lost cells of skin scouring the room for a host—before leaving I'd always stuck my wet tongue out into that light's honey, fishing it around in circles, hoping to feel satisfied I'd caught something upon it, even if it was too small to feel.

By five A.M. the morning of our first day at school, anticipation was making me feverish. Running the water for a shower, I lifted one foot up onto the countertop to look between my legs, inspecting my sex until the mirror fogged up and censored it from view. My nails, painted cherry squares that gleamed like red vinyl, scratched one last glimpse from the condensation, five thin streaks I could gaze into like open blinds that gave me a final vista on the damage I'd done throughout the night; my genitals were puffy and swollen. Spread open between my fingers, my labia looked like a splitting heart. I tilted my pelvis and hoisted up on the grounded foot's tiptoes to get a better view. It was impossible not to feel a sullen panic as their folds closed and tasted only themselves—no fresh, squirming insect of thin adolescent fingers against their cheek. I tried to take relief in the shower's warm surge of water. Thinking about the boys I was hours away from meeting, the fruity syrup of body wash I slathered across my breasts seemed to ferment to an intoxicating alcohol in the air. I smiled imagining them breathing the fragrance of the green apple shampoo I worked into my blond locks; despite the chemical bitters its scented foam belied, when one frothing swath of hair slid down against my face I had to force it into my mouth and suck. Soon I felt so dizzy that I had to kneel down on the shower floor; I clumsily extracted the showerhead from its holder and guided it between my legs, the same way one would put on an oxygen mask that dropped from the plane's ceiling due to an ominous change in cabin pressure, feeling nothing but a frightened hope for survival.

My heart sank when I checked the weather channel before leaving the house: we were due for record-high humidity. I cringed thinking of my makeup feathered and my hair frizzed by the end of the day. As I cursed, Ford sauntered out of the bedroom with a half erection and gave a large, stretching yawn in front of the window facing the sunrise. "Good luck, babe," he called. "What a beautiful morning!" I slammed the front door on my way out.

Not surprisingly, the temperature inside the faculty lounge was nearly unbearable. We'd gathered at the behest of Principal Deegan, who wasted no time launching into a tepid pep talk. Like all of his public speeches, it heavily relied on the rhetorical device of repeatedly asking *Am I right?* after every sentence. "Gosh," Mr. Sellers, the wiry chemistry teacher next to me, muttered, fanning himself. "Like the kids don't have enough ammo already. Now I have to walk into class with wet armpits." Janet continued making loud crunching noises; I assumed she kept eating handfuls of granola, but after a few investigative glances I realized it was actually aspirin.

I wanted to run from the room to my class; the earliest pupils would be gathering there now. There was a vague burning at the spot where my spine connected my neck and head; my whole body yearned with the tincture of possibility. I felt like an optimistic bride the morning of her arranged marriage: I was feasibly about to meet someone who would come to know me in every intimate way. "They are not the enemy," Principal Deegan stressed; the rest of the teachers erupted in pithy laughter.

"Could've fooled me," Janet barked. A knowing nod of sympa-

thy made Mr. Sellers's hunched neck begin a series of short, conciliatory parakeet head bobs.

Suddenly, Janet's eyes were pinning me to the wall. The polite laughter of agreement in the room had softened to background
static between Janet's ears and she'd heard my silence in response
to her joke echo forth like a scream; worse yet, she'd picked up
my expression—a snide look of unmistakable contempt. Years of
teaching junior high had likely bestowed the derision sensor in her
hearing with supernatural powers. Upon seeing her stare at me I
immediately melted my face into a grin, but she didn't return it.
"Bathroom cigarette monitoring cannot just be an occasional afterthought," Deegan continued. I watched the clock and pretended
to think on his words with contemplation. After thirty seconds I
looked back and Janet was still staring at me. When the bell rang
she dropped several more aspirins into her mouth like cocktail pea-
nuts but didn't blink.

"Go Stallions!" Principal Deegan finally called out, his well-
formed words brimming with manufactured passion. With the
sound of hundreds of students pouring through the hallways just
beyond the door, for a moment it seemed as though his call had
actually summoned a livestock stampede. I gazed back at his smiling face, his hands enthusiastically raised above his head. "Go Stallions!" He repeated this a few times with a near-animatronic flair.

I was the first faculty member out the door. In the hallway, the
air had taken on the pungent weight of teenage sweat. Loud peals
of laughter and shrieks, the type associated with forced tickling,
came from every direction. As I made my way to the exit doors,
foggy pockets of overzealous cologne hung low amidst herds of
swaggering friends; the startling aluminum bangs of lockers being

opened and closed and reopened caused me to occasionally flinch. Soon the hallway population formed into a moving herd. A competitive speed was set as students headed to outdoor extension classrooms like mine moved toward the door in a rushing swell; it seemed as though a popular band was about to go onstage. I took the opportunity to pin myself against the back of a male student whose ankles revealed a tan line from athletic socks—likely a cross-country team member. "I'm sorry," I whispered hopefully into his ear, "I'm being pushed." Was it fate; was he the one? But the face that turned to greet mine was acneic; I quickly extricated my chest from his warm back.

My heart sank as I watched two goofy girls entwine hands and run up to the door of my classroom. From the roster, I knew I had ten boys in the first period, twelve girls. I tried to steel myself—even if there weren't any suitable options in the first period, I had four other classes, and each one brought more opportunities. That was not to say that it would be easy: my ideal partner, I realized, embodied a very specific intersection of traits that would exclude most of the junior high's male population. Extreme growth spurts or pronounced muscles were immediate grounds for disqualification. They also needed to have decent skin, be somewhat thin, and have either the shame or the preternatural discipline required to keep a secret.

The door to my classroom took a great deal of force to pull open—the suck of cold air from the window AC unit formed a resisting vacuum. Inside it was dark and cold. Two boys, prankster types, were standing in front of the air conditioner; they immediately ran to their seats with smiles, expecting some kind of chastising line (*You two know you're not allowed to touch that!*) that would set them apart and declare them more audacious than their peers. I didn't get a good look at their faces, but from what I'd spied of their bodies already I knew I wasn't interested: they were a hodgepodge of pre- and post-puberty. The silhouette of one's biceps was visible from several feet away. The other had mannish curls of dark arm hair. But the room held others.

I walked straight to the AC unit and stood there, feeling my nipples harden to visibility. For a moment I closed my eyes. I had to stay calm; I had to regard the students like a delicate art exhibit and stay six feet away at all times, lest I be tempted to touch.

"Are you the teacher?" This voice was also male but slightly too deep. I turned, letting the AC cool the back of my neck.

"I am." I smiled. "It is really hot out there." I fingered the pencil inside the twisted bun of my hair, but scanning the room I knew it wasn't yet time to let it down—he wasn't present, he wasn't in this class. Yet there was eye candy aplenty. I managed to hold it together during my opening spiel until a young man in the second row who figured no one was looking reached down between his legs and spent a generous amount of time adjusting himself. This caused a brisk tightening in my lungs and chest; I gripped the side of my desk for support, working hard to speak just a few more words to the students without sounding like a labored asthmatic. "Introduce yourselves," I managed to say, "go around the room. State your hobbies, your darkest and most primitive fears, whatever you want." But as my arousal slowly came back down to a controllable level, a new sort of panic gripped me. All the alluring males in my class seemed unusable—too boisterous, overly confident.

By the end of the second period, when it became clear that class held no winners either, I found myself wondering whether or not to bail entirely over the lunch break. Had I simply thrown myself deeper into torture with no hope of release? Now I'd have to interact with them, see them daily, yet none of them seemed promising enough to attempt anything further with. Perhaps I'd be better off substituting during the fall and trying my luck again in the spring elsewhere. "So we don't have any homework?" one student asked as the bell rang. Due to the sallow smallness of her eyes and nose, her retainer was her most prominent feature. I wanted to forcibly hold her in front of a mirror and question the image: *Can faces actually look like yours?*

"Why would you ask that?" I said. "Do you want homework or something?" She gave me a helpless blink; I'd spat blood upon her face amidst the sharks. The other students immediately began launching insults at her during the group exit from the classroom in a way that pleased me. I knew I'd find it hard to cut the girls in my classes any slack at all, knowing the great generosity life had already gifted them. They were at the very beginning of their sexual lives with no need to hurry—whenever they were ready, a great range of attractions would be waiting for them, easy and disposable. Their urges would grow up right alongside them like a shadow. They'd never feel their libido a deformed thing to be kept chained up in the attic of their mind and to only be fed in secret after dark.

Finally a last group of three male stragglers, whispering and laughing, passed my desk.

"See you all tomorrow," I said. This direct address gave the loudest one the final hint of courage he'd been looking for.

"Kyle thinks you're hot," he rattled off, quick words immediately followed by laughter and Kyle aggressively pushing the speaker. Kyle himself managed only the gruff confessional phrase

"Shut up." While he might've been suitable physically—he wasn't yet too tall or muscularly thickened—he was far too self-assured and aggressive; the most willing boys were off-limits. They'd also be the most willing to talk.

In the minutes before third period, each time the door opened to reveal a new student the outside noise and sunlight poured in and anticipation closed my throat. Because they were coming from the bright outdoors, upon entering the darkened classroom their bodies were backlit, their faces featureless and shadowy, and their outlines seemed angelic—every tiny wisp of hair illuminated—in a way that made each one appear to be materializing from a dream. But when they came into focus, most were disappointments. I actually didn't catch Jack's entrance; some terrible creature whose chin and feet were elephantine in comparison to the rest of his body had approached my desk to talk at me about the books he'd read that summer. But I saw Jack soon after the bell rang, already seated. He seemed to be a larger, stretch-limbed version of a younger boy—chin-length light hair, unimposing features and a mouth that was devilishly wholesome. He was looking in my direction, though not in an overt way. Occasionally a friend would whisper something to him, make a comment, and he'd turn his head and nod or laugh. But then he'd shyly glance back up front. There was a hesitant politeness to his movements; he started to grab a notebook from his bag, second-guessed himself, looked around to see if others had taken out notebooks and only then bent over to unzip his backpack. I could imagine him pausing with the same demure reluctance as he took down the side zipper of my skirt, his alert brown eyes frequently returning to my face to check for a contradictory expression that might indicate he should stop, at which point I would have to goad him on, say, *It's okay, please continue what you're doing.*

I realized with a bit of embarrassment that it was the first time I'd remembered to take roll all day. Suddenly I was actually curious about who someone was. His name was ordinary yet peculiar—two first names.

"Jack Patrick?"

He gave a timid smile, more polite confidence than self-awareness. "Here," he said.

Rapunzel, Rapunzel, I thought. Reaching up to the nape of my neck, I shook out my hair and brought the pencil's lead tip to my tongue.

When I stepped outside after my last class, the unfiltered afternoon sun was blinding. The bedlam atmosphere of the day's end made the stoic brick walls of the junior high and all its false markers of imposed order—the perfect geometry of the landscaping, its immaculate semicircles of wood chips bordered with green hedges and palm trees—seem like relics of a recently invaded and devoured civilization. Youths walking home screamed jungle cries and sprinted past one another like feral carnivores, running together toward some invisible, felled big-game carcass just outside the boundaries of school property. I squinted against the bleached-out concrete walkway that served as an umbilical path to the school; it contained some type of mineralized rock that made it glitter in the light. Holding a stack of manila folders against my chest—student informational surveys, including all of Jack's emergency contact information—my eyes narrowed against the reflective flash of the ground and my pumps made scratching steps across its granular surface. It felt like a daydream, like I was walking to my car across a trail of luminous sugar.

"Every summer gets shorter," a throaty voice called.

No sooner had I heard the words than I smelled the cigarette. Turning, I straightened the fingers of my right hand and raised them to my forehead, half visor and half salute. In the faculty parking lot, Janet Feinlog was sitting down on the foot ledge of her blue conversion van's opened door. She was looking straight ahead; a small stump of burning cigarette served as a gravity-defying bridge between her fingers and two inches of suspended ash. Unsure if she'd been speaking to me or to herself, I pressed the remote in my hand and disabled my car alarm with a pronounced beep.

"Do you know what I'd give for one more week of summer?" she asked. There was a shake in her voice that told of inner conflict in full motion: I pictured all her internal organs bouncing as they tried to keep the unfulfilled rage beneath her floppy stomach pinned down. Hers was an anger steel-strengthened against the stone of joyless decades. She coughed and let out a low, round fart that she didn't acknowledge. "Just one more goddamn week of being teenager free." Though the rest of her body stayed hunched in place, I watched the balls of her eyes shift in my direction: two exploratory rovers sent out to appraise if I was worth the exertion of turning her neck. I felt sorry for the young men fate had assigned to her course rosters. I couldn't imagine being at an age where I was trying to grapple with the difference of the female body and having to somehow work Janet Feinlog into the matrix.

The moment I let out a nervous laugh, the long worm of ash from her cigarette fell to the ground. "Maybe you'll have a better group this year?" I asked. The thought that her classes might be filled row to row with boyish, shy young men was unbearable. During her career, how many perfect specimens must have passed through her room without notice? Ogre linebackers and delicate-boned waifs would all register as the same unwanted note to her sexually deaf ears. From the looks of her glasses, she was so blind she likely wouldn't notice if all her students were replaced with crash-test dummies except to note that their classroom behavior had improved.

When her head swiveled my way, I could almost hear the grinding sound of a long-standing boulder being moved. Her asymmetrical eyes locked onto my body in a laser stare of appraisal that began at my feet. This diagnostic continued so slowly, with such methodical rigor, that my skin began to itch.

"How old are you anyway?" she finally croaked. My head kept unconsciously turning toward the queue of packed buses; it was hard not to hear the students' excited, youthful screams as an invitation to come join them. She inhaled a long suck from her cigarette and blew out more smoke than seemed possible; it hovered all around her and drifted along the van's body, appearing to be a cloud of exhaust. "You definitely haven't given birth yet."

"No." I smiled, perhaps with too much pride. "I don't think I'm going down that road."

"You old enough to drink?"

"Of course." I cleared my throat. "I'm twenty-six."

She nodded. "That's the best way to get through the year." Janet stood and began a wide navigation of turning one hundred and eighty degrees to enter her vehicle, her slow toddles calling to mind a sleepwalking badger. Her weak forearms often came alive to shoo away invisible hindrances, pawing the air with disgruntled choler. Before beginning the climb up the van's two carpeted steps, the most athletic portion of her adieu, she unceremoniously dropped her cigarette butt to the ground without extinguishing it. I got the feeling she hoped it might roll beneath the vehicle's gas tank and give her a true Viking burial.

She gave the long grunt of a walrus bearing a load of breech pups and ascended one stair deeper into the van, then sharply called out, "Hey!" It seemed like she was yelling at someone inside the vehicle since I could no longer see her face; perhaps she had a trespasser aboard. Hoping this was the case and she was now distracted, I turned toward my car with a rush of adrenaline but I didn't manage to get to the door fast enough. "Why are you teaching middle school anyway?" she called out.

I looked over my shoulder. The side door to the van was still open, but Janet had now lodged herself at the helm, behind the wheel. She was gazing at me through the windshield. I had no doubt that if I gave the wrong answer, the van's engine would immediately roar to life as her cankle, currently resting atop the gas pedal, pressed fully downward.

The question was normally easy enough to dodge—*I just want to make a difference,* I might say, or *It's so great to watch a child learn, to actually look into his eyes the moment the lightbulb comes on,* but these canned responses would neither appease Janet nor dampen her suspicions. They could, however, get me killed in a hit-and-run.

Shrugging, I scanned the main road behind us for passing cars. Would there be any witnesses when the bottom of her rusted muffler scalped me of my blond bouquet of hair?

"Summers off and everything," I said, trying to sound casual. The heat above the parking lot's asphalt radiated up all around us like a calf-high field of quivering wheat. How horrible if instead of killing me her van merely laid me out on the tar facedown, scarring my skin forever with a series of third-degree burns. I looked back up but she was no longer behind the windshield. Rising onto my toes, I realized she'd reclined the driver's seat to lie back.

"Me too," she bellowed out. The sweat from my fingers was warping the crisp manila folders in my hands; I began fanning my face and chest with them. "Seems like a real good idea, huh?" she continued. "Work nine months, get three off. What they don't tell you is that you spend all summer waiting for the hammer to drop come August. Have you read that story 'The Pit and the Pendulum'? Me either, but I teach it every year with the Spanish Inquisition. It's like that. Here I am on my back, staring down another year of teaching." I thought about Janet lying in bed, her wiry upper lip twitching as she sensed a metaphorical blade inches above her face and smelled the imagined stink of its metal.

My phone came alive with a text summons from Ford. *Gift for you at home!* it announced. I suppose he could sense the wane of my pretended attentions now that the job was finally starting; he was so desperate not to get left behind.

"Really nice chatting!" I called to Janet. "Gotta get home, duty calls." I waited a few seconds for a good-bye to emanate from the blue van, but none came.

I put the convertible's top down and sat upon the stack of manila folders so they wouldn't blow away. My peel-out from the parking lot was a bit louder and more theatrical than I'd planned, but so be it; I had to let off a little steam before seeing Ford. I drunkenly careened through the long semicircle drive for student drop-offs and pickups, clipped a curb and a bit of the hedge as I rounded past the entrance lane with its large sign: a digital clock and thermometer served as subtext for a scrolling marquee declaring student vaccination requirements; next to these was a large illustration of a stallion, the school mascot, kicking up on its hind two legs, STALLION POWER! it declared. I revved the engine but it was hard to speed away. My eyes kept returning to my rearview mirror, hoping the figure of Jack Patrick might somehow materialize in the middle of the road. I glanced back several times just to make sure he wasn't in the distance chasing after my car and flagging me down, inexplicably barefoot with the fly of his jeans unzipped, calling out my first name in a desperate whimper.

That evening Ford sat my present at the dinner table, in its own chair, as though a guest who'd been wearing it while eating had spontaneously disappeared: a bulky bulletproof vest.

"It's huge," I said. Ford smiled a grin of goofy pride, assuming I meant this as some sort of masculine compliment.

"Kevlar." He chewed and the word seemed a judgment on his pork chop's texture. "Beautiful protection. Armor plated inside. Some little punk comes up to you, puts a gun against your spine and says he'll kill you if you don't give him an A? Tell him to pull the trigger until his finger falls off. You won't even get a bruise."

"That is peace of mind," I said. Had my little bump against the desk yesterday made a bruise on my asshole? I sent a finger down beneath the tablecloth to inspect for tenderness. The vest would transform my body into an asexual cylinder and visibly add fifteen pounds. The only way I'd wear that vest in front of the class is if I was otherwise completely naked and accessorized it with riding boots and a leather crop. I began to imagine presenting my bare legs to the male students as I rubbed the flesh beneath my tailbone.

Ford caught my pleased expression and winked at me, masticating with wide, flapping jaws that engaged his entire face. His eyes were glazed over and tinged the slight color of yellow onion; he'd been drinking wine. The thought of his tongue leaving a sour film upon my skin was enough to make me stand and intervene. "Let me freshen that for you," I said with a smile, grabbing his empty glass. I kept a series of pre-crushed Ambien pills inside emptied tea bags at the back of the pantry where he'd never look. Ford loathed tea; it just wasn't American.

"Thank you, babe." He took a long sip that left a purple shadow on his teeth and spoke for a while about guns. "Another big day tomorrow, huh?" he finally conceded. I guided him toward bed, playing zookeeper to his tranquilized bear. His unconsciousness afforded me the luxury of getting to watch a boy-band music video on the bedroom television with my vibrator on its highest setting roaring like a speedboat.

Every one of the young singers' mouths was open in a wide O of reception as they harmonized. Due to the oily lubricants of puberty's machinery, their skin looked nearly wet in the stage lighting. It was the boxy flatness of their chests that made my wrist quicken its tempo, the effortless feather of their side-swept bangs that were just slightly too long and in their eyes. To make eye contact with the camera, the teens had to brush their bangs back by running their fingers through their hair during a close-up shot; when they did, various paths of shining forehead were exposed. These glimpses of previously hidden flesh lasted only a second but made my heart quicken just as much as if they'd collectively dropped their pants.

My concentration was momentarily broken when Ford emitted a low-frequency gurgle. The television's light made him look like a blue corpse, the white film of drool around the corners of his mouth a frosted poison.

The thought of Ford dead didn't necessarily arouse me, but the idea of pert adolescent males singing around his corpse, removing their colorful jerseys and swinging them above their heads in celebration, as though his death was a victory of sport and a crucial step to their winning a divisional high school championship—there was something greater than comfort in that image. It had the feel of Greek myth. I began to fantasize that the boys on television had been tadpoles who grew in Ford's stomach until the day they were strong and large enough to rip their way out in a violent mass birth. It was almost enough to make me feel a hypothetical sympathy for Ford. If his body, torn in half, were indeed a spent cocoon that had incubated four lovely young men, I would kiss him on the cheek and mean it. *Thank you, Ford.* But there wouldn't be time to linger. These new adolescents, sticky from their residence inside him, would need me to give them a shower shortly after arrival. I've always had the suspicion that Ford's entrails smell like industrial-grade carpet: a low chemical odor that wants to seem new but instead just announces itself as ubiquitous. A smell that says, *I am not even a little bit rare. There are enough bolts of me at the warehouse to circle the planet.*

My orgasm came in the final verse as the four boys engaged together in a scripted play of contrived spontaneity: wading into the ocean, they began to flirtatiously splash at one another. One boy took a salty handful straight to the face and bared his teeth in mock outrage; he returned the assault with a baptism, pushing the offender backward onto his butt in the water. His other two friends helped him up, each grabbing an arm. His tiny, goose-bumped nipples pushed against his shirt's drenched fabric. Every inch of him was soaked except his hair. I imagined walking to him, lifting his bangs once again to lick his forehead. It would likely taste like the sweat on his thighs, like the doughy tang inside his shorts after he'd run across the sunny beach for miles.

chapter two

Jack Patrick. Something in his chin-length blond hair, in the diminutive leanness of his chest, refined for me just what it was about the particular subset of this age group that I found entrancing. He was at the very last link of androgyny that puberty would permit him: undeniably male but not man. I loved the lanky-limbed smoothness, the plasticity of his limbs, the way his frame shunned both fat and muscle. It had not yet been wrestled into a fixed shape.

The youth of Jefferson were definitely noticing me. "There's lewd graffiti about you on the stalls of the boys' bathroom," Janet reported in a bored monotone. "The janitor's painting over it as we speak but it'll be up again in no time. Calls you a hot bitch. I don't think they've broken out the p-word yet. But give them a few months." Janet's permanently half-open eyes had a way of looking past my face when she spoke; she appeared to be gazing out into the near future and seeing tomorrow's disappointments.

"Boys will be boys," I declared, shaking my head in mock disapproval. Public displays of flattery didn't appeal to me in the least—these students weren't my target audience. Someone bold enough to deface school property certainly wouldn't be able to keep any secrets, though he'd be fantastically easy to seduce. The opposite was also true. From student teaching, I'd learned that the very boys who likely wouldn't kiss and tell were the hardest to kiss in the first place.

My time as a student teacher had been a wake-up call for how complicated my needs actually were. Initially I'd hoped that just being around them would be enough—that like coral among anemones, I could glean all needed vitality through their swirling hordes moving past my body in the hallways. Within a week, I knew this to be a lie.

In a matter of days at my first institution I'd developed a heady crush on a young man named Steven—an unfortunately moral boy. He was president of that school's Fellowship of Christian Athletes and wore a small gold cross upon a necklace; I couldn't help but imagine him naked wearing only this sacred object against his thin flesh. When he'd raise his hand I'd make sure my fragrant hair fell down against his arm as I leaned over to address his question; I frequently gave his back and shoulders a reassuring touch when passing by his desk. After he missed a test I volunteered to stay after and proctor a makeup: finally, it was just the two of us alone in the classroom. When he finished I asked if I could give him a ride home and suggestively leaned across my desk.

His eyes froze with appalled disbelief. Perhaps it was a rush to judgment, but my first inclination was to blame his faith. He was suddenly looking at me as though he'd seen a demon appear on my shoulder or watched hidden expletives carved into my forehead become visible. I wanted to remind him that desire was only human but figured that was probably just what he'd expect the devil to say. "M-Mrs. Price," he'd stuttered, the tone of his porcelain voice shivering with eggshell cracks, "I think we should pray together."

"Yes!" I'd exclaimed, my enthusiasm surprising him. I'd jumped up from the desk and walked toward him, palms outstretched. "Let us join hands." I smiled.

He'd stepped backward with one foot, and then another. The incredulous look on his face told me I'd already lost him—somehow he'd seen through me, or perhaps he was skilled at foreshadowing. I'd imagine a pious avoidance of sin requires that. "When you play football, do you prefer offense?" I asked.

"I should go," he finally managed to say.

"Before we pray?" I'd licked my lips and twirled a long stretch of blond hair around two of my fingers.

He'd kept glancing back at the closed door, perhaps hoping someone else would enter. "I'll pray at home." He'd nodded solemnly. "For both of us."

"You're such a good boy, Steven." I began appealing to his sense of propriety. "I love that about you. You're different, you know. From the others." I'd stepped out of my high heels, placing my bare feet onto the tile so that the top of his head was level with my eyes. When I followed his eyes to the ground I realized that he was looking at my painted toenails. "So do I get a good-bye hug for staying late so you could make up your quiz?" Pretending that my request for permission had been granted, I'd leaned into his body before he'd answered, pressing myself hard against the length of him. Next I'd placed my hand over the back of his head, holding him close, then ran my lips against the hot skin of his neck when I pulled away. I didn't look back at him, didn't confirm or deny that anything had happened; I just walked back to the desk to pick up the papers, and when I turned around again he'd left.

I knew he'd never let me be alone with him again. I'd immediately pushed a student desk up against the door, sat down and began to finger myself while my tongue ran a slow clockwork pattern around his faint taste on my top and bottom lip—he had an earthy scent: a little grass, a bit of unsweetened tea, some salt. After I came I cried in mourning; I'd fallen for the wrong boy, an inaccessible one, and my time at that school was drawing to a close. For the three remaining weeks, he sat near the back of the class with friends and never raised his hand. Only once did he look at me as he was leaving, a glance of pained confusion that I encouraged by not giving him a smile.

On my last day, the froggish male mentor teacher I'd worked with had all the students sign a card for me. He'd included a bullshit note on ruled paper that tried too hard to play it cool and included his cell phone number, which I made a point of keeping in my purse until my next bowel movement. This happened to be at a midprice Chinese chain restaurant where Ford had insisted we meet for a celebratory dinner. "Excuse me for a moment," I'd said, "while I go use the powder room." Before grabbing any toilet paper, I made an initial swipe with the note, making sure the side bearing the teacher's handwriting was facing upward. Then I looked again at the card. While most students had left mild phrases of encouragement peppered with misspellings, Steven had written only his signature. I stood, feeling my underwear drop to my ankles, and tore down the card to his name, ripping it out in isolation, then stared at the tab of paper sitting on my finger like a square of acid. I let my head hit the side of the bathroom stall as I shoved his name as far up inside me as I could. This alone gave me the strength to walk back out to the table and greet Ford, who was drinking yet another blue cocktail overflowing with flora garnish.

"Honey," he'd called from a distance, seeing me headed back toward him. "They call this drink a Tall Blue Balls!" I'd given him an appreciative smile, as if to say, *How appropriate; you are foul to me and I just wallpapered my cervix with the name of a teenage boy.*

Jack had already passed the test of not having any outward affinity to Christianity, so I began assigning personal essays and in-class writings designed to give me more personal details about him.

"For today's journal," I announced, "I want you to take ten minutes and write about the celebrity you find most attractive. Harness the power of description—pretend I've never seen him or her before."

Most of the male responses revolved around a reality star's ample buttocks, but Jack was noncommittal. *I don't really have a favorite celebrity,* he wrote. *Usually if there's a good movie I like then I will also like the main woman in it, or if there's a singer and I like the song and the video and she's also pretty.* Friday of the first week, I decided to keep him after class to ask about the lack of detail. I planned to go shopping over the weekend and cater to his proclivities.

When I called him up, he waved good-bye to his friends—a nice gesture, I thought, making sure they wouldn't wait outside for him. Then he slowly walked up to my desk. His hands were clutched to the straps of his backpack, holding it tightly as though it were a parachute.

"I'd like to chat for a bit about your writing—do you mind missing a little of your lunch?"

He looked at the ground, his sneaker tracing a line across the tile, and shook his head no. The puffy styling of his athletic shoes made his legs seem even thinner—there didn't seem to be one ounce to his body that wasn't essential. I loved the precarious way his cargo shorts drooped on the elongated hanger of his pelvic bones, the way they'd likely fall down at the slightest tug. His kneecaps, barely sticking out from the bottom of his shorts' hem, would make perfect, nearly circular imprints if he knelt down in the sand.

"So how's your year going? What other classes do you have?" *More important,* I wanted to add, *when did you last touch yourself?*

Shrugging, he finally looked up at me. "The usual I guess. Biology, World History . . ."

"Mrs. Feinlog?" I laughed. "Dear God, I'm sorry."

He smiled. "Yeah." He started scratching his arm, then began looking at me intently while he continued, as though he was vicariously relieving an itch on my body.

"So I wanted to talk about this journal you wrote." My oversized desk was a large gulf between us, so I rose from my chair and motioned for us to head out to the student desks. "Here, let's have a chat for a minute." When he sat, I scooted another desk directly next to his so we could each stare at his notebook at the same time.

Suddenly I was closer to him than I'd ever been before. I could smell the faint sporty body wash and deodorant he used. It was nearly cruel, the apathetic way his cotton T-shirt fell on his body, not seeming to care where it clung and where it sat loose. His clothing in general had a very inconsequential feel to it, like an afterthought, as though he'd been walking out the door to go to school in his underwear but then his mother had said, *Wait, get dressed first,* and he'd shrugged and obeyed.

"So I think you took the easy way out here," I chided. "I don't know that you used one single specific adjective." I put my hand on top of his just for a moment, a reach of understanding and sympathy, then realized an opportunity to linger. "Look," I said. "Hold out your hand. I think our hands are the same size." He stretched out his palm and fingers, then gave a wide grin when mine, placed directly overtop, were indeed an exact match in length. It seemed like we'd just found a key that unlocked something.

I smiled as our hands pressed against one another in midair, as though we were pretending to touch through invisible glass. We managed a long stare before Jack finally blushed, retracting his hands. "How old are you, Jack Patrick?"

"I turned fourteen this summer," he said. I gave an impressed nod, indicating this was no small accomplishment.

"Well you're certainly old enough to know what you like." Principal Deegan's first-day speech came back to mind; I had to bite my lip not to jokingly add in, *Am I right?* "Here, let me give you some examples. Do you like it when girls wear lipstick?"

He blushed and nodded. "Yeah." His voice had an embarrassed tone, like he'd just made a vile confession.

"Good—do you like lighter lipstick? Darker lipstick? Red?" I wanted to grab his hand again. It took every ounce of self-control I had not to slide my fingers beneath the desk and touch the bare skin of his leg.

"Um," he said. His hand began to scratch at his scalp.

"Wait," I said. "I have an idea." I walked up to my desk and grabbed my purse and a box of Kleenex. "So what I'm wearing now is called fuchsia. Kind of a bright pink." I sat and wiped it off, then took the fuchsia tube of lipstick out of my purse along with two others. "Okay, ready?" He nodded with sudden animation—we were about to play a game.

I locked eyes with him. "Watch my lips," I instructed. I applied the red and rubbed my lips together. His hands left the desk and folded in his lap. "Do you like this more or less than the one I had on?"

He smiled and gave a small shrug. "I like them both."

"Let's try option three, then." I winked at him and cleaned the red lipstick off with exaggerated strokes, using far more Kleenex than necessary, as though I'd just eaten a very sloppy meal. I loved having his full attention. "This last one is coral." I applied it then rubbed my lips together and parted them with a playful smack. "Which one's your favorite?"

"They all look good." His stare didn't break from my mouth; he spoke in a hypnotized monotone.

"Jack," I said, leaning toward him, "you can't go through life being shy with your opinion. Say that right now, you were making the decision as to whether I had to wear red lipstick every day of my life, or fuchsia, or coral. It's your decision and you have to choose. Which one?"

He swallowed. "The red is pretty."

"Perfect." I smiled and grabbed the other two tubes of lipstick, then walked over to the trash and threw them in loudly, one at a time. "I value what you think." I looked up and saw his lips parted, muted around the space of something unspeakable and subconscious lodged between his teeth. The lunch period bell rang in the distance. "Here," I offered. "Let me write you a note for the cafeteria monitor."

I sat back down behind my desk and scribbled onto a piece of paper, then pursed my lips and blew on the paper while fanning it back and forth to dry the ink. "Here you are," I said. As he walked up to get it, each step of his sneaker was a magnified sound in the quiet classroom. I looked at him in a shameless way as he approached, wondering if he would turn his eyes or look away. He didn't.

Before giving him the slip of paper, I held up my palm in the air again. "High-five, friend." He placed his hand on top of mine once more. This time I pushed his fingers slightly apart with mine and slid them forward, entwined and clasping. His eyes wouldn't stop questioning but he didn't speak or pull away. "Have a good week-end," I finally said. Then I gave a small squeeze and temporarily let him go.

Ford's poker night provided a perfect cover for my first stakeout. Every Wednesday after work several of his fellow officers would come over to the house for cards. Even though this was now rou-tine, returning home to the sight of eight squad cars parked in our driveway still caused me to feel an instant and roiling vertigo; a few months ago I'd nearly swerved off the road and clipped a fire hy-drant when I saw them all there. My immediate thought was always that my Internet search history had been discovered, or a latent re-port had been filed—perhaps about one of the indiscreet hallway gropes I'd tried to pass off as accidental clumsiness during my student-teaching days. There was even the illogical panic that the police had somehow managed to read my mind.

The cigar smoke was reason enough to make myself scarce dur-ing the gathering. Through the sliding glass door, its grayish cloud nearly looked like a second mesh screen. Ford liked to joke that ci-gars keep away mosquitoes. I found the smell vulgar and fetid. It just made Ford seem even more ancient, as though he was smok-ing his very own future cremains. How opposite to the bouquet of smells on the mouths of adolescent boys, which is an honest mixture of good and bad: bubble gum, Red Hots, cola syrup, stale sleep, rub-ber bands for braces, the occasional cigarette that leaves a taste less like tobacco than something very damp and mossish.

I slid the patio door open theatrically, dressed to the nines in exercise gear. The more I did for Ford's ego publicly, I'd found, the less I had to do to satisfy him privately. "Hello, boys," I called. They all looked up with too-large approving smiles, the alcohol having given their facial muscles an increased range of movement. "I'm gonna hit the gym for a bit, Fordsie."

"Take my wife with you, will ya?" Ford's partner Bill called. At last year's police fund-raiser he'd gotten blackout drunk and put his hand on my ass shortly before vomiting behind the DJ table. "Her idea of working out is putting new batteries in the remote control." The men chuckled into their beers, the guns strapped around their waists and chests gleaming in the setting sun. "Get her working on that ab machine thing," he specified. I shut the door and waved good-bye at Ford, who made a show of watching my ass as I walked away. This was the reason Ford married me, and why I could make the argument that I was a better wife for him than a woman who was actually smitten: love makes people feel accepted, and like Bill's wife they then begin to break the rules. I had a far clearer picture of our marriage contract's unspoken line items than most women: Ford wanted me to stay in shape, look good in front of his friends, and make him look good in return.

Outside I passed our neighbor Mr. Jeffries watering his plants, holding the hose flush with his groin like a bad practical joke. I waved and he looked up at me for a too-long ogle that resulted in the hose turning on the crotch of his pants and wetting his entire front. He pretended not to notice. "If you need any fire ant poison, I bought enough to send every one of those damn biters straight to hell," he offered.

"There are actually a few fire ant questions in the natural science section of the eighth-grade state proficiency exams," I replied. Mr. Jeffries's eyes squinted up as though I was a sign he was struggling to read. "Their queen lives for six or seven years," I continued, "but the male drones only live four to five days. Their sole purpose in life is to mate with her and then die." I couldn't help but imagine an equally preferential scenario played out by several fourteen-year-old boys and myself. I wondered what percentage of the Jefferson Junior High students—if I came to them in the middle of the night, naked—would agree to have sex with me even if it meant they'd die forty-eight hours later. I guessed there would be at least a small few.

Mr. Jeffries bit the inside of his cheek and turned the hose pressure down to a low, impotent trickle. Despite his fervent watering of the plant bed, the three shepherding garden gnomes at its centerpiece remained covered in bird shit. "That is an unholy arrangement," he declared.

I'd memorized the directions to Jack's house; an old online listing divulged it was a one-story five-bedroom home with vaulted ceilings. The upper-middle-class purchase price from a few years ago was encouraging: I hoped for a set of working parents who didn't have time to decode lies or do micromanagement parenting. An online map reported a 5.3-mile drive. Before starting my car, I was sure to reset the odometer to double-check the distance. Any fact or statistic related to Jack felt like progress.

Due to a series of overprotective stoplights and explosive suburban growth, the short drive took fourteen minutes, which felt both too convenient and painfully distant all at once. I was able to park just across the street from Jack's house at an angle that allowed a view of the sliver of backyard between his home and their sole abutting neighbor. My car and the AC had been off for no more than a minute when my skin began to slicken. But each bead of sweat that grew on my lip was a pleasant sensory experience; in high school, as I had to date increasingly awful boys for social reasons, I often preferred sex in a hot car for the ways the hermetic steam made me light-headed and added a pleasant shade of autoerotic asphyxiation to an otherwise lacking encounter. Tonight I'd wanted to drive to his house after dark so the heat wouldn't be so violent, but I hadn't been patient enough to wait. Close, though. The sun had dropped low in the sky; through the tinted windows it seemed formed of brass. I imagined Jack's body made gigantic standing before me, the sun in the sky becoming the hot metal button of his jeans. If his enormous fingers reached down from the clouds and unbuttoned it, if his horizon-colored pants began to bunch and fall and his teenage sex of skyscraper proportions was freed, I would drive my car into his toe so he would kneel down to investigate and accidentally kill me when the sequoia-sized head of his penis came crashing through my windshield, all in the hopes that the last image seen before death is the backdrop to our eternity.

Drips of perspiration soon covered my body; as they began to independently crawl across my skin I had the uncomfortable sensation of being covered in ants. *Here I am, Jack,* I thought, *sitting through the heat of hell for you.* I gazed longingly at the fence protecting the home's backyard, complete with a screened-in pool. My stomach dropped with the familiar memory of how unfair life is: I couldn't simply wait in the car until nighttime, then sneak into his backyard, go for a swim in a white bra and panties and then appear at his window, knocking on the glass gently until he woke from an erection-inducing dream and peeked through the blinds to see me there, soaked and dripping, and let me in. Wasn't that exactly what every straight teenage boy wanted? It struck me as particularly selfish, the way the world was ignoring Jack's need for pantied women to knock on his window at night. Restless, I reached for the gym bag I'd used to conceal my supplies: binoculars, a vibrator, a Polaroid camera, a towel and a water bottle.

Focusing the binoculars, I gleaned what I could through windows. Many of the blinds were closed, but the square of frosted glass on the home's left side told me the location of a downstairs bathroom. The living room's light was on, though its couch appeared unoccupied—perhaps Jack was home alone? I didn't know him well enough yet to risk knocking on the door and saying hello; if he reacted badly or questions were raised the wrong way, it would blow everything—although he was the clear standout of his classmates, I reminded myself that he could still prove to be a dead end. It wasn't worth it to do anything risky. There was a flash of light in one of the back windows and I focused in further, suddenly letting out a long sigh of gratitude at my luck: there he was sitting in front of a television, low to the ground in a beanbag chair—another bright flash confirmed it was him. His alert posture and proximity to the TV suggested he was playing a video game rather than watching a program. I tried to zoom in further, but the lenses were already at maximum view.

Although a passerby would have had to press his nose fully against my car's tinted window in order to see inside, masturbating in public with no cover seemed inelegant. I grabbed the towel, unfolding it across my lap as though I were about to eat a personal picnic, then slid down my running shorts beneath it. Unsticking my legs from the seat, I expertly opened them into position—since they would immediately bond with the hot leather of the car's seat and fix themselves in place, it was important that my orgasm wouldn't require any thigh movement. It took me just a moment to perfectly balance the binoculars in my left hand and steady the vibrator in my right. But just as I was about to begin, I heard voices; looking up from the binoculars I saw two power-walking women turn the corner, swinging hand weights.

I looked back into the binoculars and waited for the women to pass Jack's house, the blurry, magnified jersey fabric of their clothing momentarily eclipsing each lens. Once their footsteps faded, I turned on the vibrator and began.

Occasionally Jack would lift the game controller up from his lap for a few seconds and I could see his clenched hands. He was wearing an undershirt, but I couldn't make out the bottom half of his body. Perhaps that could be a treat for him sometime—I could have him play a video game in the beanbag chair while I removed his pants and lay prostrate on the carpet fellating him.

Although I could hear the voices of the female walkers rounding the cul-de-sac and coming back closer toward the opposite side of my car, the thought of Jack's engorged penis in my mouth made my tongue quicken across my lips. Even in the oven of my closed convertible, I thought of his sex organs in terms of heat. I didn't doubt that some strain of magical thinking on my part would actually render this true when the time came—the flesh between his legs would likely feel warmer against my lips than anything I'd ever felt before.

I still remembered the pleasant tactile aspect of my first teenage blow jobs, before they became a forced chore: the slickness it all took on after a few minutes always made me feel weightless—it seemed like my mouth produced a different saliva that seemed to shirk density and made my bones as hollow as a bird's. When I thought of the bitter taste that would descend as Jack got closer to climax, the

unmistakable earthy harbinger not so different from the air just before a rainstorm, my leg started to kick as though I was having my
reflexes tested.

"I *swear*," a woman's voice protested, "I made the whole thing in
my Crock-Pot!" I flipped my vibrator off as the power-walkers neared
the back of my car. I noted how the breadth of their thighs stretched
the athletic logos on their spandex shorts out into fun-house-mirror
enlargements. Their silhouettes eclipsed my binocular view and I
looked up to watch them saunter off, elbows out, rowing through the
air like impotent wings. Were there souls left inside these women?
It seemed doubtful. The soul had always struck me as being a tricky
thing to keep with the body: an easily bored aristocrat with the means
to leave whenever it wished. What temptations, what vistas were their
lives of folding socks and online diet-plan message boards offering?
The goosey flesh of their limbs was not in rhythm. What facile cages
for a spirit hell-bent on sneaking out, the bodies of these women.

I resumed my view. Jack had entered a segment of greater
difficulty—his brow had creased with focus; two strong, white
teeth now pinned down his lower lip. This detail of self-domination
made me come easily, far more quickly than I wanted. To reset my
thoughts, I tried beating my head against the steering wheel a few
times before halfheartedly starting to masturbate again, but soon
sweat from the binoculars' seal began to rub into my eyes and made
them sting. Taking my hand off the vibrator, I let it buzz numbly in
place as I wiped my face off with the lap towel. The pitch of heat in
the car suddenly seemed dangerous. I turned the car on so the air-
conditioning could blow its well-intentioned breaths that wouldn't be
truly cold for several more minutes, but I didn't like to stay too long
inside a vehicle with its engine on if I wasn't driving. I'd heard—

probably urban legends, but frightening ones—about people who'd died of carbon monoxide poisoning even though their car was out in the open air; it was some unlucky accident eventually blamed on a mechanical error laypersons couldn't understand. I realized that it wouldn't be the worst exit ever to die young and beautiful with my pants down inside a Corvette, even if I was parked alone on the side of the road with a sex toy. Still, better to avoid it if possible.

A sluggish couple walking a basset hound turned the corner to come down the road and circle back. They moved at a pace their bodies would have been unable to discern from rest. I felt like a child when I saw middle-aged partners and remembered they had sex together—there was still that initial sense of horror and denial. What aspect of either one of them could be pleasant to touch or to see, even in the darkest room? Sex struck me as a seafood with the shortest imaginable shelf life, needing to be peeled and eaten the moment the urge ripened. Even by sixteen, seventeen, it seemed that people became too comfortable with their desires to have any objectivity over their vulgar moments. They closed their eyes to avoid awkward orgasm faces, slipped lingerie made for models and mannequins onto wholly imperfect bodies. Who was that queen who tried to keep her youth by bathing in the blood of virgins? She should've had sex with them instead, or at least had sex with them before killing them. Many might label this a contradiction, but I felt it to be a simple irony: in my view, having sex with teenagers was the only way to keep the act wholesome. They're observant; they catalog every detail to obsess upon. They're obsessive by nature. Should there be any other way to experience sex? I remember taking my shirt off for a friend's younger brother in college. The way his eyes lit up like he was seeing snow for the first time.

Suddenly a gray Buick pulled into Jack's driveway and the garage opened to a jumbled arrangement of home-improvement tools and sporting gear. A man of banal stature emerged from the garage's shadow; his belted dress pants sat slightly too high on his waist and his square plaid dress shirt, impervious to time, could've been from any one of the past three decades. He was an obvious multitasker. One hand held a phone to his ear; the other wheeled an oversized green trash bin behind him casually, like a suitcase—he could just as easily have been walking through the airport terminal. There was something repulsive (and revealing) about talking on a cell phone while handling garbage. Why did anyone pretend human relationships had value?

Seconds after he parked the bin on the corner, I turned and spied two joggers, each one coming from an opposite direction in a way that seemed synchronized, round the corner and advance down the street. Moments later a third appeared. It was as though they were racing toward the garbage, had been waiting all day, raccoon-like, for it to be set out. For a moment I imagined the bin filled with nothing but weightless, wadded-up puffs of Kleenex: the week's toll of Jack's feverish masturbating. There could, I reasoned, actually be such a treasure inside the trash—one tied, recycled plastic shopping bag of waste from Jack's bedroom: candy wrappers, pencil shavings, awkward starts to homework assignments that were crumpled up in frustration, and then, perhaps, a sweet ball of tissue or paper towel, crisped at the center, smelling of metallic salt. I'd happily have dug through rancid coffee grounds and tufts of middle-aged hair extracted from brushes in order to find it if the hour had been later, the street more isolated.

Jack's father walked back inside the garage, a trailing burst of laughter seeming to activate the sprinklers on his lawn as the automatic door protectively lowered. One jogger, a thirtysomething woman whose exertions of breath were thundering, stomped by. She had the haunted look of someone who'd come from a dire place and was on her way to an even worse destination to deliver awful news. This expression contrasted sharply with her caffeinated ponytail, which was perched in the top center of her skull like a plume on the hat of a Napoleonic infantryman. There was no way for women, for anyone, to gracefully age. After a certain point, any detail, like the woman's cheerleader hairstyle, that implied youth simply looked ridiculous. Despite her athletic prowess, the jogger's cratered thighs seemed more like something that would die one day than something that would not. I didn't know how long I had before this window slammed down on my fingers as well—with diligence, and avoiding children, perhaps a decade. The older I became, the harder it would be to get what I wanted, but that was probably true of everyone with everything.

Another jogger lapped my convertible, his face the color of sunburned meat. His chest was sweating the way a fatally wounded stab victim might bleed. A wave of desperation coursed through me that nearly made me jump from the car and run—shorts still around my ankles, buzzing vibrator dropping onto the asphalt from between my legs—to Jack's window, to rap on it loudly with my fist, then press my buttocks against the glass and turn behind to look at him with one panicked fish eye on the side of my face and offer no command or explanation beyond, *Take me right now, through this window. You're too young to realize we don't have much time.*

I stared back into the binoculars, but Jack was no longer in the room—summoned by Father, apparently. I scanned all the front rooms I could see into for activity, but Jack wasn't visible. With a sigh I removed the vibrator, placed it into the car's center cup holder and let its droning buzz fill the vehicle. It was time to flip down the driver's-side visor and perform a quick check in the mirror. I looked deceptively satisfied—sweating, flushed, rosy-cheeked. "Patience," I said out loud, "is a virtue." It was so funny I started cackling. A very unattractive, near-snort of a laugh, to be honest. I found that sometimes it was a relief to do something unattractive in private, to confirm that I'm deeply flawed when so many others imagine me to be perfect. People are often startled by my handwriting; because I'm pretty, they assume everything I do is pretty. It's odd to them that I write like I have a hook for an arm, just as Ford would be startled to learn I have a hook for a heart. Shitting is good this way as well. Occasionally in college, my roommate would enter the bathroom right after I'd done some business and scream out at the lingering smell with a sense of shock that left me deeply gratified. With her square, Germanic jaw and wide-set shoulders, it was easy for me to picture her hearty dumps—I pictured them to be somewhat orthogonal, favoring the rectangular. But I had a face that denied excretion.

"Good-bye for now, Jack," I called. One good thing about returning to the house in sweaty aerobic gear was that Ford had to believe me when I claimed to be too tired. The concession was always that I'd lie down on my side for him and he'd get to lower my spandex shorts to reveal my buttocks, pull down my sports bra so a profile of nipple was showing as well, and masturbate standing above me while I closed my eyes and pretended to have fallen asleep.

chapter three

Seeing the students' actualized youth up close made me dou-
ble down on my age-preventative spa visits and my purchase of vigi-
lant creams and potions. I cycled through the weeks of the month
with oxygenating facials, DNA-repair enzyme facials, caviar illu-
minating facials, precautionary Botox, microdermabrasion, LED
light therapy. To unite body and mind for the best results possible, I
always tried to envision myself literally getting younger during the
treatments: I pictured my fourteen-year-old self standing off in the
distance, waiting for me to come repossess her body; each one of
these sessions allowed me to take one step further toward reaching
her by turning back the clock a few months. Though often, well-
intentioned compliments on behalf of the aestheticians would derail
me from such vision quests.

It was not uncommon while I was receiving a glycolic peel (I
don't find its biting sting unwelcome—in general with beauty treatments, pain feels like an assurance of progress to me) for the aesthe-
tician to gush, "You know? You really could be a model."

"I'm too short," I'd quip. "Five foot seven." Though I'd flirted
with doing print ads for a small time during college, I couldn't stand
taking direction. I also had the fear that with the right photogra-
pher, the real me might accidentally be captured—that in looking at
the photo, suddenly everyone's eyes would widen and they'd actually
see me for the very first time: *Oh my God—you're a soulless pervert!*

The lobby of the plastic surgeon's office had a clinical asceticism to it; with its white pillar columns and brushed chrome accents, it seemed to be part church and part laboratory. I suppose that was the message they were trying to convey: staving off decrepitude combined the miracles of religion with the progressive advancements of medicine. Yet the elderly patients in the waiting room made it clear what a pseudoscience the whole thing was. They'd often look up at me, raising vast draperies of throat skin that hung above their crepe chests like crumpled ascots. Knowing the miseries of my future body, most of them couldn't help but give me a smile filled with sadistic delight. "You have beautiful skin," one told me once. She seemed to squirm with relish as she said the words; it was no different from kicking me in the ribs and saying, *Everything on you will one day sag.* But for now, every inch of my flesh was perfectly taut—if I were to run out to the lobby midtreatment and shed my bathrobe, the sight of my immaculate abdomen would likely have caused these withered creatures to fall to their knees crying and break a hip.

Spa days were usually paired with shopping sprees. These were a necessary cushion against the realities of my pretend marriage: buying nice things helped me temporarily forget the vulgar angle to which Ford's stubbled jaw hung open while he was snoring, the moist smacks his tongue made when he chewed a steak, and even my rare though inescapable duties in the bedroom. But they certainly couldn't help divert my thoughts from Jack. Lately I'd begun packing my closet with body-clinging tailored suits and silk shells with low-cut backs: this way I could wear a jacket into the classroom, then remove it so only the students could see my exposed flesh, never the other teachers; occasionally I also wore long sateen scarves that covered my chest. Only upon entering the class would I wrap them up around my neck or sling them back across my shoulders so the air conditioner paired with my open-nipple bra could put on a show. Until I was engaging in true contact with Jack or another student, I needed the boys' hungry stares for sustenance: these young men were so new to life, they didn't yet know how to mask the direction in which their eyes were peeking nor their wonder and delight at what they were looking at.

Even in this competition of the involuntary gaze, Jack proved himself to be far superior to his peers. While others looked upon my chest with a gleeful smirk or pleasant shock, Jack stared in the way one might watch a waterfall—there was something profoundly hopeful in his glance, an optimism that the world held more wonder than he'd ever thought to guess. It was a feeling I tried to encourage in him with an affirmative glance or a nod, one that told him, simply and plainly, *You're seeing exactly what you think you're seeing.*

In retrospect perhaps it was also his name that set me on his trail—I hoped Jack Patrick's two first names meant he was two boys in one: public Patrick, a regular fourteen-year-old schoolboy, and private Jack, who might willfully submit to every smutty thing I wanted to do to him.

His behavior in the classroom was promising: self-doubtful but alert; laughing when I or one of his classmates made a joke, but not making them himself or asking for the class's attention. Each day he wore a T-shirt and sportlike mesh shorts that fell just below his knees, but his lower calves suggested that his upper thighs were covered in a thin layer of blond hair. In the light these tufts seemed like a gossamer confection; if licked, I imagined they would dissolve on my tongue.

The reading list for the nonadvanced eighth-grade English classes was preselected and not to be deviated from: *Romeo and Juliet* began the fall semester, then we would be moving into *The Scarlet Letter* and *The Crucible*. To begin I had students draw names from a bucket: in each class, we'd read Shakespeare's play aloud to kill time. Jack drew the character of Paris, and visibly blushed when Marissa Talbet, an annoyingly theatrical redhead who on the first day of class asked if she could, from time to time, make pertinent student council announcements, spoke of Paris's legendary attractiveness in her role as Nurse. Marissa was the first student to modulate her voice for the part, raising it several octaves higher and attempting a British accent. Her classmates found this hilarious, but Jack never doubled over with sugar-induced laughter. Instead he simply smiled, all the while looking at the text of the play, hardly ever raising his virginal brown eyes—but when he did glance up, he found me watching him, and we'd lock into a stare for the briefest second before his head lowered back toward the safety of the book.

Reading aloud, his voice was steady overall, though he stumbled a bit between antiquated words and spoke with the misplaced stressors of one who doesn't fully grasp a line's context. "Thou wrong . . . sit . . . wrongs . . . it . . . more than tears . . . with that report," he spoke to Juliet, whose name happened to be drawn from the bucket by the exacting Frank Pachenko (when the teasing about this role immediately began, Frank was quick to remind his peers that in Shakespeare's time Juliet and all of the female characters would have indeed been played by male actors). In general

Frank's appearance and organized demeanor bucked the stereo-
type of the typical fourteen-year-old male: his hand always went
straight up in the air when a question was asked, and his glasses
had lenses too large and too circular for his age. Occasionally I
saw him speaking with Jack, usually a quick question or two that
Jack answered with a low, short phrase, but there was a familiar-
ity between them that suggested they'd known one another since
childhood despite the different paths the social jungle of adolescence was beginning to put them on: Jack was an accepted outlier
in the circle of the popular jocks, while Frank took geeky solace
in social failure by channeling his energy into academics. Frank
wasn't an outstanding mind—his response papers formed simplis-
tic arguments with an average vocabulary—but he looked the part
of the young academic: his shirt tucked into his slightly too-high-
waisted shorts, his bulky white sneakers that somehow didn't appear to ever have been worn.

Since lunch directly followed Jack's third-period class, I made
it a habit to drop into the lunchroom and take note of his where-
abouts, even watch him eat if the opportunity presented itself. Less
than a month after school started, I'd already begun to shut his
peers out with the myopic blindness a focused goal brings. I've
no doubt there were others, throngs of students not in any of my
classes, who were watching me as I stood in the humid fog of the
cafeteria and sipped a carton of chocolate milk through a straw,
placing myself in front of one of the large industrial fans positioned
at each corner of the cafeteria and letting it lift stray hairs from the
gathered bun at the base of my neck. A sound-based traffic light
at the cafeteria's front entrance registered how loud the collective
sound in the room was: green meant the students were talking at

an acceptable volume, yellow was an intermediate warning, and red would sound a bell that meant a punishment of total silence would be invoked—once the light turned red, a staff member sounded three whistles, and anyone caught talking afterward was given detention. But I stared into the green light—*The Great Gatsby* was assigned to the ninth graders but not the eighth—and thought about being inside my convertible with Jack, the top down, both of us completely undressed, me flooring the gas and letting the wind hit our bodies as a type of foreplay.

Janet liked to ruin these daydreams—I could've wrung her neck the day that Jack brought a pack of Twizzlers in his lunch. I had a clear view of him, framed between the hunched shoulder blades of two small girls, likely sixth graders, who were sitting at the table in front of Jack's. One at a time, he bit down onto the red rope of the candy, pulling a little, revealing just a bit of aggressive tooth, and then he would slowly chew, his lips flushing with wetness. I was so fixated I didn't even hear her until she was right next to me, her respirator-like breathing falling upon my ear.

"Rosen is on a goddamn witch hunt," she declared. I came out of my trance, suddenly vulnerable to all the room's wretched smells and sounds. It was chili day, and massive yellow trash bins around the room were brimming with garlicky waste. Janet began a series of wet coughs, reaching into the pocket of her wide elastic pants to bring out a stained handkerchief. "He dropped by in the middle of my class this morning. Totally unannounced. I'd given them a group assignment and the little punks were all over the room. A few were climbing on the desks like baboons."

"Hello, Janet." I looked back up and felt a bolt of panic in my stomach; suddenly I couldn't see Jack. I desperately began a right-to-left scan of the room; I had to swallow repeatedly to avoid the urge to yell out his name.

"I'd like to see Rosen try and teach them about the former USSR. It's not exactly flies to honey. He sits in his big air-conditioned office half the day, never has to manage a classroom. He couldn't walk a mile in my shoes."

I nodded, solemnly looking at her feet. If I gifted her a pair that weren't Velcro, would she wear them? Likely not. She frequently removed her shoes in the teacher's lounge—"Letting the dogs breathe," as she called it—and when she put them back on there was no need to bend down and tie anything. She simply latched the Velcro back up by running the opposing foot's callused heel along the straps.

When she stood in front of the industrial fan, Janet's sacklike clothing pressed against outlying regions of her body normally hidden by baggy fabric. "Just play his game for a little bit, Janet. Let him see what he wants to see, get him to stop breathing down your neck." The charcoal frizz of her perm hovered above her scalp like a rising cloud of smog. With one eye open farther than the other, she looked like a stoic survivor: pillaged by the elements but still here against all odds.

"Says he wants me to 'foster an environment of mutual respect.' What a bag of horseshit. These feral little dogs wouldn't know respect if it bit them on the privates."

"Would respect really bite them on the privates?" I asked.

"Just look at them out there. It's like *National Geographic*. The future is hopeless." Janet's caustic remarks were drawing the attention of a husky student eating alone at a nearby table. A chili dog rested limply in the side of his mouth, his mastication paused so he could stare straight ahead at Janet.

"Perhaps this conversation is best reserved for after hours," I whispered. Out of the corner of my eye, I caught a familiar blip of gray shirt and turned—Jack and his buddies had moved outside to the courtyard and were now sitting along the edge of a brick planter. The guys in the center were talking to two girls in short-shorts, saying something that was making the girls slap them on the forearms with pretend outrage as they all laughed. Jack sat at the corner, not speaking to the girls directly but in on the conversation. "Excuse me, Janet." She was still talking, still continued to talk as I walked away and unbuttoned another button on the front of my shirt. Heading through the doorway out to the courtyard and looking straight ahead, I did my best strut, veering as close to Jack as I could without brushing against him on my walk by. His crowd of friends grew silent; I could feel all their eyes transfer to me as I passed. When I was several feet away, I heard one of his friends whistle. "She is smoking hot," he said. There were laughs; next came the overenunciated voice of one of the girls. "Oh my *god,* Craig," she chided. "She's a *teacher.*" This was the attitude I knew I had to conquer in Jack's mind: he had to be convinced that I was more like him than like his mother.

In my afternoon classes I sat as close to the window AC unit as possible in an attempt to stop the electricity circulating in my body, so close that one side of my face grew nearly numb. I knew it wasn't good to be hung up on one specific student so early on, that I shouldn't feel a sense of desperation just for him. My obsessing over Jack meant I was growing increasingly willing to try to speed up contact. These urges might blind me to warning signs or cause me to engage in unnecessary risks. I needed to stay objective, but it seemed like a losing battle.

Hearing the first acts of *Romeo and Juliet* read aloud for the fifth time that day, my head began to slump back in my chair. The AC was icing down my scalp but failing to cool the incessant tingle that caused me to cross and uncross and recross my legs again and again. At times, I wished that my genitals were prosthetic, something I could slip out of. They were a constant drone of stimulation; their requests hummed aloud throughout my life like a never-ending soundtrack. And everywhere I looked there were young male bodies. I had to watch their fingers idly drum on desktops, their nascent biceps flex as they raised a hand to their ear for a scratch, the pink buds of their tongues emerge to wet the corners of their mouths. By the end of the day, the stink of pheromones clung to the walls of the classroom like wet paint and made me dizzy.

But despite the pleasant view, I saw few real options. Goody-goodies like Frank would deny me, and the overly confident type would find it impossible not to brag. There was only Jack—my second choice, Trevor Bodin, had a vast assortment of imperfections; deciding between the two of them was like being asked to pick a dance partner and given the option of a trained choreographer or an epileptic with a wooden leg. Trevor was an artsy sort whose hair was a wiggish crop of curls. A pensive journaler, he'd already asked if I'd look at some of his poetry. Since he walked home from school and didn't have to rush to catch a bus, he often came up to talk books and writing with me after class. But he had a girlfriend; most of his poetry was devoted to professing his love for her—Abby Fischer in my second period, memorable for her chunk of dyed purple hair. Being the romantic type, if Trevor ever did stray, he'd undoubtedly confess to her minutes after the act, likely through a series of frantic text messages that peppered statements of regret with frown-faced emoticons. He also came off as clingy, which could prove to be downright toxic. Trevor seemed like the type who would be ever more demanding, who would accept nothing less than symbiosis. Plus, based on his clothing, his parents were extremely lenient. He had no fear of authority, which meant he wouldn't be worried enough about getting caught and wouldn't act with the necessary level of caution. Trevor was too outspoken, tried too hard to impress. But he kept tempting me— he loved staying to talk to me alone in the classroom after everyone else had left. That afternoon as soon as the final bell rang, he came straight up to my desk. I suppose it took a while to get my attention; I was looking through a slit in the window blinds, seeing if I could identify Jack amidst the horde of students pouring from the main building out to the bus lot. As they kept coming it seemed like they were multiplying, splitting off and begetting others in a mass act of asexual reproduction.

"Mrs. Price?"

I answered but didn't break my gaze out the window. "Go ahead, Trevor, I'm listening."

"Don't you think *Romeo and Juliet* is unrealistic? I mean, how they kill themselves? Why would they kill themselves if they're actually in love?"

Suddenly I spied two boys beginning to wrestle on the lawn in front of the bus line. They clenched one another's waists until one finally began to reach around and take the other in a hold, pulling his shirt up above his ribs; I could make out the movements of his bare chest panting with exertion. I brought my lips closer to the window, feeling the sun's intensified heat through the glass. Wasn't it possible, as their fighting escalated, that they might remove their shirts entirely? My mind began to entertain the fantasy that they weren't on the grass of the school grounds at all but the dirt floor of a Roman coliseum, fighting to the death so I could copulate with the winner.

"I doubt they're really in love anyway. I mean, they hardly know each other, right?" Trevor mussed his cropped hair, awaiting a response that lauded his insight and maturity.

"Probably not, Trevor." I had a brief urge to suggest to Trevor that he and I play a copycat game of sorts, watching the boys' movements, then repeating them. If I lunged at Trevor and wrapped my arms around his waist, would I be able to stop myself from going further once I felt his sides contract in a fit of nervous giggling?

In a matter of seconds the outdoor scuffle turned from light-hearted to serious; the two had toppled over in the grass. The boy on top was trying to pin down the other's arms; kids on the nearest bus were now hanging out its opened windows and cheering them on. I had to get myself in the middle of their brawl—I'd be able to touch the hot, moist skin of the top student's arm as I pulled at him in a phony attempt to stop the fight, to smell the boys' pungent musk of hormones, and possibly more. Anything could happen—I could get pulled to the ground and sandwiched between their squirming torsos; my clothes might be ripped from my body in the fray.

"Two guys out there are going at one another like idiots," I said, turning to reach for my purse. I hurried toward the door as Trevor followed alongside me in a running walk.

"Hey!" I called out to them as loudly as I could while still sounding friendly. The top boy looked over and the bottom boy took advantage of his hesitation, lunging upright and managing to grab the kid's neck. "Okay, guys, enough already." I ran up and grabbed both arms of the choker, letting my hands roam upward into the damp pits of his T-shirt.

I expected them to pull me into their mix of interlocking limbs and continue fighting but they didn't—the choked student backed away and stood immediately, rubbing his neck. Perhaps he feared getting suspended. "We weren't fighting for real," he explained, catching his breath. His friend began to stand as well, twisting too soon from my grasp. *No!* I wanted to hiss at them, *Don't stop touching each other!* When it became clear that there would be no further physical contact between any of us, my disappointment was so intense that I experienced it as a shift in gravity; I squatted down to the grass for a moment to catch my breath.

"Yeah," the second boy added, his voice slightly deeper. "We were just messing around." There was a tense pause of silence as I closed my eyes and raised a steadying hand to my forehead; the feel of the boys' eyes looking down upon me was as intense as the sunlight on my neck. "Are you okay?"

I nodded and cautiously took my time standing back up. I looked over the body of each one with a longing for what might've been if I'd had to insert myself between them as they rolled together on the ground—the sharp chin of the top boy could've painfully buried itself in my shoulder; the flexed hand of the other could've slid across my ass in a feverish search for leverage as he tried to escape. "I get it," I said, placing my hand along the red exposed skin of the choked boy's upper shoulder. The collar of his T-shirt had been stretched out. My fingers drifted a few inches across his slick skin until they felt sufficiently wet; I hoped the wind wouldn't dry them before I had a chance to take a quick taste. "Now get out of here before the AP sees you."

"Yes, ma'am," they answered in unison, grabbing their bags and jogging just beyond the buses before slowing to a walk. I turned to find Trevor still there waiting a few feet behind me, his black T-shirt and jean shorts making him sweat profusely in the sunlight.

"Jerks," Trevor said, trying to give me a knowing smile. I squinted, reconsidering everything about him. His cheeks were rosy with heat, his hair almost entirely dampened. I'd gotten myself worked up in the hopes of a three-way wrestling match that hadn't developed—was it so improbable that the universe was now giving me Trevor as a consolation prize? He was surely too hot in those clothes; shedding them would feel divine.

But I reminded myself of all the ways he was likely dangerous— I tried to imagine that the glossy sweat covering his body was actually venom. "I'll see you tomorrow, Trevor." I gave him a perfunctory smile, then turned and started walking toward the parking lot, but my voice wasn't entirely dismissive. I suppose I wanted to see if he'd follow me to my car, and was pleased when he did indeed bound along up beside me.

"I saw this TV program . . . I mean it was on TV but it really happened in real life . . . these kids were forbidden by the girl's parents to see each other, so she and her boyfriend killed her mom and dad." Trevor nearly whispered this, trying to infuse the story with the excitement of a secret.

"Attraction creates powerful feelings," I mumbled. "It overrules intellect."

"Yeah," he agreed. "I guess that's, like, the point of the play, right?"

"You could argue that's one of the themes." When we reached the yellow line marking the edge of the faculty parking lot, I spotted AP Rosen moving alongside the string of buses with his walkie-talkie. I couldn't lead Trevor to my car in front of other faculty members, no matter how badly I wanted to see what might happen if I did. He was like a puppy dog that needed an invisible fence, and I had to train him that this was the edge of his yard.

"Last question." He smiled. "Is *Romeo and Juliet* your favorite Shakespeare play?"

I laughed far louder than I meant to. When I glanced up to see if any of the leaving faculty were staring over at Trevor and me, no one seemed to be looking. "No. My favorite's *Hamlet*. It's the most realistic."

His hand shooed away a buzzing insect that had come to inspect the salt and oil pouring off his face. If we were alone, I might have offered to wipe down his sweat with my hair. From certain angles Trevor was indeed very cute, but I had to resist him—he was low-hanging fruit. With a dull roar, the buses began rolling by and my eyes followed them like I was watching a shell game at a carnival: all of them looked identical, but one had a prize inside. Which bus was Jack's?

"Doesn't *Hamlet* start out with a ghost? How is it the most realistic?" Trevor wouldn't shut up. I badly wanted to reach out and place a finger against his lips just to see what he'd do—would he simply quit talking? Or would his lips then part just a little, letting my finger slide between his teeth and move across his tongue?

"Because everyone acts disingenuous," I said. "And then they all die." Trevor continued talking even though the tandem sounds of bus engines drowned out his words. My eyes switched back and forth between his mouth and the hovering exhaust smoke from each bus. The haze was gathering together to create a singular black cloud that I hoped Jack might appear from like in a magic trick.

I had to admit that Trevor was all wrong for my purposes. But the roar and the stink of the passing buses made me feel like Trevor and I had been placed inside a dangerous war zone together and needed one another to survive—I was impressed by the way his lips managed to look pristine, like inner meat, despite the smog filling in around us. I could feel the growing wetness between my thighs in the wind. The way Trevor was looking at me now, his wry smile, made it seem like he was reading my mind. Perhaps we were sending one another chemical signals. His growing body surely smelled upon me the dank catalyst of experience that could take him from theory to practice.

"Good-bye, Trevor," I whispered. I could feel the start of tears stinging my chest; it was hard to turn down such certain pleasure. How easy it would be to stand and chat with him just a bit longer until the parking lot emptied out, then offer him a ride. He'd sit a bit awkwardly in the car at first, his legs bent up too far as he tried to avoid touching the tender skin behind his knee against the seat's hot leather. After two blocks, we'd be on one of the main roads leaving town; after ten minutes we'd be outside of town completely, surrounded by the undeveloped grass expanse of land fenced off for future suburbs. Then I would turn down the radio and tell him to pull off his shorts, stressing that I was serious. At the first rural stop sign we came to, I'd instruct him to say my name when he saw a car coming from any direction. Then I would turn the radio back up and bend over into his lap, filling my mouth with him until I felt his tentative fingers brush my head, heard his voice say, *Mrs. Price*— quietly at first, a conflicted admission, and then again more loudly with panic, *Mrs. Price, I see a car.*

"Mrs. Price?" Trevor had his cell phone out; he was trying to show me something on the screen I couldn't see in the bright glare of the day. I pretended he was trying to show me a photo he'd taken of his penis held up against the length of a ruler and gave him a smile filled with gratitude.

"Till tomorrow, Trevor." I turned toward my car and didn't look back. The rage of lust was like an IV drip in my veins; I felt it beginning to spread inside me with the helpless awareness of someone realizing she's been slipped a drug. I tried to gain some release by pounding my heels into the asphalt as hard as I could. I felt like I might rip my car's metal door off its hinges if I wasn't careful. Inside, I lifted my hair up into a quick bun and let the seat burn at the back of my neck. With a shaking hand, I reached up to the rearview mirror and turned it to face me directly. "You will go home and snort a small amount of the cocaine you keep in the Altoids tin in your pajama drawer. You will robotically fuck your husband until your box feels like a gaping wound. You will be so aggressive that he will be frightened, and his fear will keep you from being completely repulsed by him. You will get this bothersome spark out of your system for long enough to buy you a little more time with Jack. Jack needs to know you before he can trust you. Jack needs to trust you before you can trust him. You need to trust him before you can fuck him. The end."

"Hey, hey, Celeste!"

I jumped in my seat; Janet's pork-chop fist was suddenly raining down on my window in a repeated knock. Had she heard any of what I'd just said? I quickly turned on the car and rolled down the window. She leaned her head inside until her long tapestry of neck was guillotined below from the windowpane. Taking a few congested mouth breaths, her eyes began to rove in an exploratory survey of my car's interior. "This thing is in mint condition," she warbled. When placed into direct sunlight, I'd noticed, Janet's major systems began to shut down almost immediately. Her mouth now involuntarily hung a bit open. From her vitals it seemed like she'd just been shot in the back.

"So I don't know, my van won't start. I guess I should've seen this coming. They say bad things happen in threes."

Rather than ask about the universe's other two injustices against her (her looks and personality?), I decided to cut to the chase. "What do you need, Janet?"

"Triple A will spend upward of an hour just trying to pull their heads out of their asses. Can you give me a ride? I'll call from home and have it towed. From my air-conditioned living room. I can't even think about it until I get into the air-conditioning." Our faces were so close they were almost touching, yet she managed to look past me instead of making eye contact. Did she have cataracts? I was in awe of her as a creature in sum; every one of her parts had its own individual defect, yet here she was, a basically functioning unit.

"Sure, just get in." I reached over and gingerly unzipped my gym bag, trying to worm out the towel without the dildo springing out too. "Let me put this down so the seat doesn't burn you."

I felt the car ominously lower as she transferred her weight inside. Her abdominal bumpers extended out against the gearshift. When we began to drive, each time I went into third, my hand disappeared into the borders of her stomach. "Excuse me," I mumbled. Janet shrugged.

"I can't even feel that side of my body," she said.

Although Ford's affinity for gender roles meant he hated women smoking ("Nothing's more masculine than puffing smoke. That's the business of men and tailpipes"), after sex he'd consent to just about anything, and if Ford had touched me for any length of time I usually needed a good half a pack to calm down.

He gave me a cheerful spank, followed by a satisfied wink. When I noticed the ring he'd left on, I crammed a second cigarette in my mouth and began smoking two at once. There had been a time in college when I'd told myself, as a cardinal rule, that I'd never have sex with any guy who was wearing a man ring. Ford had plenty—high school, college, fraternity, police academy, gemstone. It was a purely adult form of male sleaze and I abhorred it. "Babe, I know I give you shit sometimes for not giving it up more," he announced. "But when you do, goddamn."

"See," I said, my face expressionless. I felt like I'd sufficiently beaten him up and gotten beaten. I'd managed to choke out, just for a few hours, the angry desire inside. "When I say 'no' I'm just protecting you. You need time in between to recover." I blew a long puff up at the light on the bedroom ceiling, remembering the weightless shine of Trevor's lips. I'd have to start being crueler, less encouraging to Trevor. I couldn't let him tempt me that way again. Today in the parking lot, I'd gotten the feeling that he was pursuing me. And if he could pursue, he could tattle. He could barter and leverage and blackmail. Some student chasing me down wasn't what I was after. What I needed, what I desperately hoped to find in Jack, was a student whom I could wear down. One who, even if he initially felt like running, would gradually slow his pace and let me catch him.

chapter four

By the time fall open house arrived at the end of September, I felt like I had a legitimate virus. Every erogenous spot on my body was inflamed and aching. Between classes I often went to the faculty bathroom and stood, one knee resting on the toilet seat, to dully finger the already sore heat between my legs. *Romeo and Juliet* provided an outlet to talk about sex in the classroom, and I often sat behind my desk and pressed the swollen nest of my genitals against the chair with a friction that nearly made me moan. Most of the kids, drunk on the freedom of speaking about the subject aloud with openness, were eager to discuss. Marissa, for example, was certainly a vocal ringleader. Her teeth stained in ombré shades of red from a fruit punch drink, whenever she thought of something to say she'd boost herself up in her chair, sitting on one leg, her arm waving with the desperation of a plane crash survivor hailing a rescue chopper.

"I think, like, if they'd never . . . you know . . . *done it* . . ." She paused, smiling with glee as the class erupted into giggles. Marissa was an instigator, pushy. If Jack ever became her target, I recognized her as the type who might relentlessly pursue.

"Had sex, you mean," I added. More giggles.

"Right. I think if they'd never had sex, they wouldn't have killed themselves and stuff. I saw this video about how sex can, like, release stuff from your brain and make you crazy."

"Interesting." I surveyed the room; most students were now taking the conversation to its less-appropriate further conclusion in whispers to friends. "What do people think? Does sex make you crazy?"

A variety of jocks eager to imply they had firsthand experience spoke up. "No doubt," Danny's low voice boomed from the back of the classroom. His meaty face had drawn upward into a not-so-subtle grin.

"I dunno," another football player said. I confess I didn't trouble myself with learning their names or distinguishing one from another. Physically, they were far too developed to be appealing—their growth spurts were finished, their muscles already wrought into the structured mold of the finished male form. "I think *not* having sex is what makes you crazy." Shrieks of faux disbelief sounded through the classroom; when the bell rang moments later, it seemed like an alarm set off by the high-pitched screams.

Jack's face was flushed when he walked by me toward the door, his eyes trained shyly down at his shoes. I stood and said his name very softly—so quietly that he easily could've failed to hear me, or could have pretended not to hear. But he turned. I beckoned him over as the class emptied, staring warmly into his eyes but not speaking until the door shut for the final time and we were alone.

I continued to speak in hushed tones, enunciating, exaggerating each movement of my lips as I spoke. "You're very quiet in class, Jack Patrick." I gave him a wide smile to show it wasn't a criticism.

He scratched the back of his neck and grinned while his face blushed to a deeper red. Perhaps he continued looking at the ground because the heat in his cheeks embarrassed him. Reaching out, I placed my pointer finger upon the tiny cleft at the bottom of his chin and raised his head upright until he was looking directly at me. In heels I was taller than him; the top of his blondish hair was level with my mouth. "There," I whispered, barely speaking, trying to simply exhale the words. "That's better, isn't it. So tell me, Jack, since you don't speak up in class and leave me guessing at the thoughts inside that head of yours. What do you think makes someone crazier—having sex? Or not having it?"

His eyes widened; it seemed to take a moment for his brain to confirm I'd really asked him that question. He laughed and lowered his head a little, shaking it nervously.

"Ah-ah," I cooed, this time using all my fingers to cup his chin in my hand and guide it back upward. His fuzzy cheeks had a downy softness. If I squeezed, I would be able to lift apart his top and bottom jaw, open his mouth and lower mine down to meet his. "Here," I offered, "I'll hold your head up so you don't have to worry about eye contact." Staring at him, Jack returning the stare as the pulse of his throat began to strike against my finger, I felt as though someone were licking my inner thigh.

"I . . . um," he started. When he swallowed, his throat strained against the gentle pressure of my fingertips.

"I know you have an opinion," I teased, my words silken. "Everybody does."

He cleared his throat and sent vibrations up my wrist. "I just wouldn't know about the having-sex part," he said. Then, with an afterthought that nearly made me move my hands to his neck and force him against the wall, he added a foreshadowing phrase. "I mean," he added quietly, now speaking even more quietly than me, "not yet."

I let out a long breath; it was involuntary. Nearly a whimper.

Worried he'd seen too much in my reaction, my hand slipped from his jaw and I took a step back. "Of course." I nodded. There was a long beat of silence. "But the not having sex, just between you and me—I'm curious. Does it make you crazy? I forget what it's like to be your age. You're fourteen, right?"

"Yeah." On his brow I noticed the beginning of the slightest glimmer of sweat.

"Juliet was going on fourteen. You can tell me, I won't judge you. Does it make you crazy?"

Perhaps fearing my guiding hand again, he did his best to continue looking me in the eye; ultimately, though, he couldn't do it. His glance wandered to the left. "I guess it feels that way sometimes," he said. "When I let my mind run with it and stuff."

My composure regained, I stepped forward, closer now than even before, touching my face against the side of his head as my lips found his ear. "And when you do let your mind run, Jack Patrick," I whispered, asking him in secret so that not even the walls of the room could overhear his answer, "when your mind is running as fast as it can . . . do you ever feel like if you don't get relief you could physically die?"

Placing my hands on his shoulders, I lowered my head and moved my ear against the warmth of his mouth, awaiting a response. For several moments I could hear nothing but labored breathing that sounded like an answer in itself.

"I don't know," he said, his breath hot upon my hair. When he stopped talking, I pulled more tightly on his shoulders, drawing his mouth so that it actually pressed against my ear. "It can feel intense," he admitted.

Just as my right hand began to move from his shoulder down his left arm, the tardy bell for lunch rang; in the silence of the classroom after our whispered voices, it sounded so loud as to seem internal. We jumped in unison. It felt as though the noise had just caught us there, standing too close. He looked up at me, worried—late to lunch meant a write-up, three write-ups meant in-school suspension. I gave his shoulder a final squeeze, then quickly moved toward my desk as though nothing had happened.

"Don't worry," I said, my voice back at normal volume, "I'll write you a pass. I appreciate you staying and sharing your point of view with me." He was silent as I wrote, but I could feel him looking at my body in a revised manner, his assumed boundaries having just been proven wrong. "Do you already have any write-ups?"

He shook his head. When I handed him the pass I felt an enjoyable sense of commerce, like I was giving him a check for his services. "Good boy." I smiled.

But the moment he left the room my smile faded. I reached up my shirt and pinched my nipples as hard as I could, my fingernails digging in until my eyes began to water.

It was impossibly difficult, but for the next two days I managed to ignore Jack completely. I wanted him to miss the attention, crave my furtive glances even though he always looked away in seeming shame, as though he'd walked in on a scene inside a room he had no business entering. Instead I lavished praise upon his blockhead counterparts (*Yes, Heath, that's very perceptive—we could in fact blame Romeo and Juliet's parents!*) and encouraged the foulmouthed girls of the class in their lewd comments, hoping he'd feel ignored when my glance avoided his direction. If it was safe to cross lines with Jack, I figured open house was where I'd find out. An appearance by his mother or father (or worse, both) voicing some concerns about my keeping their son after class would mean I'd somehow have to write our planned future together out of my loins for good. I was afraid that if things fell apart with Jack I'd have to grab Trevor and pound him in the PE storage shed, then flee town immediately—surely, Trevor wouldn't be able to keep the secret longer than an hour. There'd be no other choice than to take a bus across the state line and try to assume a new identity.

At home, Ford was noticeably reeling from our decrease in face time since school had begun. Due to a leap of fortune I never would've had the optimism to imagine, the second week in September he got reassigned to an afternoon shift with alternating weekends; it started around three P.M. and got him home near midnight, by which time I made every effort to already be, or appear, asleep. He often tried to wake me upon entering bed, and in the morning while I got ready for work Ford never failed to ask me a barrage of interrogatory questions, barking them out while he lay unmoving with his torso covered up like an invalid. Nearly every other day he threatened to ask for a reassignment back to his old shift, but I'd do my best to strike this thought from his mind.

"Now, honey," I'd say, pausing from brushing my hair to walk toward him in the too-white early brightness of the bedroom. My hair was something he'd fixate on—I always joked he must've been one of those boys who would cut ponytails off of girls in elementary school. I'd take special care to be interested, bending down and sitting next to the blanketed worm of his shape, my hair falling next to his face like a scented curtain. "If you do that you'll knock yourself out of line for that promotion you're trying so hard for."

Ford wanted to advance but it didn't seem to be in the cards; written tests in particular drew a poor showing from him. Still, I tried to keep the flame of hope going strong inside of him. The last thing I needed was for him to decide his job was a dead end and begin playing detective in our personal life. "It's just temporary," I'd coo, leaning down as close to him as I could manage—that horrible adult male sourness exuded from him most in the mornings—and kiss his temple. When he did intercept and make me kiss him on the lips, I had to be sure to get him squarely there and not a millimeter to the left or right. The feeling of my lips touching stubble brought an instant and dropping hotness to my bowels, a sensation I can only liken to a forced enema.

"You're right, peaches," he'd finally say. Then I'd smile and pat his form beneath the blanket, get up from the bed and start back toward the bathroom. He'd grab my hair when I did this, but he wouldn't hold on—he just liked to feel it slip through his fingers as I walked away.

The night of open house we had to report for duty at six; rather than leave and return I stayed in the classroom and used a set of needle-nose tweezers to carve a message into the desk Jack Patrick sat at: YOU WANT ME, placed in small, squarish letters at the very top, a border that would hover above his textbook when he read and his notebook when he wrote. Around five I went to the teachers' lounge to eat a quick bite; several of my colleagues were also there milling around, including Janet. The moment I arrived they wasted no time explaining to me how the evening's events would be an Armageddon of parent ass-kissing. The feelings that would surface as I agreed to be complicit in such debasing events year after year, they warned, might eventually trigger a midlife crisis.

Daniel Tambor, a soft-spoken math teacher whose model of prescription glasses had not been manufactured for the past two decades, put down his Ziploc bag of Nilla Wafers and turned to me. "Well you've heard about Gary Felding, right?"

I shook my head.

"Oh. Well, that kind of shows you. We like to remember Gary each year today."

"Complete crash and burn," boomed Larry Keller, a speech teacher who wore splashy bow ties and liked to shake his right index finger with abandon. "The man taught biology for twenty-six consecutive years here, and the night of his twenty-seventh open house, he snapped." Larry sat down on the corner of a table, his back straight with perfect posture and his eyes fixed ahead, as though he were being interviewed for a documentary film on the subject. "Went batty. Some parent was complaining that her son found the lectures in his class to be unintelligible. Gary just began screaming. Asked the mother if she was aware that her son had drawn an illustration of a hairy boner on his mitosis-video response worksheet.

"But Gary didn't stop there. He lit up a Bunsen burner and began stripping. Set his tie and shirt on fire, then his pants. Parents ran from the room screaming. By the time the cops came, Gary had turned out the lights in his classroom and put on an old-school filmstrip about the atom bomb. He was sitting in one of the student desks, crying and watching mushroom clouds fill the screen."

Mr. Tambor reentered the conversation, his eyes wide and his quiet voice imbued with the vibrato of the haunted. "The saddest memory I have is of Gary being taken away in handcuffs. Though they did let him put on one of those black chemical aprons the kids have to wear during experiments before they led him out. I guess he felt a little exposed when he realized his clothes were burned up."

Janet slowly pushed herself up from the couch and made a frustrated groan. "We're just circus animals here to give the taxpaying parents an entertaining evening." She hunched her back over and bowed her arms into the shape of exaggerated parentheses. "Monkey dance for you," she grunted in a low voice. "Me monkey. Monkey jump high if parent say so." Encouraged by a light pattering of laughter from the other teachers, she shuffled over to the fruit bowl next to the coffeemaker and grabbed a banana. "Monkey ass itch," Janet proclaimed in a throaty growl, "monkey scratch!" Her hands reaching backward, she began to laboriously lift each orthopedic Velcro shoe a few inches off the ground to mimic a dance.

"Stop . . . stop!" Larry hissed under his breath. Suddenly the cause came into view: Assistant Principal Rosen was standing just outside the doorway looking in. Janet removed her hands from in between her butt cheeks but did not turn around to face him.

"Ned," Larry greeted him, extending his coffee cup outward in a type of salute. "Don't mind us. Just blowing off a little steam before all the pomp and circumstance." Ned Rosen nodded, then wandered away. He seemed confused and a little sad, the way the last caveman to accept the wheel might, wondering how others could possibly appreciate something he found to be so useless.

I wasn't looking forward to meeting the parents for a different reason—to me they were libido kryptonite. I liked to imagine the students as an independent resource, new creatures of their own design. Day to day, it was easy to think of the junior high as an island of immortal youths who might never age, but seeing the parents killed that fantasy. Suddenly I'd be aware of what nearly all my students would look like two decades down the road. And after I'd seen them, it was impossible to get those images out of my mind.

For example, I learned that Trevor's physical destiny involved the generous distribution of hirsute facial moles, in addition to a series of broken nasal capillaries that had a near-infected red glow. Michael Ronaldo in my fifth period, though currently lanky and weightless, was destined to inherit a third-trimester paunch. Though the night included a few creepy fathers (*I sure would've paid attention if my teacher had looked like you*) and overcomplimentary mothers who seemed to be skirting the line of possible friendship (*Dana told me after the first day, "Mom, my English teacher is the prettiest person I've ever seen!" Isn't that sweet? You know, a few of us mothers have a scrapbooking circle on Wednesday nights . . .*), the only bona fide nut who showed up was Frank Pachenko's mother, who introduced herself simply as Mrs. Pachenko, though I knew she was Frank's mother even before she spoke—the two of them had the same bulging eyes. Their resting expression was one of squeezed panic, like a ferret dressed up in a miniature corset. Frank was a hopeless dork with the haircut of a fourth grader; meeting his mother, it was easy to see why.

"Mrs. Price, good evening." She addressed me like I was a Japanese businessman with whom she'd previously had a long and profitable, if not personable, relationship. "Did you receive the written inquiries I sent with Frank? According to him, you have yet to send home a reply." My mind raced—written inquiries? After a moment I finally remembered odd offers, written on floral stationery, of volunteer-aide classroom assistance that Frank occasionally handed me. I'd read the first one all the way through, worried it might be some personalized warning about a specific food allergy or attention disorder, but when I realized their unchanging contents I began to throw them away upon receipt.

"Of course, yes—I figured we could just chat in person since I knew I'd be seeing you soon at open house." Mrs. Pachenko's pursed lips flexed slightly tighter.

"Well I've always started the week classes began," she stressed, lamenting the great inconvenience I'd brought upon her. "But I'm a quick study. If you can give me the lesson plans and assignments for the next few weeks, I'll simply work double-time to catch up. I'll have no choice."

It took all the muscle control in my body to keep my eyes from growing large with perception of insanity. I wasn't sure what we'd be doing in class tomorrow, let alone several weeks from now. "You know, Mrs. Pachenko, the reason I waited to talk to you in person is that we have a somewhat sensitive situation I think you'd be a perfect fit for." I lowered my voice to a confidential volume, taking her by the arm and guiding her toward a corner of the classroom.

"I have a colleague," I continued, "who could really use the assistance of someone with expertise. Now, I know you've probably always helped out in Frank's classes, and I get it. You're invested in your child's education. But I have to say, Frank is really holding his own in my course—he's a star. With your skill set, you could do a world of good—the most good—helping out a teacher who's frankly . . . well, she's at risk."

Mrs. Pachenko folded her arms together. "I was certainly counting on being in Frank's class," she began. "But I don't want to refuse someone if I'm badly needed."

I put my hand on her shoulder. The low thread count of the garment was nearly prickly. "Mrs. Pachenko, I wouldn't request this if it weren't an emergency. I feel like you're the only one who could help." The flattery worked; at the end of the night I walked her down to Janet's room and made an introduction.

"You're a godsend," Janet exclaimed. For a brief moment she became distracted by a patch of eczema on her upper arm, but after a few scratches her joy returned. "I've been waiting for the cavalry to come. Do you know how many times I filled out an assistant request form?"

I left the two of them to acquaint themselves while I ran back to the classroom for a final peek—were there any stragglers, any parents working late shifts who'd only been able to arrive five minutes after open house ended?

There were not. That meant Jack Patrick's parents hadn't shown. I couldn't help but see it as an omen; as I drove home that evening, every intersection's signal was green for go.

After the open house, a pilot light of inevitability lit up inside me; it wasn't possible to think of anything beyond when things would begin in earnest and I would have him. I felt like a scientist whose years of research had finally brought him to the cusp of the discovery he'd been seeking all along: I could feel the payoff about to hit, and waiting any longer made me want to scream at the top of my lungs.

The day after open house was a Friday; the kids were mentally checked out and I was looking forward to the possibilities of a first weekend with Jack. Perhaps we would drive through Dairy Queen, then park and explore the differences of each other's bodies with ice-cream-cooled tongues. Or drive out to the country fields, strip down naked and run together like deer, each taking turns being the follower, the one who gets to watch the active mechanics of the running body in front. I was hopeful his parents were easily lied to, that an excuse of a sleepover would allow an overnight romp, the sun rising on our sticky bodies, me introducing Jack to his first taste of gas station coffee as I dropped him off a safe walking distance from his home, then went to the gym to shower up. I could tell Ford I had an all-night yoga retreat. Any excuse relating to physical maintenance would float with him. But what if Jack's parents weren't so lenient? If needed, anything was possible. Jack could sneak me into his window at night and we could fuck on the floor with clean socks stuffed in our mouths to muffle the sound. Nothing would keep me from him.

But he was absent. His very first absence. I was so dumbstruck by this development that for nearly a minute after the start of class, all I could do was stare at his empty chair without speaking. The rest of the students began to whisper and check their phones, wondering at the delay but also not wanting to snap me out of a trance and initiate schoolwork. Finally I stood and wordlessly started to put on a video of a modern adaptation of *The Scarlet Letter.* "Are we moving to that red-A book now?" Danny asked.

"Yup," I answered. I found myself chewing at my nails—a repulsive habit from my childhood that I'd taken great pains to break, repeatedly applying a bitter-tasting custom polish; to this day, candy with that same specific, tangy odor will turn my stomach.

"I've already read this," a young girl—I believe her name was

Alexis—said. "It's like a *Romeo and Juliet* where Juliet gets caught and punished and Romeo doesn't." She paused briefly before adding, "I read all the books for this year over the summer."

"How impressive," I remarked. I couldn't stop looking at his empty chair. Had he, in fact, told his parents about our whispered exchange? Perhaps he'd confessed just before open house and his parents, who then consulted their lawyer, were told that any contact with the soon-to-be defendant was a bad idea. Worse yet, perhaps one of his parents was a lawyer. Perhaps both of them were. Were they plotting their case right now?

"Our society is still this way," rattled Gash, whose real name was Jessica. She dyed her naturally blond hair jet black and wore black lipstick and clothing assaulted by several hundred appliquéd safety pins. "When women hit it they're labeled sluts, but with men it's just expected."

"That's true, Gash." I nodded, pausing the video. "But it was not 'just expected' from Puritan ministers, like the character of Arthur Dimmesdale. Let's think about social context for a moment, and social roles. In today's society, whom might we expect sex scandals from?"

"Priests," yelled Marissa; the class erupted in laughter as she looked around nodding. "For real," she giggled.

"Athletes," said Danny, self-referentially pulling at his football jersey with a smile on his face.

"Good," I responded, "celebrities especially. But like Marissa mentioned, we're most scandalized by relationships where someone breaches the boundaries of a given social role. The culturally agreed-upon role of a priest is to be chaste and holy, whereas the culturally agreed-upon role of a celebrity is to be entertaining."

Marissa's hand shot up again but she didn't wait to be called upon before talking. "Plus with priests it's kids and stuff."

"Good point. Can someone else tell us why that's significantly more scandalous?"

"It's, like, double illegal," said Heath.

Jack's seat seemed to nearly be glowing; the glinting chrome buttons on its backrest kept flashing darts of light against the window. "Are there any social roles in our society where it's okay for an adult to have sex with minors?" I asked.

"Well like in some redneck states adults can marry minors with the parents' consent and stuff," Gash said.

"Yes." I smiled. Never had I imagined my later years unfolding in a holler of West Virginia, paying the families of young men reverse dowries to marry me for their fourteenth year of life and then divorce on their next birthday. Perhaps, if I managed to stick with Ford long enough, past when his father died and he received the bulk of his inheritance, I could gain the type of alimony settlement that would make this arrangement possible. It might not be so bad: the shirtless overalls, the Mountain Dew–fueled sex marathons. It could be a far smarter route than staring at an empty seat in a classroom wondering if litigation was brewing.

Suddenly I realized I'd been looking out the window with a grin on my face. "So the point being," I continued, "where legal, an adult and minor can take on the roles of husband and wife and have the consensual sex implied in that relationship. We mentioned religious officials. What are other social roles where sexual impropriety is taboo?"

"Politicians," one student yelled. Then, from the front row in a very quiet voice, Frank Pachenko called out, "Teachers."

"But, like, that's exactly what we expect now," Danny said. The bass and enthusiasm of his voice gratefully drowned out Frank's comment, which I pretended not to hear. "I mean, like, look at past presidents. JFK was a player. Clinton got it sucked in office." The room exploded with shrieks of laughter that made my ears ring; the vocal chaos in the aftermath of the comment made the twenty-five students sound like a full auditorium.

"Okay, okay," I called out. "Let's settle down. If we want to talk about grown-up subjects we have to act like grown-ups."

"Mrs. Price," Marissa chided, her acne-riddled face suddenly full of ancient knowledge. "We are so not grown-ups."

"But can't you act it?" I said encouragingly. "Can't you pretend?"

They were a room full of reality TV hopefuls; in that moment, they swore that they could.

chapter five

I waited all weekend for the hammer to drop: the summons
to be served, the call to come in. But Friday night passed unevent-
fully—I rented a movie about a thirteen-year-old who had to learn
how to operate a motor vehicle when his intoxicated older brother
needed to be picked up from jail: the two of them then ran a series of errands around shady parts of town to figure out where his
brother had left a bag of drugs. To make sure I'd be asleep by the
time Ford got home, and for most of Saturday as well, I bought a
box of wine, removed its bladderlike sack from the cardboard shell
and took it with me to watch the video in bed. Several hours later
I woke to Ford holding the emptied container up in front of the
night-table lamp. Next to the light, with its amorphous shape and
merlot-dyed plastic, it vaguely resembled a placenta.

"Jesus, Celeste." Ford let out a whistle that wasn't void of admiration. "Those little brats stress you out today or what?"

My mouth felt taped shut with the sleepy film of the wine. "Can
you turn off the light?" I suggested.

"It reeks in here. Did you know this bedroom smells like a hobo,
Celeste?" I sat up and Ford immediately began laughing. "Oh my
god, look at your face. I think you need to brush your teeth before
they fall out."

It was true; my smile had taken on a darkened sheen of purple. Around my mouth, where pigmented drool had journeyed and

dried, there was a reddish stain that recalled clown paint. Stumbling from bed, I was at least able to tuck the vibrator beneath the pillow so that the portrait of my solitary hedonism wouldn't appear to be quite so complete. "We had a 10-31 that some wino was breaking into the bathroom of the convenience mart tonight," Ford called as I rummaged through the medicine cabinet, downing a small hand-ful of what I hoped were Tylenol PM. "But the perp got away. That wasn't you, was it?"

By the time I was up and showered on Saturday afternoon, I had little energy to do anything but sit at the kitchen table and stare at the phone, hoping not to receive a call from AP Rosen or the legal team of Jack's parents. When it finally did ring, I jumped in my seat. I was suddenly paralyzed; it felt self-proclaimed—if I hadn't been watching it, it would not have rung—and I cursed myself and let the machine pick up. But it was just Ford doing a sobriety check on me.

"Hello, dear," I said, picking up to the loud beep of the machine recording stopping. My voice had the gravelly sound of someone wearing a bathrobe well into the day. "I have not touched a single bottle and I've prayed to the Lord for strength."

"Ha," he muttered. I heard a car horn.

"Isn't it against the law to be on your phone while you drive?"

"Not when you're driving the cop car, sweets." He then entered into a long story about a domestic dispute he'd interrupted that had the following punch line: the chosen weapon of assault was a fly-swatter.

"I'll catch you later, hero," I said. When I was hungover, the sound of Ford's voice made me unbearably nauseous.

Unable to go back to sleep for a nap, I decided I'd wait until dusk settled, then drive by Jack's house again. Surely, if the family was in pandemonium from a revelation Jack had made, I'd be able to detect something from the exterior: the dining room aglow long after dinnertime, the family seated around the table in a strategy meeting, Jack's head held between his hands at an angle suggesting emotional anguish while his parents bickered about how best to proceed.

There was nothing to do but wait. Baking myself seemed like the ideal activity; the feeling of sun on skin would serve as a fitting distraction. Slathering myself with SPF and wearing nothing but a wide-brimmed straw hat, I lay nude in our pool's floating chaise lounge for the better part of the afternoon and evening, bobbing and staring at the clarified sky through polarized sunglass lenses. I thought about Jack there with me, the scent of chlorine and coconut on his skin, his balls tightening in my hand as he eased into the cool water. How great it would feel to be lying on the warm concrete and have him leap from the water, taut and dripping, and lie on top of me, outlining each of my limbs with his own cold counterpart.

I kept hope as well that instead of the worst possible outcome— seeing his parents interrogating him on the couch, large yellow legal pads in both of their hands—I might plausibly encounter the best: Jack mowing the lawn at dusk for his weekly allowance money, freckles of blown dirt sticking to the sweat of his shirtless torso, his mesh basketball shorts slung down below the boxers on his hips. No one else home. In that case, I might be able to park the car and gradually happen upon him, feigning surprise: I'd just made a wrong turn looking for a friend's house, and then I thought I recognized him out cutting the grass and decided to say hello. Would he mind taking a break, letting me in to have a glass of water? I'd been running around all day; I was parched and he likely was too.

Should this happen, I wanted to be dressed accordingly. When I got out of the pool, I towel-dried my hair and added sea salt spray for messy curls. The sunblock had left a soft beachy fragrance on my skin. Shirking underwear, I put on a pair of terry-cloth lounge pants that sat below my belly button, a push-up bra and a T-shirt that would show just enough midriff. My hangover was causing me to crave starch, so I stopped at a drive-through on the way to his house and got a large order of French fries. I had a certain method of eating them. I liked to clamp down my lips on each one, pulling it through like a straw to get all the salt off, then rub the grains between my lips to make them raw and redden them. By the time I arrived at Jack's house, my lips stung badly enough to feel poisonous. I parked and the sound of my car's engine dying was immediately replaced with the harried drone of crickets everywhere.

The garage door was closed; no cars were parked in his driveway. But someone could have been home—a single front room was lit up and the curtains were open. I took the binoculars out of my glove compartment and moved to the passenger seat to see around the cluster of giant palms in the front yard. A closer view showed a middle-aged man passed out asleep on the sofa, a pizza box and two beer bottles on the coffee table. I searched every inch of the room I could view, but there was only the man—Jack wasn't there. It was Saturday night, I reasoned; it had been silly to get my hopes up. But there was still much to celebrate: the unconscious father figure meant the house wasn't locked down in any sort of emergency mode. Clearly, Jack hadn't said a word. I moved the binoculars over to Jack's darkened window and immediately dropped them.

I couldn't pick them back up fast enough. My chest began to surge; trying to find them on the floor, I felt like I might suffocate with adrenaline. Had I actually seen him?

When I finally got ahold of them beneath the seat, I thrust them up to my eyes so violently that I felt a volt of pain when their hard plastic hit the bone of my left brow. There, within two seven-centimeter circular lenses, I could see the shape of a body contrasting against the darkness. I focused the lenses further, my fingertips sweating. It was indeed Jack. His right arm rose and fell in repetitive motion, tugging against his crotch. The windowsill blocked me from seeing below his pelvis—the tip of his penis was visible, but nothing beneath it. Yet there in full view was the entirety of his torso, his flexed arm. What caused me to nearly scream as I shoved my fist into my underwear and began grinding my clit against my knuckles was the oddity of his posture and gaze; I came immediately, then continued to push against my pubic bone with the full force of my wrist, as if to try to muffle the insanity-producing sensation and stay in a state where I could, with full mental faculty, observe him as a specimen. He was staring out the window, straight up at the moon, wildly jerking off to a distant celestial body.

Watching him was so taunting that I felt like I was being injured; the longer I looked, the deeper the hot wound inside of me grew. When he finished he closed his eyes for just a moment, resting his forehead on the glass of the window. Then, suddenly, his head turned, and in a singular panicked motion he seemed to reach to his ankles for pants and disappear within his room. A quick rove of my binoculars over to the living room showed that the sleeping father had awakened and left the couch.

I felt like I'd been kidnapped and now had to escape while drugged—a fuzzy, sharp paralysis swam through my limbs and made it difficult to turn the key and start my car; my vision was blurred and a dull nausea churned in the back of my head. My body petitioned that my actions made no sense—everything I wanted, stripped down and clearly ready, was right there in wait, yet I was driving away in the opposite direction, an oxygen-deprived climber traveling farther up the mountain instead of making a descent. My feet were too heavy on the pedals; I pictured Janet's swollen feet grafted onto my ankles, the prosthetic hooflike shoes she wore tangling on the clutch and brake; at the first stoplight I arrived at, I stalled out. It was several minutes before I realized I'd left his subdivision through an alternate exit. Getting home would require many corrective turns. For a harried moment, with the fluorescent lights of the road and the strip-mall business swirling around me, I wondered if I could find my way home at all. Supposedly I knew exactly where I was—these were roads I drove daily. But there was a confusing pressure at the base of my skull and it was pulsing a blood rhythm not unlike the sound and speed of riot police striking their shields with their batons; it was a sound that thought and memory seemed to find threatening. Reason had evacuated my body. I felt like nothing more than a bomb with a steady timer attached, my heart counting down to an unknown hour of disaster.

When I finally found my street, I parked sideways in the driveway and stumbled in the door. My clothes felt like scratchy wool; I disrobed and stood in the dark, leaning against the cool drywall, panting. Moments or hours later when I heard Ford arrive home— the slam of his car door, a frustrated expletive because he had to park on the street due to my vehicle's position—I fell to my knees in the dark, squatting down like a dog in the hallway with my ass facing the door.

There was an incoming flood of light, then the hurried slamming of the door's screen.

"Celeste, Jesus, *hello*! Good thing I didn't bring Scottie back for a beer . . ." The sound of his locking the doorknob and dead bolt, drawing the chain.

"Can you turn the light back out?" I asked softly. Darkness. The sound of his belt being undone, his weapons coming off. My view as he took me from behind was the glass patio doors, through which I could see the full moon hanging in the sky, reflecting off our pool as if it was its point of origin. I stared up at it imagining not the brutish strength of Ford thrusting inside me but the inquisitive determination of Jack's body exploring the instinct of touch. The moment Ford finished I began to crawl away to the patio door, his semen dripping down my thighs like blood from an injury. Wordlessly, I jumped into the pool and sank to the very bottom, blowing every ounce of air in my body out with all the force of my lungs. The moon seemed to take up over half of the sky. I continued to stare as my lungs began to twinge with panic, my abdominal muscles struggling not to heave in for air, until a naked Ford, one hand cupping his genitals for fear of a nosy neighbor peeking over the fence, eclipsed the view, his mouth overenunciating. "What the hell are you doing?" read his lips. Then I slowly glided up the pool's slanted floor to the shallow end and surfaced.

I went back to Jack's house again Sunday night. Hoping for a repeat performance, I took great pains to leave the house at exactly the same time, park in the same spot. I fought the superstition that nagged me to wear dirty clothes I'd worn just the night before, step back into the doubtlessly hardened crotch of the terry-cloth pants I'd had on when I'd seen the erect and glistening tip of Jack's penis, his budding chest and arms in the full motions of exertion and his mouth parted to channel additional oxygen.

But he wasn't there; his window was closed. All I could see of his bedroom was a long, draped curtain, fallen as if to announce the show was over.

chapter six

Monday morning the sky was pouring rain to opacity. Students arrived with wet hair and soaked textbooks that had served as impromptu umbrellas. By third period muddy footprints leading from the door to the desks and back had formed the circular pattern of a complex dance diagram.

"There should be a tunnel or something, from the school to the outdoor classrooms," Marissa protested. Her shirt was soaked through, clinging to her breasts and the side rolls of her stomach. Jack came in a few moments later, a tracing of rain around his shoulders; he'd used a folder to shield his head and his hair had managed to stay nearly dry, but the calves of his legs had been showered. I watched each one of the drops snaking down his legs, some of them traveling all the way from above his knee in a manner that recalled urine. The innocence of that thought—a frightened Jack in the middle of the classroom, wetting himself; me undressing him from his soiled clothes, his damp tender skin cold to the touch—briefly clutched me in a fantasy of erotic mothering and made me long, oddly and briefly, for a more developed personal relationship with Jack. There was a turn-on to the suggestion that I might one day see him troubled, perhaps crying; that I might soothe and reassure him with a sympathy that could lead to a feeling of gratitude on his behalf. One that he would repay sexually, his eyes smiling up at me during cunnilingus. I gave the students a quick character-study quiz about Dimmesdale and his physical response to the guilt of his actions and then stared at the clock: I simply had to make it to the end of the class, mere minutes, and then my wait might possibly be over.

"So what can we learn about the poor, sad character of Arthur Dimmesdale?" I asked. Frank Pachenko raised his hand. Today he wore an actual raincoat, an oversized, red and shining version of the type a kindergartner might wear. It was a hideous color, like the erection of a dog.

"Secrets will fester inside you and make you sick," Frank reported. At all times, he had the cheerful air of being completely pleased with both himself and the world around him. I pictured him standing in that jacket with that same grin amidst several hundred buckets of fish entrails at the back dock of a busy seafood market. The kid simply wasn't one to let reality spoil a good time.

"Guilt will eat you alive!" Heath called from the back of the room with a dramatic flair, extending his upturned palms to the sky. I felt a pang of worry in my stomach at the effect the content of today's class might have on Jack—would it taint his view of the proposal he was about to receive? When I looked over at him he was watching the rain outside the classroom window, the glass pane alive with a metropolitan energy of moving water.

"Do you think he'd feel as tortured if Hester hadn't gotten pregnant and then been caught and punished?" I asked. "What if no one had ever found out—if they'd stayed two consenting individuals who simply got together outside the view of the uptight townspeople? Couldn't it have been kind of fun for them—an invigorating secret instead of a poisonous one?"

"Like when you're dating a girl on the down-low," Danny said.

"Right . . . sometimes the whole crux of the excitement is actually based on the fact that it's a secret," I added enthusiastically, hoping some of the conversation was filtering through Jack's daydream. "Unfortunately, pregnancy revealed Hester's half of the secret. Now Dimmesdale is suffering with a sort of survivor's guilt for not being taken down in the scandal as well."

A discussion ensued ("This one time, I was dating this girl but I also kind of technically had a girlfriend . . ."), though I was careful to stay in the vicinity of Jack's desk at the back of the room; I had to be next to him when the final bell rang. When it sounded, I stopped right next to the entry side of his desk so it wasn't even possible for him to get up. "Jack," I said, standing utterly still amidst the bustle of the students around us rallying to exit. "Stay behind for a moment so we can talk."

He nodded, imperceptibly at first, but then he looked up and gave me a slightly worried smile.

"Thank you, Jack." I took a seat in the desk directly behind him, staring at the blond trail of hair on the base of his neck that swirled discreetly to the right. When the room had emptied, part of me wondered if I should skip the pretense of words entirely—simply stand and disrobe, then ask him to follow suit.

I cleared my throat. "What I need to say to you is a little embarrassing, Jack. I think it's best, at least at the beginning, if you keep looking forward and I talk directly to your back, just like we're doing now. Is that all right with you?"

His head nodded. I eyed the waistband of his baggy shorts; my hand could easily slip down their back and touch the base of his tailbone. It was hard to continue talking. But I needed to establish for Jack that our actions wouldn't be wrong; I also needed to see if Jack would put out any verbal warnings. I kept reminding myself that if he didn't respond to my advance, if he told, I could simply deny it—I was only speaking words; they couldn't be proven. "Good. I need to ask one favor from you before I even begin. No matter what I say, no matter what it makes you feel or think, I need you to promise me that you'll stay in your seat."

He nodded again, the muscles of his back tensing rigidly upright. Outside, the rain gave a long, windy gust. I wanted him to feel like he wasn't simply keeping my secret—that I was keeping one of his as well.

"I was driving by your house on Saturday night," I admitted. "When we first got our rosters, I recognized your address. A friend of mine lived on your street once. So when I was over by your neighborhood, I just decided to drive past your house and see if the subdivision had changed much. I didn't actually expect to see you, but I did. I slowed down to look at the houses and I saw you in your room." I took in a deep breath, hoping what I said next wouldn't make him run. "You didn't have your clothes on. You were touching yourself."

His hands slid up to his face and over the back of his head. "God," he said. His breathing broke into an unusual pattern; for a moment I thought he might cry. "You can see into my bedroom from the street? But it's so far back on the side . . ." In a perfect world, I could've assured him that without binoculars one probably couldn't see inside very well at all, but discretion warranted I keep this detail to myself. "Are you going to tell my dad?"

"Of course not, Jack. You weren't doing anything wrong." Now I leaned inward toward him, wishing I could fast-forward past my words to his reaction. "But since I saw you there, doing that without your clothes on, I haven't been able to think about anything else." I paused for emphasis but there was only silence; Jack was frozen. No part of his body moved. "All I can think about is touching you. I want to touch you so badly that I've decided to just ask you if you'll let me touch you." The tardy bell sounded, a sharp quick cut into the static of the rain. I let the shock of its noise dissolve, then continued. "What I'm saying is that you turned me on."

It wasn't possible to read an answer into his unchanged posture. "You can look at me now," I finally said. He turned, expressionless, and I decided to play at a lack of confidence. My eyes drew toward the floor. "You probably think I'm old and gross."

"N-no," he finally stuttered. "I don't at all. You're beautiful, I mean." He looked directly at me, studying my face as if to make a medical diagnosis. "You could be on television."

I gave him a pleased smile. "You really think that?"

He nodded with an unfiltered, strictly adolescent sincerity. "Yeah. All the guys talk about you. Everyone was, like, blown away when you showed up on the first day."

I reached one hand toward him and began moving a finger lightly across his arm. "I'm not interested in all the guys. I'm interested in you, Jack." I'd said enough about me; it was time to shift the blame of desire back onto him. "Have you ever thought about me? The way you were thinking at your window Saturday night?" When he didn't answer I paused so as to seem embarrassed and decided there wasn't harm in leading him even further; he didn't look frightened or outraged. "I've thought about you," I said quietly. "Since Saturday I've thought about you a lot."

"Yes," he finally answered. His voice was shaking. "You're really pretty."

"Can I please kiss you, Jack?" I closed my eyes and found his silent mouth with my own. His lips were perfectly sized, almost exactly the length of mine, his mouth not so large, like Ford's, as to make my own tongue seem insubstantial inside of it. I pushed my lips hard against his teeth, gripped a section of soft hair on the back of his head. Minutes later when I opened my eyes to pull away, I saw that his were already drawn wide—they'd been open and staring the entire time. I moved my hand up his leg and he squirmed a little, ashamed.

"I got kind of . . . ," he started.

"I know." I smiled. "I want to feel it. I love that you're hard." He nodded and I traced my hand along the firm length in his cargo shorts. I noticed he was peeking down the dip in my blouse at my breasts. "Do you want to see them?" I whispered. I squeezed his erection; despite the dense canvas of his shorts, I could make out the circumcised shape of his tip beneath my fingers.

His wet lips fell slightly open as he nodded. "Let me go lock the door." I walked to the desk and grabbed my purse; to avoid faculty accidentally getting locked out of their classroom, the knob could only be locked with a key. The sound of the clanking metal as the bolt shut into place felt like a small, perfect kick in the center of my loins—here we were, locked up and perfectly free.

I unbuttoned my shirt as I walked back to him, removed it and placed it carefully on one of the desks. Standing for a moment in my bra and my skirt, I let him take a long look at me before I unhooked it and placed it on the desk as well. "Come touch me," I said.

He stood and walked over very carefully, as though the offer was some spell he might break with loud footsteps. He stopped a few inches away from me and stood, paralyzed and transfixed, until I grabbed his neck and pulled his mouth back to mine. Soon I felt his tentative hands sliding up the sides of my stomach.

His tongue grew still inside my mouth as his hand cupped my breast and found my nipple. Rubbed arbitrarily by the uncertain strokes of his lost fingers, it hardened to the point of aching, and gripping his head in my hands I forced his lips from my mouth to my chest. He latched on and my eyes closed; for a moment the sound of the rain was so loud that it sounded like the roof had opened; I gave a short scream as a quick orgasm bit down through the center of me. It hardly lasted a second after I perceived it, ending with the abrupt halt of an unplugged current the second Jack's lips fell away. "Are you okay?" he asked.

My appetite was roaring; the incomplete contractions had awakened every sensory cell in my body. In seconds I could've hoisted my skirt and slid my panties just a centimeter over, unzipped his pants and felt exactly what I needed, his anatomy's tentative push delivering a wave of release that in that moment might've truly felt endless. Yet I knew our first time couldn't be right there—I had to give him a little space, even if that meant only a few hours, for things to sink in and the next step to become his idea. I couldn't smother him in unexpected sex, then send him off to chemistry having feelings so strong and confusing that he had to do something horrible like go and talk about them.

"I'm fine," I answered. "It was a good scream." I glanced up at the clock. "Look, I've gone and made you miss nearly all your lunch. I'm sorry."

His face was the most earnest thing I'd ever seen; it held a near-alien amount of honesty. "I don't mind," he said.

I pushed my breasts against his chest, feeling the hardened tiny buds of his own nipples through his shirt. "I hope you realize how amazing you are," I whispered, kissing his bottom lip. "We're only able to do this because I know I can trust you not to tell anyone."

"I won't tell," he said, his arms holding my waist with an amateur stiffness. I smiled, thinking about the lover he'd become and all the things he'd try with me for the very first time. I'd be the sexual yardstick for his whole life: Jack would spend the rest of his days trying but failing to relive the experience of being given everything at a time when he knew nothing. Like a tollbooth in his memory, every partner he'd have afterward would have to pass through the gate of my comparison, and it would be a losing equation. The numbers could never be as favorable as they were right now, when his naïveté would be subtracted from my expertise to produce the largest sum of astonishment possible.

"Of course you won't. Not even to your very best friend. That would mean that all the fun would be over." Topless, I walked to my desk and sat down to write him a note, giving him a new daydream image for the boring minutes of our class together. Now any time I sat at my desk he could vividly imagine me naked. I handed him the note, then began to put on my bra. "Don't worry"—I winked—"you'll see them again soon. If anyone asks where you were, remind them you were absent Friday and say you were getting notes. We can't do this too much at school; we don't want to push our luck. Is there a time after school you can meet me somewhere else?"

"Yeah," he said. His brow knotted with a worrying thought; for a moment he tried to shake it but eventually asked, "Aren't you married?"

"Adult relationships are complicated, Jack. All you need to know is that we can do anything we want if no one finds out about it."

"My parents are divorced," he offered, picking up his backpack.

"Then you have some insight about the great range of human

behavior." I gave him another kiss; I meant it to be quick but his cushioned lips pulled me in and soon I was rubbing my leg across his erection. The bell signaling the end of lunch sounded and I let out an audible groan. "Just go straight to your next class," I said, heavy breaths slowing my words. "No one will know you missed lunch except your friends."

"I have to get rid of this," he said, looking down.

"Hold your backpack over it." I placed my hand on his shoulder and began walking him to the door. "That will go away when you start walking. There's nothing sexy about hurrying to class."

Now I had to reveal a bit of planning on my part; I hoped it wouldn't make things seem too contrived. I reached into my purse and handed him a prepaid cell phone. "Take this. My number is the only contact programmed in. Only use this phone to text me. No one else. Don't call anyone else on it, don't text anyone else on it." The number was for a matching prepaid in my car that I'd bought with cash over the summer—an optimistic venture that helped me manage the long wait for classes to begin.

He looked at the phone in his hand like it was a living thing, a small animal he hoped might wake up soon.

"Put it away," I urged. "Never bring it to school. Text me later if you can meet up." With that, I gave him a kiss on the neck that ended with a small lick upon his pulse point, unlocked the door and watched him stumble out into the rain.

In that day's remaining three classes, time seemed to stretch and bend. I found myself constantly looking to the clock, then back out to the students' faces. By sixth period my extended suffering led me to audibly lament my predicament. "Do you ever feel like the school day will never be over?" The classroom became a landscape of nodding heads.

"You're, like, the only adult who gets it, Mrs. Price," Trevor said. My eyes found him in the back of the room and I smiled. He'd hooked up with a new girlfriend, a quirky thing named Darcy who hadn't the faintest idea how to correctly use a comma. They sat together in the back, holding hands across the desks and playing footsie while passing a notebook of inside jokes back and forth. Now as I watched Trevor's fingers rubbing Darcy's palm with rhythmic small circles, I found that my jealousy at their ability to touch openly in the classroom was a nice torture, like running my finger through a lighter's flame just a little too slowly; I liked the way it drove me crazy thinking about what could be in store with Jack tonight. Were Darcy and Trevor having sex yet? At least oral, I figured. Like two human leopards, their necks, as well as Darcy's upper chest, were spotted with a series of hickeys ranging from maroon to a twilight purple.

When the bell did finally ring, all the students save the happy couple ran from the classroom. Trevor and Darcy were always the last to leave, each bogged down in the fog of consideration, imploring one another with offers of assistance and questions about after-school plans. Then they headed for my desk, where Trevor liked to make a comment that aimed to be impressive while Darcy stood by him silently like a conjoined twin. "Have you seen the movie version where Hester and Dimmesdale do it in a pile of wheat?" he asked.

I nodded. "It looks good but I don't know if nudity and grain particles mix. It seems kind of like beach sex, right? There are some places where sand can be downright painful." The shock on their faces was sweet to devour. They began to laugh as the door swung wide, an opened drain that sucked all the levity and oxygen from the room. Assistant Principal Rosen walked in. Oddly, my first thought wasn't of Jack at all but the joke I'd just told—had he been listening at the door? But then it came to me in a single blow that felt as though I might have an accident in my chair; my stomach twisted hot and sharp and the sound of my pulse swelled inside my ears. I licked my lips, feeling my armpits begin to dampen. "Trevor, Darcy, I'll see you tomorrow."

Rosen scowled at the pair, examining their necks with a look of repulsion. His wing-tip loafers moved back a few steps to allow them a wider berth by which to exit. He seemed to think their hickeys were the contagious sores of leprosy. "No holding hands," he called after them. "All students signed an anti-PDA contract on the first day of classes, remember? Page two of the conduct handbook?" Their hands fell apart momentarily, then rejoined with the force of attaching magnets the moment they stepped outside the classroom. I gave a nervous laugh.

"Young love," I joked. He began an assessing loop around the classroom, stopping to examine each lame poster the textbook companies sent that I'd half-assedly taped to the walls in an effort to blend in. There was a timeline of Shakespeare's life, the text of Edgar Allan Poe's "The Raven" printed in microscopic lettering to form the overall shape of a large black bird.

"Celeste," he began, his tone sullen, "I'm afraid we have a problem." Scanning my desk, my eyes fell on the metal body of the industrial stapler. It might be possible, if I hit him hard enough with it on the back of the head to knock him unconscious, for me to escape if the police weren't yet there. I pictured them leading me away in handcuffs as Ford, having heard the location of the arrest on his CB, pulled up and ran toward me, suspecting there'd been a misunderstanding his connections might easily clear up. I stood and gingerly walked over to the window to peek through the blinds for cop cars.

"This is an awkward conversation for me," he admitted. "I don't enjoy this part of my job at all. No administrator wants situations like these to come up. But when they do, they fall on my plate."

I didn't see any vehicles on the east side of the building. Crossing the room, I looked out the blinds of a west-facing window. Perhaps the police hadn't been called yet? Since it was one of the better school districts, I realized it was quite possible they didn't want the arrest to take place on school grounds. Maybe things hadn't reached the point of arrest—maybe they'd only heard hallway talk from a few of Jack's friends, enough to summon Jack down to the office, but he'd denied it; nevertheless, such allegations had to be taken seriously and I'd be suspended pending an investigation. The fact that Jack had told others, and had told them immediately, was infinitely problematic. Could my instincts about him have been that wrong? Blinded by lust, I supposed, anything was possible. Perhaps what I was most guilty of was impatience.

"I know you're new here," he continued. "And I don't want you to get the impression that this is a common occurrence. In fact this is one of the only situations of its kind we've ever had to deal with." He walked up to my desk and rapped the knuckles of his balled fist against it a few times. "I'll be honest with you," he said, turning his back to me. "It pisses me off more than I can even say."

The classroom door was close—mere feet away from where I was standing. I had the urge to run, though that would merely prolong the inevitable. It would also seem a positive admission of guilt. Perhaps things weren't as bad as I feared; maybe Rosen didn't believe the rumors at all. It could actually be the students he was pissed at, the randy boys who'd let their imaginations go wild over the attractive young teacher during her first semester on the job.

"Janet Feinlog has got to go," he said flatly.

"Janet?" Relief flooded my chest with a mentholated cooling sensation; I found myself smiling uncontrollably and even let out a little laugh. He turned his stern face to me and wrinkled his brow. "I'm sorry," I said, trying to recover, "excuse my reaction. It's just that Janet is such a strange bird."

He nodded. "Strange isn't the half of it. She's a horrible teacher. Her students' section of the FCAT has been the lowest of the district for the past decade. Her classroom is unruly; we get more parent complaints about Janet than all the other teachers combined. She has no rapport with teenagers. Do you know what she told one of the parents at open house?"

"Oh no," I said.

"Oh yes. She told a parent, a *mother,* that she has fantasies of working in a juvenile detention center where they make the kids wear shock collars."

Objectively, I could see how Janet might excel in such a position.

"She can't continue here. Now, this is pathetic seeing as you've been with us for all of two months, but I think you're the best friend Janet has on staff. You're the only one I've ever heard her say good things about. Apparently you pushed some volunteer help her way?"

"I just want Janet to be as effective of a teacher as possible." I smiled. "For the kids."

"Well I truly appreciate that. But I think our efforts are lost on this one. I need your input on breaking the news to her. We'll have security escort her from the building, of course, but I'd still prefer to make as small a scene as possible. I just can't read the woman. Do you think she's capable of doing something violent? Returning to the campus with a weapon?"

I winced at how easily I could picture Janet holding an automatic rifle while wearing an oversized yellow smiley-face T-shirt. "Well . . ."

"Sorry," he said. "My mind tends to go dark. On the brighter side, Janet's departure will free up a classroom in the main building, and you'll have seniority over whomever we hire to replace her. No more stepchild in the attic." He smiled. "We can move you on up to the big house."

Suddenly all the panic inside me that had recently drained gushed back in full force. The main building meant doors with glass viewing panels, other faculty constantly dropping in unannounced with their petty needs. Everything said in class would be audible from the hallway—no more sex talk veiled behind a thin veneer of literary studies. No more swearing. No more private flirtations with Jack after the bell rang.

"Mr. Rosen"—I smiled, running my fingers through my hair with a slow thoughtfulness—"I do absolutely agree with you that things have got to change. But I wonder if Janet might be able to turn things around with the further help of some mentoring. My student teaching days generated such . . . energy in me. And this Mrs. Pachenko who's working with Janet . . . I'm really excited about that partnership. Mrs. Pachenko is completely by the book."

He took a seat on my desk, his pants rising up to reveal trouser socks patterned with rows of tiny rainbow-trout icons. "Go on."

"What if every few weeks I started observing Janet's classroom during my grading period? I could give her feedback and submit reports to you of her progress, or her lack of progress. And maybe I could get her to come observe my class during her grading period. It might give her a new perspective. Like you said, she and I have a good working relationship. I think she'd be open to it, coming from me."

He shrugged. "Well that's very generous of you. I'm ready to throw in the towel and burn it. But she certainly can't get any worse. If there's a way to avoid the headache of having to fire a longtime union worker, I'm all for it."

"Thank you." I smiled. "I'm glad for the opportunity."

He tilted his head and gave a pleased nod in my direction. "If even a quarter of the faculty had your spirit, we'd have the best school in North America." Standing, he offered his hand, which I embraced between both of mine. "We're very lucky to have you here."

On his way out, he stopped and pointed his arm across the rows of empty chairs. "But luckiest of all are all these kids. You're fantastic with them. I know." He winked. "I've got my ear to the ground."

chapter seven

That night at 7:23 P.M., I picked Jack up for the first time in front of a combination Taco Bell/Long John Silver's. It wasn't dark yet, but in the low light of sunset, eyes could easily be mistaken— passersby thinking they saw Jack entering a red Corvette might have to admit that it could've been any boy his size who looked similar, and though they were nearly certain of the make and model of the car, perhaps the color, tinged by the sunset's pink glare, had only looked red in that moment.

"Thanks for coming." I smiled. "Buckle up."

He'd changed into a different, preppier outfit than he'd worn to school; in fact he looked ready to go to a casual job interview at a supermarket—khakis and a striped polo shirt—and the very ends of his hair were slightly wet, telling of a recent shower. His skin bore a soapy-sweet fragrance of cologne; I smiled thinking of the bitter flavor its spice would leave on my tongue. "I like your car," he offered.

I began to head out of town toward the nearby bay area and its long rows of mangroves where we could park undisturbed. The traffic soon began to perturb me—it was an unwelcome contrast to the adolescent morsel strapped into my passenger seat. We immediately became trapped behind a livestock truck of chickens; when I was finally able to pass, a hideous woman simultaneously operating a station wagon and cramming a Whopper into her mouth came into view. "Aren't people revolting in general?" I complained.

Jack offered back a polite smile. I noticed him eyeing the car's center console, my hand gripping the top of the gearshift.

"Can you drive a stick?"

He shook his head. "I wish. I can't drive at all. I can get my learner's in February though."

"Well we'll have to give you some lessons," I offered. This seemed to please him a great deal, although it wasn't a genuine proposal. But I followed it up with a more earnest suggestion. "Jack?"

"Yes?" He was so nervous that it was hard for me to gauge his level of horniness.

"You can touch me, you know. Anywhere you want while I drive. My windows are tinted." He swallowed and looked straight ahead for a moment, rubbing his sweaty palms against his pants while giving himself an inward pep talk.

"Okay." He finally nodded. He placed a sweaty hand on my bare knee, then sat motionless for a minute before his fingers began to gently move in one direction and then another, sliding incrementally farther up my thigh. I began to moan but my enthusiasm was slightly dampened when we passed a graphic pro-life billboard, then an advertisement for septic repair service whose mascot was an anthropomorphized plunger. I sighed—Jack and I needed a highway all our own, devoid of reminders about life's daily vulgarities. Even the rusted exteriors of the jalopies we sped by seemed ominous harbingers of unwelcome news, announcing that my time with Jack, that our bodies and everything we'd each ever known, would all inevitably decay and fall apart.

In an attempt to get his hand closer to my genitals, I lifted my pelvis off the seat, pushing it forward against his fingers in a way that forced me to widen the placement of my legs on the floor and the gas pedal and hunch over the steering wheel for balance in a crablike pose. I reminded myself not to scare him at first with outright demands for more; instead I praised the very restrained motions he was managing. "That feels so good, Jack." I stole a quick look at his face as I peered behind my seat to change lanes and get on the highway; his eyes were fixed wide upon my airborne lap. Not once did Jack ask me where we were going. He had a perfect sense of what wasn't important.

Eventually his fingers found a rhythm of stroking my thigh, which made it hard not to close my eyes in pleasure for seconds at a time, but the distractions of the road did finally seem to fade. I didn't feel like I was driving or even knew where we were going; instead it seemed the vehicle had been programmed to whisk us off to privacy and I was there merely to steer. Each time Jack's slippery fingers massaged my leg I contemplated stopping earlier and choosing a closer place, but I knew I had to let strategy override lust for just a while longer—what we were about to do was dangerous enough; impulsive decisions would open the door to a whole new set of risky variables. I stayed on the highway until the planned exit, keeping my needs temporarily reined in, and made every single turn required to arrive at an outpost of the lost. Jack's shaking had risen from a shiver to a tremor. "Are you cold?" I asked. Jack didn't seem to know how to respond.

"I'm not sure," he finally said.

Roughly half an hour after I'd picked him up, we pulled into the overgrown tree-lined drive of a long-abandoned farm. "It's safe here," I announced. He nodded back at me, eyes filled with eager uncertainty, looking briefly out his car window into the pitch-blackness surrounding us as if to scan for predators. "No one's going to interrupt us," I stressed, my voice a honeyed invitation. "We're in the middle of nowhere."

With that I took off my shirt, watching his eyes lock onto my bra. There was a Christmas-morning feel to the way I slid off my shorts to reveal lace thong panties, then crawled over the console, purposefully arching my spine to push my left butt cheek inches from his face as I jumped into the backseat—every step of the process seemed like a new gift being given. "It's a little cramped, but we can lie down." I motioned to him. "Take off your clothes and come back here with me." He removed his shirt, then his shoes and pants, lifting himself toward me with a visible erection beneath his blue boxers.

"You have a great body," I told him. His build was the slender, undeveloped wiry sort whose tautness revealed the shadowy promise of muscles not yet arrived.

"I'm too skinny," he began, but I quickly placed one hand across his mouth to avoid further speech and with the other began rubbing across his chest and down his stomach, dipping a finger inside the elastic band of his shorts to stroke the starting delineation of his pubic hair. I felt his lips part beneath my hand to breathe more heavily; his eyes were traveling a vertical circuit from my crotch up to my breasts. "Have you ever taken off a girl's bra before?" He shook his head no. "They're mysterious little contraptions," I said, turning my back to him and raising the veil of my blond hair over my right shoulder to clear his view. "Go ahead and give it a try." His hands shook as he stumbled with the tiny metal hooks; he was nearly panting as he bent in closer to my back, struggling to see the bra's petite mechanics in the dark. I could smell the mint chewing gum on his breath—he'd indeed prepared himself for a make-out session. Could consent have been any more transparent? Eventually I felt the release of its pressure and Jack gave a victorious sigh.

"Bravo." I smiled at him from over my shoulder, then dropped the bra to the ground and turned back to face him bare-chested. "You've got me pretty worked up, Jack." His hands were down at his sides, bracing; he'd scooted back over to the right, as far away from me as the tiny backseat would allow. I got up on all fours and crawled over to him, my breasts hanging level with his face. "Feel how hard my nipples are." He started to reach out his hand but I pulled away and gave him a teasing smile. "Not with your fingers," I said, correcting him. "With your tongue."

Nodding, he scooted closer and stuck his tongue as far out from his lips as he could manage, as though he'd just been dared to lick a metal pole in the winter. His eyes were open wide, visually taking in the target—he seemed to be worried that he wouldn't be able to find my breast if he closed them. I lowered my head and watched the pink-on-pink contact, my nipple beginning to glisten with Jack's saliva. Dutifully, he fully wetted one, moved over and wetted the other, then sat back and looked up at me with eyes that awaited further instruction. "That felt perfect," I said encouragingly. "I knew you'd be really good at this." I sat down in front of him with my legs bent open; the thin lace string of the thong covered the tip of my clitoris but not much else. "Have you ever put your fingers inside a girl?"

Even in the dark I could make out the hot blush that was covering his cheeks. "I haven't done much," he said. The sound of his breathing suggested he was running away from something.

"Why is that?" I asked. "You're certainly good-looking." My

hands wrapped around the jersey of his cloth-covered penis and began to stroke. He folded a leg up and sat on it, squirming with nervous energy as the speed of my fingers increased. Compliments seemed to freak him out more than relax him.

"I'm just shy with girls I guess," he said. I watched him swallow three times before speaking again. "I never know what to say."

I lifted my hands from the wad of fabric swirled up around the shape of his erection and found the panel opening of the crotch, then slowly moved it down to reveal his penis. Lowering my head so my hair fell across it, I spoke just above it like it was a microphone. "You can relax, Jack," I said, bathing its tip in my warm breath. "You don't have to say anything." With that, I licked my lips, then slid them down over him, slowly arching my neck and extending my throat until my mouth came to the base. He made a gasping noise and bucked a little, writhing in a disoriented way that bumped the head of his cock against the roof of my mouth. I gave him a quick thirty seconds of advanced sucking, my tongue fluttering against his underside until I could taste the salty bitters of pre-ejaculate, then sat back up and wiped my mouth off on my arm.

His face had transformed into a foreign mask of disbelief. He looked down at his erection as though he was trying to confirm it was still attached to his body. I grabbed his right hand, which was clammy and limp, bereft of all resistance. I felt like I needed to continue talking to him, the way one would a victim of hypothermia, to keep him conscious and prevent him from going into shock. "You've seen pictures of girls on the Internet, right?" I began moving his fingers across the sides of my exposed labia. "Did they have hair down there or were they shaved?" He closed his eyes for a moment, flipping through his mental catalog and trying to remember in earnest, and I took this opportunity of blindness to guide two of his fingers inside me, pushing my hips forward to meet them. When he opened his eyes again, he did so slowly, like someone who's seen an apparition and tried to make it go away by tightly squeezing his lids shut, hoping it might disappear if he gave it a chance to escape unwatched. "Well?" I smiled, my pelvis bucking up against his fingers in rhythmic movements. "Shaved or unshaved?" I couldn't believe how close we were to actually doing it. I had the growing paranoia that some bizarre act of nature was about to intervene and prevent our sex from happening—lightning was going to strike down and bisect the car, throwing Jack and me to opposite, smoking ends, or a sinkhole to the center of the earth was opening just below the convertible, about to send the vehicle plummeting. I pictured us, airborne and naked in the backseat of the falling car, trying desperately to crawl toward one another against the forces of gravity so he could stuff his penis inside me for just one moment before death.

"I guess I've seen both," he whispered.

Lifting off from his fingers, I stood upright on my knees and braced against the ceiling, gripping the garment hook above the door for balance. "You know what's fun?" I asked, squaring my vagina in front of his mouth. "If you take my panties off with your teeth." He glanced down at his wet fingers for a moment, taking in the reality of them, then brought his mouth to my underwear and grabbed at their elastic, lightly scraping the skin around it with his incisors. His head slowly lowered, his nose grazing my pubic bone, and I let out a relieved shout of ecstasy as the top of his head moved down my leg, my thighs nearly straddling the back of his neck. When my thong fell loose to my knees and he sat back, only a slight tilt of my pelvis was required—I leaned forward and in a single moist click-and-lock was sitting atop him, fully impaled by every inch he had to offer: it had happened. It had actually, finally happened. In many ways, I realized, this was a bigger first time for me than it was for Jack. Sliding back, I pulled his torso down until he was lying nearly flat along the backseat, grabbed his hands and placed them on my breasts as I began to push against him with slow, rocking-horse motions. For an instant I felt like spontaneously crying at the release of it—in that moment I had everything I wanted; every action of my adult life had been engaged in setting up a situation that would allow me to feel exactly this: the slim, curious pressure of a teenage boy pushing into the center of my being.

Our orgasms were almost instantaneous. I looked down into his face and saw both ecstasy and loss—the running comprehension of his brain, always one long step behind his body, attempting to tally what had happened, what was happening, and what was almost over. His eyes registered a sense of bewilderment at his lack of control, then an involuntary and guttural noise of surprise left his mouth. The unpracticed wince of his face as it contorted tipped off my own; I dropped my hips and pushed into his erection with all my force as he began to spasm. Several moments passed before I looked down again at his eyes and saw fear—when I came, I'd probably screamed in a manner reserved for the fatally injured.

But my breath soon returned. I dismounted and felt the leather seat lock onto my wet skin. My crotch was a hot pool of spent pleasure; the slow drip of his fluid leaving my body felt like a deep ache inside me that had finally been purged. My mind immediately raced forward to after I'd drop Jack off at home—there would then be the additional delight, perhaps an act that would become part of the ritual, of stopping in a parking lot to wipe our fluids off the car seat.

The windows of the car had fogged up; I reached into the front seat to grab my shirt and first wiped Jack's brow, his sweat clinging the small bright curls of hair against his forehead, then wiped the sweat from my own face and between and beneath my breasts before clearing off the two windows on the driver's side of the car. Finished, I passed the shirt to Jack, and he wiped down the two on his side.

"That was the best sex of my life, Jack." He smiled; his eyes bashfully dodged my own but his face held a definite glow of pride.

"Mine too," he said, then, realizing his own joke, began to giggle. Now that it was over, the lust no longer there to suppress his modesty, Jack seemed embarrassed of his body—he'd lifted his knees up to his chest.

I reached up into the front seat and turned the key, blasting a cool stream of air-conditioning back onto us, and looked at the clock. It felt like we'd been there for hours, but it had only been twenty minutes.

"Are you hungry? Do you want to go to a drive-through?" Jack nodded. He reached to the floor and pulled his underwear back on, and I climbed up into the front seat to grab our clothes, hoping he was staring at my ass and the glossy spill covering my thighs. I knew it would be a while before he stopped being too timid to do something like mount me from behind and have me again. I looked back to see—if he was erect, we could easily have another session in this new position. But his penis was flaccid and he was looking out the window. And yet, I reasoned, it was hard for him to want what he didn't know he could have—it probably didn't cross his mind that sex again already was possible.

"Jack," I called softly. When he looked up at me, his eyes immediately fell right where they should have. "I want you to feel comfortable with my body," I said, turning my head around so he was left unsupervised with my backside squatted toward him. "Why don't you have another look?" I asked. When he still hadn't touched me after a long minute, I gave him direction. "Spread my cheeks apart," I whispered, turning to watch him. He sat for a moment, contemplating, like a child who had once touched a hot stove and now wanted to overcome his fear by daring himself to place a hand on its burner when the electricity was off. Gradually his thin fingers slid up my legs and across the patches of drying cum between my thighs, then he gripped the flesh of my cheeks at their fullest point and pulled them to opposing sides. My asshole immediately tightened as I felt a cold shock of air from the side vent upon it. Reaching one arm back, my hand landed on his knee. "Come closer," I urged. Now that I might have him again, it seemed I hadn't had him at all—every ounce of my original desire returned. My fingers crawled up his leg to the nexus of his crotch, and with a small bend of my elbow, I was able to grip the base of him and gently pull. He obediently scooted up closer to the edge of his seat. When I balanced on my knees, I was finally able to straddle over him backward and sit down on his lap.

There were a few awkward limp thrusts when I wasn't sure he was responding, but soon his nascent erection began to quicken. He even grabbed my hips for better leverage as he lifted himself up and down. I turned my head and began kissing him more violently than I meant to; I couldn't restrain myself. He was simply right there for the taking. "Do it as hard as you can," I breathed, and he did, the speed making him feel larger inside me as he strove toward climax. When he came his teeth involuntarily clenched together, nearly catching my tongue between them; I slid his right hand around from my hip onto my clit and pubis in broad, mashing strokes. It was the thought of his small fist punching up into me that made my whole body begin to shake until I'd slid off the seat; soon my spent limbs were splayed between the floor and the front passenger seat, my ass unceremoniously positioned upward in the air. For a moment the car was filled with nothing but the sound of our panting breath; desire had chased us long and hard.

"Do you need help up?" he finally asked.

My position on the ground suggested I'd been tossed from my seat in a car accident. I took a deep breath and uncrumpled my limbs, pushing my damp hair from my face. Wordlessly, I reached up and grabbed his shirt and pants and my shorts. We dressed in silence and said nothing as we moved back into the front of the car, though the soreness between my legs when I spread them to climb over the console was such a pleasant sort of ache that I nearly swore. A hurried urge to get him back home suddenly came over me—I wanted plenty of time alone with my own fantasied memories of the evening before Ford got off work.

Two exits outside of town we got milkshakes and burgers and parked in front of a closed appliance store to eat. There was a clear eroticism to every action Jack made—ripping open the ketchup packet with his teeth, taking the top off the milkshake cup to attack the whipped cream with his tongue; I didn't know if it was an intentional tease or if his actions normally held such innuendoed physicality. "We don't have this restaurant in town," he commented. "Their milkshakes are really good."

"You'll see me again, won't you, Jack?" I'd taken the cherry off the top of my milkshake to suck, holding its stem between my lips as I looked at him with imploring eyes. He used his arm like a napkin on the whipped cream in the corners of his mouth and I smiled. "Besides in class, I mean."

He nodded eagerly, then ran his fingers across the grooves in the top of the gearshift, reading it like Braille, turning to me with a hopeful expression. "Can we do this every night?"

His forehead was still sweaty. I brushed at it with a napkin, pausing to tuck a fold of hair back against the side of his head. "Probably not every single night. Hopefully most nights though." I started the car but turned the radio down low as I pulled out of the parking lot; from Jack's tentative expression, it seemed like he had more to say.

"Should I drop you off at the same place?" I started.

He gave a small nod. "It's going to feel really weird being in class tomorrow." We pulled up to a stoplight and I noticed a shoddy hotel, the Toucan Inn, on my left. I imagined checking into it with Jack and the shroud of anonymity we'd have to function under, the way the coming months would force us to date like criminals on the lam, shirking anyplace public, any activity that might require ID.

"Want to go to that motel sometime?" I pointed. "It won't be clean enough to get under the sheets but I'll bet there's a nice setup of mirrors in each room." His face took on a blank expression, like his mind had to unfold new and never-used corners to process what I'd just said. I placed a reassuring hand on his upper leg and squeezed. "Don't worry about class. You're always daydreaming in there, anyway. What are you thinking about?" He shrugged.

"Stupid stuff, I dunno. Whatever comes into my head. I don't usually even remember. One minute I'm staring off into space and then suddenly a teacher's calling on me." He bent over and began putting his shoes back on. "Mrs. Feinlog is the worst about that. She pretends like she's NASA or something. 'Jack, Jack, you're lost in orbit.' She's such an idiot."

"I'm sorry she picks on you. She doesn't have many advantages in life." I pulled back into the Taco Bell lot and felt a deep sense of normalcy: here we were right where we'd started—it had actually happened, and no one else knew. Jack sat casually slouched in the passenger seat and continued to make small talk for a few minutes. He certainly didn't seem traumatized or the victim of something harmful—in fact his expression was alive with a dewy glow. Far more so than when I'd first picked him up, he looked spirited and engaged. He looked improved.

"So when are you unsupervised this week?" I asked. He seemed to get the joke, a thin smile spreading over his lips as he thought.

"My mom lives in Crystal Springs; it's just me and my dad. Usually he's home by six but I'm alone from when I get home at four until then." His face suddenly brightened with the realization of good news. "And Wednesdays he's never home before nine . . . he stays late to do continuing education for the new service reps. IT maintenance stuff. He doesn't really like me to go out on school nights."

"Oh? How did you manage to come meet me?"

Jack laughed. "I told him I had a group project for English tonight. But during the week you could come over any afternoon before he gets home."

I felt my crotch seize at the thought of fucking Jack on his own bed with the musky funk of early adolescence rising from his sheets, everything in the room surrounding us related to him in a way that would make his body feel magnified. His home was a better location than I'd ever let myself imagine—I'd been expecting only sex in the outdoors, in my car, perhaps occasionally breaking up the monotony with faraway venues: in darkened out-of-town theaters for a poorly attended movie to which we separately bought tickets. His home meant a bathtub and shower, a pool, a kitchen table, a host of variety. "That would be great but it could be risky. Do any of your classmates live on your street?"

Jack shook his head. "Some of the guys live close in the subdivision, but not on my same street." There was a pause as his forehead lifted with memory. "Wait, that one kid does live across the street from me. I'm not friends with him or anything. Frank?"

"Frank Pachenko?" He nodded and I fell back against my seat, deflated. "His mother is the nosiest bitch in the world. She can't see me anywhere near your house."

"Your car windows are tinted, right?"

"Yeah, but she could see me walking in or out." I could picture her thin, birdlike lips leveling the accusation now: *And what were you doing at a minor's house when his guardian was not present?*

"You can park in our garage. I can have it open for you when you're coming over, then the second you pull in I'll shut it. She won't ever see you get out of your car."

I knew this wasn't airtight: she could catch me getting into or out of my car at school and associate it with the mysterious red Corvette seen at the Patricks' recently; a pinprick of curiosity would be cause enough for her to write down my license plate and wait at home, happy to investigate, ready to match it up. But the treat of Jack in his own bed helped convince me that my paranoia required a long and unlikely chain of events to occur: she'd have to first become suspicious about a car entering another house's garage. Clearly, the families weren't close. But even in the worst-case scenario, even if she did determine with certainty that it was absolutely my car, there was no way for her to be certain of motive. What if I was a family friend? A loving relative who just happened to have my third cousin in class this semester? She couldn't be sure.

I nodded and leaned in to give him a kiss. "Okay, I'll come over tomorrow around four fifteen. Have the garage open for me. We have to be really careful though . . . I can only stay an hour, tops."

His kisses had changed already; now there was an unrestrained eagerness, almost a force. But he was still keeping his eyes wide open; they stayed trained on me the entire time. "Try it one more time with your eyes shut," I whispered. He closed them and suddenly his hands found my ribs; his thin arms wrapped around me and pulled me tight. Several minutes later we unlocked with swollen lips and glossy faces.

"It's more intense that way," he observed.

I gave him one final kiss, then ruffled his hair the way a Little League coach might—I had the urge to impart a sense of normalcy to our good-bye, make it seem casual. "Right," I said. "Now get lost. I'll see you tomorrow." He opened the door and shut it too softly, then began walking briskly down the sidewalk. I checked my phone for messages I might've missed from Ford but there were none. It had truly been a perfect night. When I looked back up, Jack had crossed the street; by the time I pulled the car back onto the road and headed toward home, I could see in my rearview mirror that he'd broken into a run.

Though I wanted to relish every patch of our mingled odors on my skin, I knew I had to take a precautionary shower before bed.

But it seemed like an act of criminal vandalism, like I was taking a sanding belt to a priceless oil painting. As I dried off, I couldn't shake the feeling that I'd been robbed of a possession of great value; it was so compelling that I actually went to my jewelry chest and looked over its contents as a form of reassurance. I passed out on the bed almost immediately afterward, drunk on my sense of accomplishment. It couldn't have been later than nine thirty.

When I woke up it was past midnight; I could hear the television blaring in the living room and was seized by hunger—I'd been too excited to eat dinner and hadn't touched my milkshake, save the cherry. I hadn't wanted to corrupt Jack's taste on my tongue.

Ford was in the reclining chair, watching a show that featured junked cars getting blown up by a series of impressive weapons. The TV illuminated a bucket of chicken on the kitchen table; I grabbed a leg, then walked up behind his chair and stood there in naked silence, quietly gnawing the meat. Had he looked up at the mirror on the living room wall, he would've seen me, perhaps made a little jump and turned with a laugh to declare that I'd scared him, but he didn't look. His simple brow was still and waxen, his eyes blinking with the flicker of the television in the dark. I ate until I was holding a clean bone, then watched myself in the mirror, standing behind Ford and holding it in my hand like a weapon.

chapter eight

The screams echoing through Janet's class were hard to bear. She was attempting a lecture on the Treaty of Paris while Mrs. Pachenko walked between the rows of desks insisting upon calm, raising a finger to her lips and whispering to individual students to please sit all the way down in their desks. In the back of the room, several kids were cheering as one of them, a young man whose shirt bore a flaming skull, stood hunched atop his desk like a motocross biker, sliding it forward in small hops. *Students appear enthusiastic and are communicating well together,* I wrote on the evaluation form.

"Kevin!" Janet yelled, her thick fingers surrounding her mouth in an amplifying oval. "You can either park it on your butt right now, or you can practice sitting still after school in detention." Kevin momentarily stopped jumping, but as soon as Janet turned around to write on the board, he stood and lifted his desk up with him, tiptoeing toward the front of the room until she turned back around, at which point he'd drop it and sit down as though frozen. Mrs. Pachenko, busy waiting on a student riffling through his backpack in a farce of looking to see if he had his homework, was none the wiser. Janet finally noticed when Kevin's desk had surpassed the front row of students and he sat islanded just inches from the chalkboard. She looked down at him through the bifocals of her thick lenses. "What is with you?" she asked. "Do you have ants in your pants?" The students immediately began to roar as Kevin, nodding, stood up and began spinning around the room pretending to reach into his pants and itch. It was about this time that I noticed the intricacy of Mrs. Pachenko's embroidered blue vest, which read VOLUNTEER across the back. Usually volunteers just donned the ID card around their necks that she also wore. The vest was a production from her own imagination. I pictured the sad scene of her making it at home one evening, dutifully feeding its fabric into a sewing machine by lamplight as Frank recited an alphabetical list of SAT word definitions in the background with audible zest.

Nonetheless, my write-up of Janet had to be positive yet credible. *Though occasional classroom management issues did arise,* I continued, *Mrs. Feinlog was able to use humor and authority to restore student attention. Mrs. Pachenko, the classroom aide, serves as a clear source of calm assistance and organization.* By the time the bell rang, Janet had given up entirely and was sitting at her desk with a look of constipated apathy as Mrs. Pachenko, reading aloud from a revised syllabus that they'd decided to institute once she began helping out, stressed how important it was that the students complete their substantial assigned readings each night at home. "If we don't get to a discussion of the War of 1812 by Friday," she threatened, a quaver of panic tingling her voice, "we will *not* be on schedule for our November unit on the Texas Revolution."

"Thank you for letting me sit in," I said to them afterward, beaming. "I think there's been improvement from a few weeks ago?" During my first observation session, one of the students had successfully used an oversized safety pin to pierce his own septum but hadn't counted on the prolific blood loss. He'd held the area and waited quietly until most of his hand and lower arm were covered, at which point he'd raised his other hand and asked, in a muffled voice, if he could please use the bathroom; the classroom had turned into an assault of screams and cell phone pictures when he walked from the room dripping a long trail of micro-splatter. As a result, Janet and Mrs. Pachenko had to fill out bloodborne pathogen exposure paperwork and hold classes in the auditorium for the rest of the day as a janitor scoured the boy's desk and the classroom floor with bleach. Although I had to make brief mention of the incident, I tried to minimize references to leaked bodily fluids and spun the event as follows: *Mrs. Feinlog fosters an environment of openness where students feel free to express themselves artistically.*

While things at school continued running smoothly, in the first few weeks after my affair with Jack began, Ford seemed to sense my further mental departure. Desiring shared bonding, he insisted upon a weekend double date with Bill and Shelley, Ford's partner and his wife, at the bowling alley. "You need to get out once in a while and have some fun," Ford insisted. "Otherwise you'll go stir-crazy."

The evening was not a success. I found it hard to focus; the place was awash with teenagers. In the alley next to us, several young boys and girls wearing glow-stick necklaces began tossing lightweight balls granny-style through their legs. I couldn't help but find watching them preferential to the stolid conversation my own party was having. Several times during the evening, I'd snap out of a fantasy—a pantsless Jack standing spread-eagle atop the lane's gleaming wooden floors, repeatedly bending over and swinging the bowling ball between his knees, his testicles coming alive with motion when he finally stood and released the ball toward the pins—only to find that Ford and the others were waiting on me to comment. I hadn't even heard the question.

Displeased, Ford drained pitcher after pitcher of beer. When the festivities reached their natural conclusion, he was drunk and clingy; he stank of stale adult sweat and kept trying to kiss me on the mouth, becoming increasingly irate each time I pushed him off. By the time we called it a night and got into the car he was ready to explode.

"What's with you? You hardly even spoke to Shelley. You think you're too good to hang out with normal-looking people or something?" By this I could only imagine that Ford was referring to Shelley's unfortunate bulb-tipped nose.

"I have nothing in common with her. I wasn't impolite." Looking over at him, I kept having the disquieting thought that Jack had somehow been sitting in the passenger seat of my car waiting for me and Ford had just climbed in and sat right on top of him. I feared that Jack was now writhing unseen beneath Ford's large back and limbs, being suffocated as we drove.

"You seemed like a stuck-up bitch," he said. He spoke very slowly, as though the words were being sent to him through an earpiece and he was repeating what he'd heard on time delay. "You have to realize that's what people will think of you if you don't act friendlier." His head rolled down and to the side and then raised again, recharged by its own kinetic movements. "And what do you mean you have nothing in common? She teaches high school for fuck's sake."

I then had the optimistic thought that perhaps Jack wasn't trapped under Ford at all—maybe he was crouched down in the backseat with a generous length of taut piano wire in his hands, about to pop up and strangle the stocky trunk of Ford's neck while I blew him a kiss and turned up the radio—what a delightful show of initiative that would demonstrate on Jack's behalf. "Do you have something in common with every cop?" I asked him. "Every single one? The deadbeats? The thieves? The traitors?"

"Enough in common to talk to them over a beer," he said. "I wasn't asking you two to go on a road trip together." I could feel his eyes train upon me at the stoplight, his demeanor softening as he admired my face in profile. "Hey," he said, reaching his hand out toward my shoulder. But I wanted none of it.

"Come on," I said, pushing his hand away. "I'm driving."

"Yeah you're driving," he said, seething. "The fucking car I bought you. What, you can spend my money but I can't touch you? You're better than me, too?"

"You're just drunk, Ford."

"No," he said, adamant. "This doesn't just happen when I drink. This is *why* I drink." With that his hand clamped down upon my upper arm. I tried to push it off but he was holding on with all his strength.

"Ford, you're hurting me," I warned him, my voice inflected with actual fear. It wasn't so much the pain as the act of restraint itself that felt so awful, the knowledge that I wasn't physically in control.

"Do you know how you make me feel all the time?" He was yelling, nearly weeping. I slowed down the car and began driving far below the speed limit. I didn't want to arrive home with him like this. He'd never actually hit me, but he wasn't opposed to using applied force—a gripping of the wrist when I wanted to leave the room and he wasn't done talking, a too-firm squeezing of the thigh when I'd said no too many nights in a row. "You're ice-cold for days, sometimes *weeks,* then suddenly I come home and you're so hot for it that you're greeting me with your ass in the air. Then the next morning it's like I disgust you again. Do you know what a mind-fuck that is?" His eyes were trained on me, staring; he wanted me to turn and look at him, to see the expression accompanying his painful confession, but I refused. The rest of the drive continued in slow silence; eventually his grip loosened and he retracted his arm. "Fuck my life," he mumbled.

When we got into the house, he opened a beer and sat in front of the television; I went directly to the bedroom. I was hardly into my pajamas when I heard his deep openmouthed snores begin. The next afternoon he showered and went to work with no discussion of the previous evening's conversation; he asked about dinner and I told him I'd make pork chops and leave a plate for him in the refrigerator. He nodded, gave me a quick kiss that smelled too strongly of aftershave, and left. One thing I could always count on with Ford, despite his occasional outbursts, was his ability to suppress the uncomfortable—his breaking point was deep and not often reached, but whenever he got there I knew that as soon as the air cleared I'd have another long stretch of time where all his angst would stay buried.

Jack's concerns were a bit more out in the open, and they included Ford. I hadn't told Jack that my husband was a cop, though I wouldn't have lied if Jack had asked. What worried Jack most was my physical relationship with Ford. The Wednesday after Ford's outburst, Jack and I were having an extended hangout at his house, which had proven a wonderful arrangement. In fact, since our first completed tryst in the car, Jack's house was the only place we'd met. His single bed was deliciously narrow, forcing us to either be fucking or otherwise pressed together simply to both fit on top of it. On Wednesdays Jack ordered pizza—we always laughed as I'd hide in the hallway when the deliveryman came to the door—then for the second course we'd eat chocolate pudding cups without spoons, dipping our tongues down into their cool centers and watching one another's pink flesh skate around the cups' plastic rims.

Today we were naked in the pool, careful to stay submerged to our necks lest any passersby feel the need to peek over his fence in the twilight of fall's dinner hour. Facing each other with twined legs, Jack and I bobbed in the warm water with a circular foam tube pressed between us to help us float.

"It sucks how we won't get to go do stuff together for like four more years," he said. Jack had already adopted the illusion that we'd date through his entire high school career and beyond, a fantasy I didn't attempt to ruin. In truth, our relationship's shelf life was closer to that of an elderly Labrador. One more year seemed to be the most realistic to hope for; two was very unlikely. He'd grow, his voice would further deepen, defining muscle would thicken and broaden him. I couldn't imagine remaining attracted to him beyond fifteen at the latest. "I mean even stupid stuff, you know? Like getting dinner or going to a basketball game."

I tilted my pelvis up and wrapped my legs around his waist, rubbing myself against the smoothness of his stomach. "But you can do that stuff with friends. We get to have the very best part of a relationship be our whole relationship. With us it's dessert for every meal." I could feel his erection beginning to form beneath my ass cheeks, so his next question surprised me—I figured his mind was drifting somewhere more pleasant.

"What's your husband like?" he asked.

I didn't have to feign indifference. "He's just a husband." I shrugged. Worried his interview might go in a direction that could derail the evening's merriment, I decided to play upon Jack's sympathy. "The other night he was drunk and swearing at me. It's more of a living arrangement. He pays the bills, takes care of all the boring adult stuff." I laced my fingers between Jack's, looking at their pruneish tips. Despite the warmth of the evening, our time in the water had given Jack's lips a blue hue and covered his body with goose bumps. I loved how timid it made him look, as though he had just been rescued from the bottom of a well.

"Do you guys still . . . you know?" Jack asked. I wanted him to say it—I loved to hear Jack use the vocabulary of lust in any context.

"Still what?"

He rolled his eyes. "Have sex and stuff."

"Not often. But when we do, it's nothing like you and me. There's no passion like there is with us. When I have to have sex with him, I just think of you." With that I swam to the pool wall, then motioned Jack toward me, grabbing his arm the moment he got close and pulling him in, pinning myself between him and a cold jet of water. "So give me some more to think about." Obligingly, Jack began to kiss my neck, an activity that, guided by my moans, he'd quickly become rather good at. Reaching down I used my fingers to guide his penis into me, helping him through the initial, awkward rubbery stage of underwater entry. The sky was just dark enough that I could make out the beginnings of a few stars, but the whole world soon reduced to the simple sound of Jack's thrusts and the water, responsive, lapping.

Jack and I were always cautious, even on Wednesdays, when our schedule was extended: his father's training night went until 8:00 and it then took him an hour to drive home, but I was always out of the house by 7:50, save for the night that Jack had begun his cunnilingus studies in earnest—it was nearly impossible to look down at him, the flesh around his lips marinated in my enthusiasm, and not grant his smiling request to do it just a little longer. That night I left at 8:15 and it was worth every second of the risk.

I'd hoped some of the safeguard restraints I'd implemented would have a secondary side effect of helping to keep Jack's emotions compartmentalized. But less than a month into our affair his shyness when we were alone together had fully retracted, and he didn't hold back when talking about his feelings for me or his plans for our life as a couple. I'd stressed early on that there could be no written notes, no text messages, no wordy ruminations of ardor. He ended up bypassing this rule though, writing terrible poems in a notebook (*When you leave / My heart falls asleep in my chest / and has nightmares of death until you return*), which he'd give to me to read after sex. They were harmless enough—if they were found, it would be obvious only that he was smitten with someone; none of them mentioned my name. He frequently told me he loved me, a behavior I didn't like to encourage with a response—I claimed I didn't want to use the word "love" because it should be felt and understood rather than said. This, too, became a point of contention with Jack.

One night I asked if I could watch him jerk off and he agreed, but explained he was used to looking out his window at the sky while he did it. "I stand to the side of the window now instead of in front of it though." He smiled. "I guess it worked out that you saw me but I sure don't want anyone else to."

"Go ahead," I urged. "Do it exactly like you'd do it if I wasn't here." Taking a seat on the bed behind him, I watched his buttocks clench and his head lift up as though he was having a conversation with God. When he was finished I told him to come rub his semen on my breasts and asked him why he liked to look out the window.

"Are you sure you're looking at the sky?" It did seem to be the only thing visible save for a few distant hedges. "Not peeping in someone's window?"

He laughed. "Yeah, I dunno. At clouds or stars."

"Why?" I cradled his balls in my hand; even their wrinkled exterior still held the incipient softness of youth. His balls, I realized, were softer than the skin on Ford's stomach.

"It just makes me feel overwhelmed or something. A good overwhelmed. Like I'm such a small part of the world that I don't ever have to worry about anything."

I gave him a wide grin. "You're really young." He play-pushed me in a teasing way; he hated when I brought up his age.

"You don't look as old as you are," he countered. "In a few years no one will even know there's an age difference when we're together. When I'm in college everyone will think you're my college girlfriend."

"Don't fast-forward," I said. "We need to enjoy every second of this." The phrase "when I'm in college" made me feel kicked in the skull. It was like seeing a plate of my favorite meal that had been left out for a week and now was rotting and festering with maggots—I wouldn't be able to enjoy a second helping of Jack tonight with that image in my head. I began to kiss his chest, closing my eyes and tucking my nose beneath his arm, hoping the odor would act like a smelling salt and wake me up from the horrible vision of Jack matured.

But he'd just orgasmed, which meant my power over him was at its lowest—he didn't want to stop gazing in his crystal ball just yet. "I say we get married the day I turn eighteen," he suggested. "We'll already have been waiting forever by then."

With this second mention of advanced age, I slumped back onto his bed, taking comfort in the faded basketball graphic of his sheets that he was already too old for. A yawn slipped past my lips.

"You do want to get married, don't you?" he asked.

"I'm already married, Jack."

A confused look came over his face. It was not an attractive kind of naïveté, just a perplexed one, like a customer who orders chicken salad at the deli but gets home and opens the container to find a pound of macaroni instead. "Well yeah," he said defensively. "But you'll leave him when I'm old enough for us to be together for real, right? I mean, you don't love him. You love me."

"This is tedious, Jack." I started to reach for my bra but he placed his hands on my shoulders, imploring.

"You love me, right?"

"What do you think?" He nodded and stepped back but wasn't sated.

"If you feel it, then why can't you say it?" he demanded. "It's not like saying it will make it untrue."

"But saying it doesn't make it true either," I reasoned. "People throw that word around all the time. It's meaningless."

He began to pace at the end of his bed in a way that made his genitals lightly bounce; their hypnotic sway made me feel slightly more favorable toward him. "It's not meaningless to *me,*" he stressed. "This is . . . it's hard what we do, how I have to see you in class without touching you or saying anything real to you. How we can't talk on the phone more than a second to make plans, and it has to be on a secret phone I keep in a box under my bed. How we can't tell anybody or go anywhere together. And you can't even say three words to me?"

"Let me show you instead," I offered, reaching for his arm.

"I know," he said, pulling back. "I know that. I just want to hear it out loud."

I didn't want him to hear it—the more he heard it, the more he'd believe it, and the more he believed it the harder it would be to break things off when the time inevitably came. But, I figured, it would be more than slightly hypocritical for me to belabor the conversation further by taking some odd stance on an insistence of honesty. There was no need to prematurely ruin things.

"Just this once," I said. "You know I don't like it. It makes us seem just like everyone else, and we're not like everyone else."

He buried his fingers in the back of my hair and brought his lips and eyes in close and level with my own. "I love you," he said, his voice stupid with hormones.

"I love you too, Jack." As soon as I said it he was kissing me. He didn't give one second of pause for analysis, had no desire to read the veracity of my expression. Before I knew it he was fully inside me, my legs balancing wearily on his shoulders like an oversized harness on a young ox.

Pictures were another sore spot for Jack—I insisted that I could have none of him nor he of me, not even a fully clothed shot of me snapped surreptitiously on his regular phone in the classroom. "I can't have a photo of you standing in the front of our class in a turtleneck?" he asked. "One picture to look at between our visits?"

I was firm. "It's just not smart, Jack. Say your father sees it, or a friend. One question leads to another. Suddenly they're watching you watch me in class, or they catch me staring at your crotch as you walk past my desk. We don't want to invite scrutiny."

But his father soon saw more of me than a photo. This also happened on a Wednesday, a bit after 6:40. Jack and I were in his bathroom, the shower still running—he'd soaped up my breasts with shampoo, rinsed them using the detachable wand, then liked the visual so much he'd repeated the lather. Jack was standing up on the edge of the tub, his hands lifted to hold the curtain bar for balance, so that he could see my squatting ass in the mirror and my blond hair trailing down my back while I gave him a blow job and theatrically touched my foamy breasts. Given the running water and fervor of Jack's escalating moans, we only barely managed to hear the sound of the garage door opening.

chapter nine

We allowed ourselves just a moment of shared disbelief, me staring up with his cock still between my lips and Jack looking down in horror, before beginning to jump into action. I killed the water as Jack threw on pants and a T-shirt. "Grab your books and go sit at the kitchen table," I ordered. "Tell him I'm here helping you with a paper and that I just went to the bathroom. Go right now." He ran. Whether or not his erection had time to soften I wasn't sure.

I put my hair up into a bun, trying to towel-dry it as much as possible. The side door opened and a muffled conversation began. When I was convinced I looked put-together enough that I couldn't possibly have been getting a titty bath just minutes earlier, I took a deep breath and walked out to meet Jack's father.

Gratefully, Buck and Jack Patrick looked nothing alike. At fourteen, Jack was already as tall as Buck, who stood squat and frontloaded with a growing beer gut that seemed to force apart his hips and made his legs seem even smaller and farther back upon his body than they really were. His light brown hair had the barbershop-haircut shape of a young boy's standard trim; it was shaved slightly too close on the sides. When I walked in and extended my hand, he made a show of looking me up and down from my head to my feet and back again. It was only then that I realized I hadn't put my shoes back on—I'd left them under Jack's bed.

"Lovely to meet you, Mr. Patrick. I'm Celeste, Jack's English teacher." Buck gave out a low whistle.

"I did not have teachers like you back in my day, I'll tell you that right now. Jack, do you realize how lucky you are?" Buck turned around and gave his humiliated son a wink. Jack's face had boiled to a crimson. "And house calls to boot!" Buck exclaimed. At this point, the titanic knot of worry inside me relaxed. Most parents would have been so suspicious to come home and find their child's teacher there, unannounced in a session of impromptu tutoring, that they'd have called the school the next day. But it certainly didn't seem to be raising flags on Buck's radar. Especially not when the teacher looked like me.

"Well," I reasoned, "I live close by and Jack's research paper is getting very close to a solid outline." Jack was sitting fully upright at the dining room table and had set up the first things he'd grabbed from his backpack in front of him to form a guise of studying: a history textbook, a chemistry textbook and a notebook turned open to a blank page. Buck didn't seem to be concerning himself with specifics though. "Jack's a very smart kid," I added.

Buck decided to equivocate. "When he focuses, he can do all right," he said, nodding. There was an uncomfortable pause as Buck's concentrated stare settled on my breasts. Jack was trying to seem absorbed with the blank page of notebook paper in front of him. To his credit, I saw that he had added the following title to the top of the page as Buck and I were talking: "Outline."

"Well, Jack and I were just wrapping up," I said. I'd need to ask Jack to check for my shoes and claim I'd left them in his bathroom.

"Stay for dinner!" Buck said encouragingly. "I was just going to order some takeout. After you coming here to help Jack, it's the least I can do. I know they can't be paying you worth a damn. Although from the looks of your car you're doing all right. That's a beauty. I can see why you didn't want to park it on the street." He gave me a judging smile, as though I'd broken the law by having something nice. "That's not a teacher's-salary vehicle." It was then, despite the wedding ring on my hand, that Buck truly began to get to the chase. "Now are you *married*-married or just married?" Buck asked. Thankfully, he didn't give me time to answer. "Let me tell you, I know exactly how it can be." He tilted his head toward Jack, as though by avoiding the phrase "Jack's mom" he was being subtle and not clearly going to say something awful about his son's mother. "A couple years back I barely escaped alive from a real nasty situation." His eyes refocused on my breasts yet again and he tried to make an impressive show of lifting his cell phone from its external holder on his belt. "Marriage can be so confining," he said, giving his lips a slow lick, his eyes trained at nipple level. "Sometimes you just need to let off a little steam." With that he placed a call to the restaurant and started to walk into the kitchen. Jack stood and began packing the books on the table into his backpack; when his father was sufficiently far away, he whispered that he was sorry.

"Your father is a horror show," I whispered back. Jack nodded solemnly. I badly wanted to give him a victory kiss—we'd done it together, partners in crime who'd managed to deceive, but Buck quickly circled in again, pointing to line items on a colorful menu for my approval; I nodded vigorously and he began to wander away once more, unable to talk on the phone and stand still. "Jack," I called quickly, wiggling my foot, "get my shoes."

When Buck returned from the call, I was stepping into a pair of shiny beige heels. "Dressing up for dinner." Buck smiled.

"I really should probably be going," I tried, playing the traditional-wife card. "I need to get supper on for my husband."

In the area of my estrangement from Ford only, Buck did seem to have an oddly intuitive streak. "He's waiting on you right now?" he asked. There was an air of conquest in his tone; he knew, some-how, that Ford was not waiting.

"Not right now, no," I conceded. "He works pretty late." Buck's face lit up like a winning pinball machine. He seemed to think the sole determining factor in whether or not I'd have an affair with him was Ford's schedule.

Jack mechanically set the table as Buck droned on about work—the large number of people he supervised, the fire alarm malfunction that had ended their training night early. Not once did his words slow in order to ponder the extended amount of tutoring Jack and I might have accomplished, all without his ever knowing, had this accident at work not occurred. He also spoke openly of lavish vacations he'd taken past girlfriends on and his knowledge of where to buy jewelry, insinuating that if I hooked up with him there could be a nice bracelet in my future. "You want some of the best emer-alds you've ever seen?" he asked coyly. "Get off at St. Thomas on a Caribbean cruise." It was hard not to laugh. Sure, Buck seemed a comfortable level of middle-class, but dating him in exchange for gifts wouldn't qualify as gold-digging; it would be more like pan-ning for nuggets.

I sat across the table from Jack during dinner, loving the way he shunned chopsticks in favor of a fork, as though sex had made him so hungry he couldn't bother with anything that compro-mised his ability to shovel food in his mouth. At one point I took my foot out of my shoe and ran it up his leg, rubbing front to back again and again along his crotch while Buck spoke of upcoming concerts that his company could get box-seat tickets to. Watching Jack eat made the conversation bearable; his lips became visibly flavored with oil and sauce, and I delighted in the torture of knowing just what they tasted like by eating the food. By the time Buck asked if I could stay for dessert, though, my patience had been sufficiently used up.

"No thank you," I said. "I have to watch my figure."

"Self-control." He smiled. "I like that in a woman. Outside of the bedroom I mean." The three of us stood there for a moment, paralyzed by the awkwardness of this remark, then Buck tried to come in for a good-bye hug. I managed to trap one of his stumpy hands and shake it thoroughly instead.

"I would really love to see you again," he said.

"Thank you for a lovely evening." They were the only polite words I could manage.

I had a near-giddy sense of optimism afterward, knowing that if Buck ever came home earlier than expected, all would be well as long as Jack could make it to the table with a notebook and a pair of shorts on.

But Jack wanted even more freedom than this. That Friday, at Jack's insistence, I took him to a drive-in movie. We went all the way out to Clearwater, about an hour away. I insisted we both wear party-store wigs since I'd have to roll the window down and be seen in order to buy a ticket. My faux hair was a short red bob, Jack's a shaggy blond mop that might have accompanied a surfer costume. "It's like we're going to rob a bank," he joked, putting his on.

We watched the film casually, his hand resting against my bare crotch with two fingers blithely inserted, my own fingers gripping the base of his penis, our limbs irregularly coming alive with motion, then hanging in stasis to watch one of the more interesting moments of a scene. "You know my dad keeps asking me to get your number for him," he finally mentioned.

"I feel for you. That guy is a boob." The movie centered on the quarterback rivalry between two opposing high school football teams; disappointingly, the youngest actor in the film still appeared to be at least twenty-six. Yet the sentiment lodged in one of the pregame locker-room speeches nearly moved me to tears. *We're high school seniors,* the lead actor gushed. Due to the passion in his voice, I was able to momentarily suspend disbelief and think of him as an eighteen-year-old despite having seen in the tabloids that he'd recently cheated on his wife with their children's nanny and fathered a set of illegitimate twins. *Tonight is all we have. This is the night we're going to dream about for the rest of our lives. Some of us aren't ever going to make it out of this town, but for the next two hours we can go out on that field and feel immortal!* It's true, I thought; the adult world has so much less to offer than adolescence does. It seemed to me that the happiest possible ending to the movie would be both teams playing impeccably and tying at the end of the fourth quarter, then the entire stadium being blown up by terrorists and their young lives ending on a high.

Jack turned to me, a sudden excitement making his words sound jumpy. "So I think I know a way that you can be at the house a lot more and it won't matter if you're there when my dad comes home," he said. "You just have to lead him on a little. All of my dad's past girlfriends have had keys to our house. They'd come over even when he wasn't there and lay out by the pool or whatever. Bring groceries over and make dinner so it would be ready by the time he walked in the door—that kind of stuff. If you pretend to date him, you could come over all the time."

My hands fell away from his penis, suddenly unsure of everything about Jack. "You want me to sleep with your dad?"

"No!" Jack looked at me like I was completely insane. "God, are you kidding me?"

"Well adults don't usually date without having sex, Jack. It's just the way things work. I'm sorry to break it to you, but those women coming over to cook for him were most certainly putting themselves on the menu too."

"Ewww!" he screamed, cupping his hands over his ears. "Stop saying gross things. I know they were, I get that. I'm not saying you actually date. Just tell him you want to get to know him better or something."

The thought of Buck's frontal-scalp hair plugs rubbing against my skin made my toes curl inside my shoes. "It's a slippery slope, Jack."

"You just pretend to be a little interested. Then if he gets home early and you're there, he'll think you came over to see him. You could even stop by on weekends and stuff."

On-screen, a tubby linebacker with a heart of gold took a concussion-inducing hit to protect the quarterback. The camera zoomed forward to follow the trajectory of the bite guard, expelled from the linebacker's mouth on impact, as it soared over a pileup of bodies and landed across the end zone with a poignant bounce. "Jack," I pointed out, "he's not interested in simply eating pot roast and watching *Jeopardy!* He'll start wanting more and more."

I thought of Buck's shining red face mid-proposition, the way his flushed cheeks would gleam like griddled ham. "Eventually I'll have to either reject him or give in."

Of course what Jack didn't know was just how temporary our own relationship was going to be. As I argued, I began to realize that several months from now, when Buck would likely reach his sexually frustrated breaking point, Jack would probably be due to hit a growth spurt—I'd need to be waning away from both of them anyhow. Buck could prove to be a perfect excuse to begin going over to see Jack less and less, and eventually I might be able to play the conflicted-conscience card with Jack: how I'd wronged them both and needed some time to soul-search, that my pretend relationship with Buck had made me realize Jack needed to be a normal kid and bound into high school without the heavy tethers of an adult love affair.

Jack was still trying to solve the puzzle I'd set before him of how I could engage Buck without the flirtation becoming physical. "I think if you just keep telling him you need more time or whatever, he'd go along with that. Say he's totally free to date other people and stuff. I know he likes going to the strip clubs. He's sick; sometimes he'll get a lap dance, then come home and tell me about it."

"That is very, very nauseating." Jack smiled; illuminated by the movie screen, his expression caused a series of micro-wrinkles to form at the corners of his eyes. Perhaps he wouldn't be opposed to starting a preventative regimen of retinol? Surely I could gently convince him of its benefits.

"I know he's disgusting. But I mean, you're so much hotter and younger than anyone he's ever dated. I think you could string him along for a super-long time. At least until I can drive and have a later curfew. Think about it—you'll be able to come over whenever you want."

The thought of unbridled access made my crotch seize up in a robust squeeze. I realized I'd be able to go over in the early hours and peek in on Jack, perhaps catch him with bedhead and a sleep erection and wake him up by putting his penis into the warmth of my mouth. This image was more than enough to let greed cloud my judgment.

"I guess we can give it a try," I agreed. "But tell him he can't call me, ever, so there's no point in giving him my number. My husband's a cop, and he's the jealous sort. We can't be too careful." I didn't clarify to Jack whether or not the cop detail and the jealous detail were true, and oddly, he didn't ask. I suppose in the same way I wanted the details of Jack's future to remain vague and blurry in my mind, he wasn't looking to cement the particulars of my home life. It could work, I figured. I'd explain to Buck that I'd never had an affair and probably never could. That I wasn't looking for anything physical and he needed to understand that. I was simply looking for a friend. And of course I'd mention he was free to date and sleep with whomever he wanted. Dating wasn't what he and I were doing, I'd explain—I was just getting some space from my husband.

One of the teams in the movie scored a touchdown; cannons filled with school-spirit-colored confetti shot into the air as football players ran to cheerleaders for congratulatory kisses. Jack slurped the last dregs of his cola through his straw.

"This is going to be so cool." He smiled and gripped my hand in a way that I can only describe as juvenile—like we were at the fair and he wanted me to follow him over to the Ferris wheel.

chapter ten

Not having to worry about being in the house when Buck came home meant more time for play—in the kitchen there were food games where Jack, keeping his eyes closed, sampled dollops of salad dressing off my chest and had to guess at the flavor, getting a hearty spank with a wooden spoon when he was wrong; in the living room we'd often play a soft-core movie from one of the racier on-demand cable channels on the big-screen TV while copulating atop Buck's electric reclining chair, operating the control switch so that it slowly shifted positions the entire time like we were riding on the back of a somnambulant horse. Although I worried the increased contact was making Jack grow too needy—he'd begun to call any time Buck stepped out, even for a moment to return a DVD—the variety and frequency the arrangement added to our exploits made it hard to turn back from, even at its lowest moments, when I didn't make it out of the house before Buck arrived home and I had to pretend I'd dropped by for a visit. To my surprise, Buck actually was simply entertained—fine with watching a few television programs together and then accepting my exit. He required only an extended hug upon departure that often morphed into a quasi-grope, his hand squeezing the flesh of my upper buttock with the probing tenacity of a fruit inspector. Occasionally as we untangled he'd plant a wet kiss against my jawline and audibly inhale the fragrance of my hair.

But the moments before he came home made this suffering

worth it—times when Jack would urgently call and I'd open the door to find him sitting on the couch waiting for me, naked and erect, wearing the baseball cap I liked (its Little League vibe made him look just a shade younger). Sometimes we knew we had only minutes alone and there was a harried and apocalyptic violence in the way we went for each other—our joined bodies slamming into the wall, quaking with a fortune of pleasure that we had just seconds to spend. I began to dress for efficiency—skirts that could be lifted, shirts that could be slipped overhead, never any panties.

It was an optimal situation, save for the additional ripples it made at home. I now saw Buck enough that he drained the reserves of patient energy I had used to spend tolerating Ford. Evenings when Ford returned home from work and came into the bedroom wanting an inspired quickie inevitably led to hurt feelings—I encouraged him to look at pictures online, to buy videos. "Teaching all day takes everything I've got," I complained; "it exhausts me wholly." But Ford's appetite was for real flesh and he'd insist that at the very least I let him look at me naked while he pleasured himself; this led to offensive scenes of Ford's face in the dim-lit shadows, his jaw fixed as tightly and aggressively as an assassin about to pull a trigger while his body hunched over me panting and dripping sweat.

Sensing that I was drifting even further away from him, Ford's mind went into overdrive. He'd recently tried to get the baby conversation going again—he wanted us to go to a fertility doctor, get the ball rolling. "If we ever have a child, it'll be through adoption," I stressed, trying to play to both his vanity and my own. "You didn't marry me for my stretch marks." I had no interest in children; even if Ford raised the thing completely by himself and we trained it not to talk to me or interact with me whatsoever, I would surely end up moving out of our home within days of its arrival. There was an impulse of self-protection surrounding the decision as well; I knew if I ever had a son, at a certain age it would be impossible to ignore him, and I never wanted to force that transgression upon myself.

"You know there are benefits," he reminded me. It was true—as soon as we became parents, we'd gain additional monthly income from his father's trust.

"What, you want more money?" I asked. He shook his head, in a cursory way at first, but then an anger mounted behind his eyes that soon forced him from his chair; he began to pace around the living room, fists closed, chest forward. "I don't care about the money," he stated, nearly a growl. "But yeah, I do want more."

"More *what*?" I asked; this was the end of the line, the brink of his rage. His fist sank into the drywall with a loud crack. "More!" he shouted, then stammered incoherently. He opened his hand and beat his palm against the wall several more times before grabbing his jacket and walking out the door—he didn't take his keys. When he returned three hours later it was raining heavily; his waterlogged sneakers made long sucking noises as he entered the hallway and walked straight to the kitchen phone, leaving a puddled trail. I brought him a towel, which he accepted but did not use. Instead he continued to drip, every inch of him from his hair down to the ends of his soaked jeans, as he called the cable company and ordered three new premium upgrade packages of digital sports channels.

I ended the fall term assigning *Lord of the Flies* to read over the holiday. "It's the perfect Christmas story," I told them. "Think of these boys when you see news footage of shoppers getting trampled as hordes of consumers race for an on-sale video game console."

"Is this book like that TV show *Survivor*?" Marissa asked. Stained red from candy canes, the students' tongues appeared to have been dyed by communal blood in a satanic cult ceremony.

"Sure," I said, opening the door and practically pushing them out of the classroom. "Happy holidays. Bon voyage." Of late, Jack had begun to exit the class with a too-cool air: not looking at me, slightly sauntering, effortfully aping casual. But today he gave me a smirk of foretold pleasure—his birthday was over the Christmas holiday, which he mostly had to spend at his mother's. As a final hurrah before his departure, we were going to make the drive to the Toucan Inn after school as a seedy holiday gift to ourselves. Seeing angel-faced Jack standing nude inside a room normally used for hourly blow jobs and heroin binges struck me as a delicious treat: the juxtaposition would vividly magnify all his boyish qualities.

I picked him up at dusk behind a gas station; when I pulled in he was wandering to and fro with a small bow-topped box in his hands, as though he was working up the courage to walk in and propose marriage to the station's attendant. I wore my red wig and had cash for the hotel desk clerk; if asked for ID, I figured I could simply claim not to have it on me and he wouldn't refuse the money, but no such ruse was required. "An hour?" he guessed, taking in the faux electric hue of my hair and the oversized sunglasses that eclipsed most of my face. He was smoking behind the counter and watching a reality cop show. The same show's crew had once visited Ford's precinct, but no footage of him was chosen. This had deeply interrupted Ford's sense of entitlement. His friends had already taken to calling him "movie star"—when the Fordless episode aired, he'd turned to me on the sofa and repeated, about twelve times, "Can you believe it?"

I wouldn't let Jack touch any of the carpeting or bedding in the room—"You could get crabs just thinking about it," I told him. Instead I had him take off all his clothes and lie down across the bathroom countertop with his penis hanging down in the sink and his butt positioned directly below the faucet.

"This is weird," he said, not judging so much as objectively noticing. He started to set his face down on the counter, then recoiled and placed an arm underneath his cheek. "The counter's kind of sticky."

"You'll survive." I turned on the water, watching his cheeks momentarily buckle together, then began to carefully wash his asshole, which made him laugh.

"Does it tickle?" I asked, pressing the tip of my soapy finger centimeters inside him.

He nodded and I rinsed and patted him dry before I started giving him his very first rim job. He made no sound or expression, perhaps equally afraid to like it or dislike it, but when I turned him over he was exceptionally hard and it took only seconds of sucking the tip of his penis for him to come down the back of my throat. For a moment he sat very still on the counter, ass in the sink and head back against the mirror, and I wondered for a second if he felt too out of control—too molested perhaps, his orgasms a seeming consent to acts he didn't fully enjoy. But then he bounded off the counter and grabbed the box he'd brought with him. "Here," he said, immediately sheepish. "This is for you." He looked so anxious that for a moment I worried it might indeed be an engagement ring— that somehow he'd gotten a diamond band, or even a cubic zirconia one, figuring it's the thought that counts—and was about to suggest that we embark upon a four-year engagement to legality. When he opened the box to reveal only a pair of gold hoop earrings, Jack easily misinterpreted my flooding relief as happiness.

"They're just so beautiful," I gushed. "Truly. These are simply perfect; I can wear them with anything."

The part of me that had once voiced concern about having any object that could be linked to Jack—that would've asked Jack if the earrings were a family heirloom or made sure he hadn't taken them from his mother, who might discover them missing and mention them to Buck—no longer fussed over such neurotic worries; our repeated contact without consequence meant I didn't sweat small details anymore. "You like them?" he said, fishing.

"I love them." I smiled.

"And you love me?" He was fishing again, his smile widening. I bent to the floor, put his cock in my mouth, and began speaking in muffled words. He laughed, pushing me off.

"What?" I smiled. "You can't understand me?" These mere seconds on the Toucan's carpet gave my knees a rash that took days to fade.

Less carefree as of late was Jack and Buck's relationship. For one, Jack's grades were suffering—Jack simply seemed distracted this term, Buck lamented, like he couldn't get his head in the game. "But his English grade is fantastic," I pointed out.

"Well," Buck said, winking at me, "that's because he has a great teacher."

Despite the arrangement being his idea, Jack likewise seemed to grow defiant whenever Buck insisted upon time alone with me. If

Buck put on a movie, he'd ask Jack to go to his room and start on homework. Occasionally Buck would even set the dinner table for two and tell Jack to eat in the kitchen. "We need grown-up time," he'd insist, and Jack would slam doors and make protestations. The worst incident happened days after the visit to the hotel. At dinner, Buck also gave me a Christmas present—earrings as well, moderately expensive diamond ones—and Jack's eyes immediately made the comparison and saw how much shorter his sword was in this particular duel.

Trying to make Jack feel better, I politely highlighted their impracticality. "I can't take these home," I argued. "If my husband saw these, he would definitely start asking questions."

Buck shrugged. "So just wear them when you're here." With that he stood and began to take out the earrings I was wearing. They happened to be the very same earrings Jack had bought me.

Jack loudly pushed his chair back from the table and threw his fork to the ground, stomping off to his room. "What the hell?" Buck asked, but he didn't dwell on it; he was too busy outfitting my lobes with his prize.

It was only because of Jack's melancholy at being outgifted that I agreed to meet him once over the break—two days before Christmas—several hours away in the town where his mother lived with her husband and his seventeen- and nineteen-year-old sons, whom Jack apparently loathed enough to prefer residence with Buck. We'd made a plan to rendezvous at the mall in one of the handicapped restrooms, where Jack alleged that one of his stepbrothers took girlfriends to fornicate all the time—a single room with a locking door, a sink and a toilet. "He sounds like a romantic guy," I'd joked. It was bold of us, but the chaos of the holiday meant the mall would be teeming and overcrowded, all security personnel busy watching merchandise instead of trying to halt any hanky-panky in the toilets. Even if we were caught in the bathroom together, I reasoned that nothing could be proven. I could allege that Jack had seen me enter the bathroom, recognized me as a trusted teacher and, being in the middle of a personal crisis, came and knocked on the door wanting to have a private conversation, which I allowed him. I doubted they could legally have cameras in the bathroom; there would be no proof that we'd been copulating against the hand dryer instead of talking.

I got a blended iced coffee drink and waited on a bench near the restrooms. The moment I saw him enter the main doors, I walked into the bathroom and locked the door. I'd come prepared for the worst—the possibility that the bathroom's previous occupant was a customer of size on a mobility scooter whose food court cheesesteak hadn't agreed with him, perhaps—and quickly took out a small can of Lysol, misting the room's corners.

When I heard the agreed-upon knock—one single rap—I unlocked the door and stood behind it, out of view to anyone in the hallway as the door swung open and Jack entered. After locking the door he immediately turned to place his mouth upon mine. We hadn't seen one another in nearly a week and a half, the longest we'd gone since our affair started. He wasn't interested in the slightest bit of foreplay, the poor, desperate creature. In less than a minute he'd unzipped and lowered his pants; I leaned against the sink and extended my ass toward him. Upon entry he gasped, the relieved sigh of homecoming, and buried his face in the back of my head, roiling his cheeks against my hair. We were done in less time than it would have taken to complete a legitimate bowel movement.

Afterward, his panting lips found my ear. "Do you want to wait a second and do it again?" he whispered. I did, but I worried a line was forming outside—the longer we took, the greater our chances of having to exit to an audience.

"We shouldn't be too long," I warned. "That'll have to hold you till you're back at your dad's."

Jack's expression instantly hardened, as though he'd been insulted. "You're not seeing him while I'm gone, are you?" There was a hint of outrage in his voice.

"Of course not. I told him I have far too many family gatherings to attend." I gave Jack a frisky poke in the ribs and he laughed with relief.

"It sucks," he said, shaking his head. "My dad is crazy about you. Usually he's kinda 'whatever' about women. I knew he thought you were really good-looking but I didn't know he'd get all gaga." He zipped up his pants and paused, hesitating to add, "He talks about you all the time."

I gently grabbed the collar of Jack's shirt, tilting my head to the side and letting my hair fall across my right shoulder in a way I knew to be flattering. "Jack," I said reassuringly, "he doesn't even know me. He has no idea who I really am."

This thought made Jack smile—subtly at first, but soon he broke out into a wide grin. "Yeah." Jack nodded. "He sure doesn't." We gave one another a final kiss, nearly choking on the force of our own needy tongues, before I opened the door. We'd reasoned that if someone else was waiting, I'd try to ask the location of a store as a distraction while Jack crept out. But the woman planted outside was squat and hunched over a walker.

"Here," I said to her loudly, directing Jack out behind my back, "let me help you." I stood in front of her, a concerned citizen, and slowly guided her toward the door while his thin teenage frame dashed out and off.

Christmas Day with Ford had the effect of his seeming to be in cahoots with Jack—every gift he gave me was some type of boudoir garment I couldn't wait to wear for Jack, from satiny thongs to lace bustiers to crotchless teddies. "Ford!" I was able to exclaim upon opening each package, my voice truly resplendent with expectant glee over the way Jack's mouth would drop. "This is downright nasty." The ice cubes in his glass of whiskey clinked as he brought the cup to his face to water his leering grin.

I knew an initial viewing session of the garments was unavoidable, so I took a great number of sedatives and washed them down with cranberry mimosas; Ford had placed himself in charge of deep-frying a turkey, so I had no real duties for the day other than to remember to continuously dab a Kleenex at the drool forming in the corners of my mouth and serve as a veritable blow-up doll for Ford to take his festive cheer out on. We both passed out after dinner, Ford from tryptophan and myself from a more complex hurricane of chemicals, and by the time he woke me up making jokes about the Cool Whip originally intended for the pumpkin pie, I was in a twilight state of cyclical consciousness. I managed to put on the French maid–inspired bra-and-panty set (Ford had included a small pink feather duster in the box that he wanted me to use to tickle his cock) and began spouting loose phrases in French I remembered from college (*Peux-tu m'aider?*). There's little else I remember about this particular celebration of Christ's birth. The next morning I woke up sore with the raging thirst that follows a night of obliteration, but with very few painful memories. That erasure was the gift I gave myself.

chapter eleven

It was a situation we couldn't have foreseen. The Sunday afternoon prior to the start of spring semester, Jack called to say Buck had taken his car in for an oil change. What we didn't know was that the wait at the mechanic's was going to be hours. Since the shop was just blocks from Jack's house, Buck decided to walk home until the car was ready. Instead of the loud and slow mechanical crawl that usually warned us of Buck's arrival and added a generous thirty seconds from the time Buck pulled into his driveway to his entering the house, there was only a tiny click of a key, nearly imperceptible, and the soft closing of a well-sealed front door. Buck was already walking through the living room by the time we heard him whistling. We were on top of the kitchen table, Jack positioned behind me in a deep thrust; there were open containers of holiday leftovers that we'd been using as body paint strewn everywhere—cranberry sauce, brown gravy, pumpkin pie—and our eyes opened wide in mutual terror as Jack jumped down and yanked on his shirt and a pair of gym shorts; his boxers were crumpled up on the floor over by the stove. I was able to put on my bra and secure one of its three clasps, get my shirt over my head, and pull up my pants. When Buck's figure rounded the doorway, he saw the disheveled appearance of Jack's clothing, my pants hanging open unbuttoned and unzipped, and the carnage of our edible foreplay atop the table.

As his gaze met mine, I felt my hands, which were holding the top of my unzipped jeans, begin to lightly shake.

No one said anything. I could see Buck's mind working—he knew what he'd just seen, but he didn't want to have seen it. He wanted a loophole, a flimsy cover story he could bury his doubts under so there didn't have to be an emergency.

Standing, I slapped my bare stomach. "You'll excuse my appearance, I hope," I said. "I had to unzip these puppies and let my gut breathe. I need to take it easy on the leftovers."

There was a brief moment when he didn't react at all, seemingly deciding whether or not to follow my lead. His left eye began to tic, as though the scene before him was simply a slideshow experiencing technical difficulties—he was trying to move forward to another image, but we were stuck on this one. I watched his field of vision move from Jack's neck and collarbone, lightly stained with traces of foodstuffs, over to the table, then finally rest back upon my unzipped pants. These were puzzle pieces Buck badly wanted to rearrange so that they formed a different picture.

"You certainly don't have a gut," he finally said. But he wasn't smiling; he wasn't fully on board yet.

What else could I have done? I walked over and placed my arms around his neck, my greatest show of affection to date, cringing as the side of my cheek landed on the wiry pad of chest hair that often spilled from the top of Buck's shirts. He seemed to take great care to always have this curly fur exposed during the daytime, as though it needed photosynthesis to thrive. "I'm glad you're home," I said to him, trying to whisper but knowing that Jack would hear no matter how quietly I talked. Jack would have to understand, though, and hopefully also feel a sense of gratitude—I was about to martyr my loins on the grotesque altar of Buck's four-post bed, all so our escapades might continue. "Jack and I were just having a snack while we waited for you. I don't have long but I thought maybe if you're free for a bit we could spend some time together . . . I could finally give you your Christmas present?"

I have to hand it to Buck; he wasn't one to sit idly atop a power dynamic and let it expire. His hands moved up to rest on my waist and the previous confusion in his face gave way to a carnivorous excitement. "You certainly can." He smiled. I looked down and saw his penis had begun to swell against his pants with an embarrassing immediacy, as if he'd just pulled a cord to initiate inflation. "I was beginning to wonder when I'd see you again."

With that, he took me by the hand and led me to his bedroom, where a prompt interchange of compromise began. My pants were already unzipped; when he reached slowly down into them and felt the absence of underwear, his mind seemed to register every permission slip he could possibly think of as being signed and sealed; seconds later he'd pulled them down completely and was kneeling in front of me, running his tongue along the connecting divide between my leg and pubis. I closed my eyes and tensed up; the feeling of his tongue didn't even register as a human body part—I felt like my thigh was being stroked with the belly of a moist toad. Foreplay with Buck wouldn't do; I had to convince him to move things along. "Buck," I managed to say, "I'm more of a get-right-to-it girl." He looked up, slightly confused, so I took the initiative and lay down on the floor facing away from him, curling my arms and knees in toward my chest in a fetal pose that would still allow for entry. It was the same position I'd assumed on my bathroom floor the last time I'd gotten food poisoning to help ease the cramping.

"You're so beautiful," he said, his stumpy hands running up and down over the circumference of my ass.

"I want you inside me," I said, but the inflection came out wrong—it sounded like I was trying to convince myself. So I managed a follow-up line so awful that I was only able to say it through clenched teeth: "Please don't make me wait any longer." I found myself wishing I'd employed a bit more strategy before we'd gotten undressed. I could've asked Buck for a minute alone to use the restroom, then guzzled down his mouthwash and aftershave in the hopes of getting a buzz off their low alcohol content.

"Your wish is my command," he whispered. I felt a gagging tug at the back of my throat but managed to swallow it down with a quiet burp. He quickly fumbled off his shirt and pants, each sound a tortuous reminder that we hadn't even started yet. There was a small slapping sound of hand on skin, the equivalent of Buck having to prime gasoline into a lawn mower engine by pulling the cord a few times, then finally, with relief and a bit of pride, he kneeled down behind me on the carpet and said, "Okay. I'm hard for you."

I might've laughed had I not felt two of his fingers, unable to resist a small checkup, do an exploratory rub across my vagina. "Let me wetten things a little," he said. I felt his face and breathing move closer toward my exposed flesh; it was all I could do to force myself not to rear up and kick him in the jaw.

"No, don't!" I yelled; my voice had all the urgency of someone calling up to a suicide jumper from the street below. "Sorry," I said, recovering, "I'm weird about that." The thought of his tongue on my genitals seemed like a contamination I'd never be able to shake off. I could already feel each place he'd managed to lick me earlier—the path of his tongue left a skein of saliva that dried a bit too tightly on my skin.

"Do you want some lube?" he asked. "I think I've got some around here, somewhere."

"Buck," I said, turning my face to his with the best portrayal of excitement I could manage. I caught a glimpse of myself in the full-length mirror hanging on the wall—I was smiling far too widely, with an unnatural number of teeth exposed, as though I was doing an impression of an overly enthusiastic game show host. But I wanted to make my impatience to finish seem like an impatience to begin. "Shut up and stick it in."

With that he nodded and placed a hand on my back, using his other hand to make joystick corrections to the left and the right as he tried to align himself and eventually succeeded.

"Is that okay?" he asked. I began pushing back toward him with an animal energy, half trying to push him off me and half trying to make him come. I reminded myself of what was at stake—by the time we finished, he needed to be absolutely convinced that it was him I wanted; I hadn't come to the house to hang out with Jack. I began performing a satirized impression of a cliché pornography soundtrack—every hyperbolized moan one would produce in order to make fun of contrived ecstasy. "You're frisky," he exclaimed, and moments later, "This is incredible." He then divulged an obvious confession: "I've been thinking about doing this since the second I saw you."

It was only then, as his thrusts became more pronounced and jerky and his hands began to slide farther and farther down my torso in an attempt to gain leverage—he wanted to somehow try to move even deeper inside of me—that my craving for escape caused my head to loll sideways and notice the door was wide open. Why hadn't Buck closed it? Did he *want* Jack to hear us? If so, I wondered about Buck's motivation. Either he wanted his son to know about his sexual conquest out of some depraved sense of paternal pride, or it was related to what Buck had walked in on earlier—that moment an unconscious part of his brain was likely still working to convince itself it hadn't actually seen.

Near the end Buck started audibly grunting, a throaty, primal groan that sounded like a marine completing an obstacle course. He seemed to be losing steam; his thrusts were more erratic and further apart, as though he had to recharge between each one. I had to close my eyes when I saw it then in the doorway, unmistakable—the top half of one of Jack's white athletic socks, his toes peeking closer toward the door's entrance than he realized.

"Jack," I whispered inaudibly, the terror of possibility causing my hands to clench knuckle-white into the ground. I immediately began the future conversation he and I would have to have in my head, preparing a list of rationalizations: I really didn't have a choice, Jack. Your father saw us together, and I was pulling up my pants. If I hadn't done what I did, I would be in jail right now.

His toes stayed fixed in the doorway until the very end, when Buck let out a protracted wail that sounded like a large draft animal readying to sneeze. The noise startled me; my head snapped upright and my eyes landed on the shelf above Buck's bed that held a series of bowling league trophies. When I looked back, Jack was gone.

I was hoping that the two of us would get to sneak a simple good-bye, no matter how small—a wave and me mouthing *I'm sorry,* or perhaps I'd even resort to the juvenile phrase he was so adamantly fond of—*I love you.* But his door was shut when we emerged from the bedroom and I worried about forcing contact before I left. If I made an excuse to go into Jack's room, there'd be the risk that Jack was inside crying hysterically. And he certainly might, in his grief, begin a loud confrontation. Instead I let Buck give me a farewell kiss on the neck—"You're a goddess," he gushed; I simply turned and opened the door to leave. The sound of the garage door lifting as I started my car felt traitorous. Where had that noise been an hour ago when we needed it?

"Hey," Buck called. "Can I get a ride up the street to the mechanic?"

I rolled my window down a crack and peered out at him. "I'm sorry; I can't. If my husband saw us, he'd put a bullet between your eyes." With that, I rolled the window back up and peeled out of the drive.

In the middle of the night I woke to the soft buzz of Jack's cell phone going off inside my purse beside the bed. Ford was snoring and didn't hear it. For a moment I looked at him as I held the glowing device in my hands—his slack jaw was open with a troutish indifference; his left arm was buried beneath his head to reveal the gaping maw of his armpit and its garden of long hairs that rose out from his body like visible fumes. I shut the phone's vibration alert completely off, then sat for nearly an hour watching Jack's repeated calls light it up again and again and again, its green glow sounding a panicked alarm that only I could hear. Ford seemed securely unconscious; I was half tempted to go out to the pool patio and actually pick up, to whisper my devotion to Jack in hushed tones and calm him down. Thinking about the very hormones that coursed through Jack's veins and made his reaction so drastic was itself a turn on—he was out of control in all the right ways, a mind steered by his body. It was almost enough to tempt me to sneak from the house and go to his window in earnest, but getting caught by Buck a second time in one night might be more than sexual bribery—no matter how enthusiastically delivered—could make him overlook.

I barely registered the first two class periods the next day; I had the students all do freewriting about their holiday break. Most of them worked for ten minutes, then began to rampantly text message. I certainly didn't care. The first class was half-asleep, used to the up-all-night schedules they'd established the past three weeks playing the video games they'd gotten for Christmas and having sleepovers with friends. The second class was a bit more alert.

"When are we going to talk about *Lord of the Flies*?" one girl asked.

"Talk away," I said. Out of nowhere I suddenly remembered the feel of Buck's sausagelike fingers upon my shoulder. An acidic stripe of vomit moved up my throat in a way that made me picture mercury rising inside a thermometer.

"None of that stuff would've happened on an island of girls. Spearing a pig in the . . . butthole?" She made a visceral "no thank you" face, as though the act were a party game we were actually playing and she was refusing her turn.

"Yeah right," said Lambert. He was a dorky kid who wrote long diatribes in his journals about how girls *say* they want a nice guy but he knew this to be patently false: *I am one such fellow,* he wrote, *and my female peers will not come near me unless they're trying to copy my homework.* "If it were an island of girls they would've cannibalized each other in days."

I sighed, an autopilot recording of base-level literary analysis rattling through my mouth. "It's an interesting book to help us think about our own barbaric tendencies, given the right circumstances." I paused, hoping the conversation might turn to sex and lift me out of my depression. "What are some times when you feel out of control?"

"When I go animal style on the dance floor," one kid offered, standing up to goofily gyrate his pelvis while the class laughed. I sighed; it was always the older-looking students who made public displays of their bodies: his upper lip revealed he'd already started shaving.

Another chimed in. "When I get into a fight with my parents."

I immediately thought of Jack and Buck. "Say more—what do you want to do, when you get into a fight with your parents?" I asked. "What about that makes you feel like you've lost it?"

"I mean," he said, shrugging, "I'd never, like, actually hurt them or anything. You know? But sometimes . . ." His fist began to grind against his closed palm with the memory of rage. "Like I just want to beat the *crap* out of them. I think about choking their lights out."

"Um, psycho?" one girl joked.

"It's not psycho," another said, "unless you actually do it."

The thought sent a cold pang of fear down my center. Not once before last night had Jack ever called me so repeatedly, especially when he knew Ford would be home. Had his fury at what he'd seen me do with his father turned into an actual, physical argument? Had Jack done something terrible after I'd gone? I now remembered the stark image of his socked foot as his father's pleasured grunts had filled the bedroom. If he'd murdered Buck and said I'd driven him to do it, would I be considered an accessory to murder? I wondered if that charge would bring more jail time than sex with a minor. How twisted it all would be if it turned out I'd slept with Buck for nothing—I was going to jail for one thing or another anyway. For a moment my stomach wrenched at the thought of a father/son conspiracy: Maybe Buck was smarter than I'd given him credit for. Perhaps he'd figured out what Jack and I were up to and Buck realized that if he caught us together I'd seduce him to keep him quiet. So he made a deal with Jack, bribing him with the promise of a top-of-the-line gaming system, or a new car as soon as he got his learner's permit: arrange it so I walk in on you two and let me have her once before I call the cops. But then the guilt and envy had been too much for Jack's teenage brain, and in a heated argument late last night he'd taken his father's life.

I had to get my mind into a better place. We were having a classroom discussion about lack of restraint—why wasn't anyone bringing up libido? "So we understand a loss of control due to anger," I summarized. "What are other times you feel out of control? Do any of you not trust your actions, say, when you're alone with your boyfriend or girlfriend?" This caused the room to fill with nervous laughter.

"I know if I ever met my favorite singer, I would do anything he wanted," one girl confessed.

"Yeah, that's illegal," her friend joked.

"Whatever." She laughed. "I'd make it worth the jail time for him."

This made me wonder—if things did all fall apart today, had Jack made the jail time worth it for me? He had done everything I'd wanted him to do, and as far as I knew had kept quiet. But no memory seemed enough to adequately sustain me through a boy-less incarceration. When the bell rang, I remained frozen in place imagining the starch-heavy cafeteria meals, the formless jumpsuits whose color resembled traffic cones.

I quickly took inventory of the worst-case scenario: Jack not showing up to class. I pictured him at home, weeping next to his father's sheet-covered corpse, trying to think of how to dispose of the body. But an abnormal break from my daily routine would seem suspect: I couldn't suddenly go home during the same class when Jack was absent. No matter how difficult, I'd have to make it through the school day, and only then, at the day's very end in the privacy of my own car, could I call Jack's phone (which might easily have a police tap on it now, if Buck had been found dead) and begin the conversation in a very straitlaced manner. I'd ask only why he hadn't been in class today, nothing more. Such a call and a question wasn't out of bounds for any caring teacher. And no one could prove I'd given him the cell phone.

But Jack did stumble in. He had the near-black eyes of some-one who'd been up all night interrogating himself. "Jack," I called to him from behind my desk when he entered, a bit perturbed at how needy I sounded—I didn't like depending on him for resolu-tion. He refused to stop or turn toward me and wore a crumpled shirt and sweatpants that he'd likely slept in. I made a mental note to ready the tin of mints from my purse when we spoke—he'd certainly forgotten to brush his teeth.

Jack went straight to his usual seat in the back and stared at the ground with a scowl. In some ways, this tantrum made him seem more juvenile, and I allowed myself the pleasure of pausing to take in his sour expression: he looked like a child who'd been forced to share a toy. His outrage, I figured, was a good sign—if he'd gotten on the bus this morning after leaving behind his father's dead body, he would likely have been antsy, guilt-stricken, wanting to talk with me immediately in private. Instead he was ignoring me. He wanted me punished for having given up a conciliatory offering to Buck. Finally I stood and very calmly walked over to his desk. "I have the essay you handed in before break graded," I told him. "Can you stay after class and discuss it?" He gave a near-imperceptible nod, then further exaggerated his scowl in a way that seemed like a challenge. I was happy to take him up on it. As soon as class ended, I would fuck that pout right off his face.

After fifty long minutes, when the bell rang and the other students dispersed, I grabbed my keys out of my purse and ran to the door, locking the knob, then quickly began to disrobe. I'd worn the French maid bra-and-thong set—the very one that had gotten Ford so worked up on Christmas that he'd helped himself to an extended session with my unconscious body. "Jack," I said, my voice slightly too businesslike, "I'm very sorry I couldn't pick up your phone calls last night. My husband really is a policeman. If he caught me talking on the phone in the middle of the night—it wouldn't matter who I said it was—he'd get suspicious. Cops have resources, Jack. He'd have me followed. I wouldn't be able to come over to your house ever again. I wouldn't be able to pick you up and go places with you. None of it." I walked over and began clearing off the top of my desk, all except for the small tabletop Christmas tree in the corner.

I made sure to face away from Jack so he could see my thonged ass as I spoke. No matter how angry he was, could he really resist looking? Could any straight fourteen-year-old boy?

"Think of the situation we'd be in right now if I hadn't done what I did." Jack's expression remained unconvinced. I realized he needed to share in the blame. "It's not like you left me a lot of choice," I pointed out. "You told me he'd be gone for hours."

Jack's eyebrows lifted incredulously. "So it's *my* fault you slept with him? I didn't know he'd come back so soon. When he gets his car worked on he's usually gone half the day."

I backpedaled a little. "I'm not blaming you. I'm just reminding you of the fact that you thought we had more time than we did."

Even before he spoke, I realized I'd miscalculated; his level of anger at the situation wouldn't allow for any contrition. "You had *sex* with him," Jack yelled. "You slept with my dad. You didn't even give him time to say anything." As he began pacing from side to side, I started to worry. It wasn't safe for Jack to be this upset at school. One offhand remark from a pimply smart-ass in the hall-way and Jack could throw a punch. Then, when confronted about his uncharacteristic aggression in the assistant principal's office, Jack would lose it and begin spilling details. "Maybe he wasn't even that suspicious. But you just started crawling all over him. You *wanted* to. I heard you guys in the bedroom. You liked it!" Jack started toward the door and I let him go; it was locked. He turned the knob a few times, then gave the door a frustrated kick when it didn't open. "Let me out," he finally said. He didn't turn back around to face me.

I needed a new plan for a truce—I had to give him a peace offering. I softened my voice, adding a new tone of apology. "He watched me pull up my pants, Jack. The human brain can do amazing things with denial, but it has to have enough incentive. Me staying for dinner and watching television with your father is a little ego boost for him, but it's not the type of leverage needed for him to block out questions of what I may have been doing with my pants halfway down in the kitchen with his teenage son."

I took off my bra, then said his name. After a long moment he turned around to face me. "Come here," I said.

Jack's eyes fell to the floor. "Are you going to fuck him all the time now?" he asked.

I couldn't help but let out a small chuckle. "I would rather be sprayed with bear mace than touch your father again." Carefully, my heels still on, I climbed up onto the desk and got on my knees. "Are you going to come here?"

"He's going to want it all the time."

"Well he's not going to get it. You and I will be more careful. I'll have to be around far less when he's home. And when he is home, I'll tell him that things are going a little fast for me and I need to dial it back a bit." Jack nodded but stayed fixed next to the door.

"Come here, I'm going to let you do something special." I wanted to tell him that the act would be exclusive to us, but doing that meant bringing up my sexual relationship with Ford—it was a risk to talk about sex with another person right now. But I wanted him to know this was certainly out of the ordinary. After a moment of debate, I decided it was worth it. "I don't even do this with my husband," I added. This wasn't entirely true of course, but I doubted that saying *We do this when I want Ford to feel indebted to me and I've doped myself to the moon on barbiturates* would have the same persuasive vigor.

The gamble paid off. Grabbing his backpack, he walked up to the desk and dropped it to the floor dramatically, like a soldier shedding his duffel bag upon entering the house after returning from war. He unbuttoned his pants and pulled them down to his knees along with his boxers. "Climb up here with me," I said encouragingly. I turned and sloppily began to lick the length of him, wetting him up as much as I could. With that I squatted down onto his penis, letting it slip securely into my asshole before kneeling down on all fours to be fucked on the desktop. It was an act I'd never enjoyed, but I figured with Jack there would at least be the pleasure of getting to see his surprise and enjoyment as he experienced it for the first time.

I was wrong. Jack wasn't gentle or slow and he remained completely mute throughout the process—there were no moans of how great it felt or expressions of gratitude at how I was subjugating myself for his pleasure. Perhaps in his naïveté he wasn't aware of the pain involved on my behalf, or maybe he was completely mindful of it, trying to repay me for the agony he'd gone through in the last twenty-four hours. Either way, his silent anger made it a true punishment. It was the first time we'd had sex that I was glad when it was over.

When he finished and slipped back out, there was a small amount of mucus and blood that I dried off with a Kleenex. I wiped myself off and readied a small plug of tissue to put between my cheeks so his semen wouldn't visibly leak out and stain my pants later in the day. Too late I realized that Jack was digging around in his backpack; by the time I looked over to see what he was doing his personal smart phone was already extended toward me. I didn't have time to move or cover myself in any way before the damning click of its camera echoed through the room. He'd snapped a shot of me completely nude, spreading apart my ass cheeks in an act of inspection.

"Very funny, Jack. But you've got to delete that. Better yet, let me do it." I held out my hand, motioning for him to pass me the phone.

"I'm keeping it," he demanded. "I've got to have more than he has."

"Come on, Jack. You've had me a thousand times and he's had me once. Think of all the things we've done together. All I did was let him tuck it in for a minute while I looked at the wall and thought about my grocery list." But he didn't appear to be in the mood for bartering, not even after the sexual concession I'd just given him in the middle of the day on school property. "Fine," I agreed. "Keep the picture." It would only be a matter of time before I had an opportunity to delete it.

When Jack left I Febrezed the room profusely, but our act seemed to have left behind a hormonal cloud that had a full-moon effect on the classes afterward. Trevor, having been dumped by Darcy over the holiday break, did a freewrite that obliquely referenced suicide and proceeded to read it out loud to the class as he stared at her across the room. When class ended he sought counsel at my desk while I tried to get comfortable in my chair; though the ache left from Jack's fury felt raw and sharp, it also seemed a reminder of forgiveness. Hopefully Jack would feel I'd done due penance and we could go back to the way things had been.

I offered weeping Trevor a tissue as I adjusted against the cumsoaked wad of it in my pants. Suddenly the classroom door opened. I worried that it would be Jack, that upon seeing me with Trevor he'd convince himself I was holding dual trysts with other students. But the sound of heavy footsteps and the labored breathing relieved me of this scare. It was Janet.

Waddling in, she tilted her head back to look at Trevor through her Coke-bottle glasses. "Someone failed a quiz, huh," she barked.

Momentarily ignoring her, I turned and spoke to Trevor in a dramatic manner I knew he'd like. "If I have any worry you might harm yourself, I'm required by law to report it," I said. "Now, you and I both know she isn't worth this suffering. You will have a long list of women in your life, Trevor. It hurts now," I said, clenching my asshole in empathy, "but that pain is temporary. What I need to know from you is whether or not you're going to be okay until I see you in class tomorrow."

He gave a long sigh and tried to stare out beyond the walls of the classroom. "Yeah," he said. "I'll make it until tomorrow."

"That's good," I declared, standing to place a hand on his back and usher him toward the door. For a moment I worried the ball of tissue had dislodged when I stood and was about to roll down my pant leg and drop onto the floor like a magic egg that Janet and Trevor and I would all look at in disbelief. "Be kind to yourself," I whispered to him. "Go home and jerk off to porn on the Internet. Have a look at other fish in the sea. Especially the surgically enhanced ones." He gave me a confused grin and blew his nose.

"Thanks, Mrs. Price." I nodded and shut the door. When I turned I found Janet leaning over my desk, bracing her weight with her elbows; her head now occupied the exact spot where Jack's erection had penetrated my rectum.

"I wanted to tell you," she said victoriously. "AP Rosen's shoe has officially been removed from my butt." For a second I worried her comment held a sort of telepathy, but I knew it was just coincidence.

"Oh good." I smiled. "I bet you're more comfortable now."

"He said your reports showed I was making . . . let me remember exactly how he phrased this. Oh yeah, 'demonstrable improvement.'" She pointed a finger at me and began to wag it. "Before you stepped in he was throwing around write-ups and termination guidelines, all kinds of bullshit." Her right hand balled into a doughy fist and pounded the desk. "Damn it," she said, nearly tearing up, "you're the only decent person who works here."

Before I was able to run or dodge her, she'd lunged toward me in a rare display of speed, drawing me close into a pillowy, slightly sour embrace.

"Well you're certainly welcome, Janet."

As she released me she gave me a firm slap on the arm. "I have to admit, I thought there was something off about you when you first came here. You didn't seem like the bleeding-heart liberal type who's out to save the world. And you sure didn't look like you needed the money. I didn't get why someone like you would want to piss away their youth and beauty in this torture chamber." I smiled nervously and let her hand meet my face in a grandmotherly pat. "But you're just a good person. Rare. The world is going to shit and flies real fast."

She moved toward the door, then stopped to wave a disapproving hand in front of her nose. "Speaking of which," she called out, "I can't stand the stench of these kids. Make our classes smell like a locker room."

I opened the door for her and held it as I gave my brightest smile. "It is a little ripe in here by the end of the day," I conceded.

chapter twelve

Though we'd escaped any legal consequences from Buck's interruption, the sex with Jack had definitely suffered. Puerile buoyancy no longer poured from him like an energy source. This had been one of my favorite things about our sessions together; I was determined to get it back. Prior to the incident, if a camera had been trained on Jack's face during intercourse, the viewer might've guessed he was jumping on a trampoline: the underwater sway of his hair combined with the wordless marvel in his bouncing face made him look nearly airborne when he was on top of me. Now there was a sullen determination to the way he went about the task. When he inserted himself, he did so with a concentrated silence, watching as though our two parts could never fit together without his direct oversight. His eyes, squinting with focus, made him seem like a burdened metalworker performing an arduous task on a lathe. "Don't scowl," I had to remind him all the time now. "It causes wrinkles."

I thought the introduction of props and toys might add some much-needed levity, but this was tricky: my own arousal was based on the juxtaposition of Jack's long-standing innocence and budding carnality—vibrating cock rings and French ticklers might pique his interest, but they would do so at the expense of my own. If Jack's requests began to grow more adult and lurid, the effect would be just as offensive to me as his body maturing.

My creative suggestions, therefore, had to be homespun deeds of inverted kink that came from the corruption of something wholesome. I tried having him wear his old Halloween costumes and sports equipment while I pleasured him—a favorite of mine was the now-too-small cup that had been part of his junior soccer uniform. It barely held him; his genitals spilled out from its edges, like a snake-in-the-can practical joke that had been halfheartedly pushed back inside after popping open.

But nothing seemed to nudge Jack back into the mode of abandon I was searching for. The problem, I soon realized, wasn't simply between us. The way Jack would flinch at the slightest noise when we were alone, the moments during sex when I'd open my eyes to find that Jack's gaze wasn't trained on me at all but on his closed bedroom door, made it clear he couldn't let the catastrophe of Buck finding us together go: it had left Jack with a post-traumatic stress disorder that was heartily interfering with my getting off. It felt like Jack and I were never alone. At every moment, Buck's leering, potbellied ghost was pressing in upon us at the periphery, threatening to suffocate the best aspects of my relationship with Jack for good.

What was needed was a dual act of revenge upon Buck—a plan that Jack and I could execute together as a team to show him that his father didn't hold any real power over us. What Jack no doubt really wanted—for his father to know that Jack alone sexually fulfilled me—obviously wasn't possible; we couldn't demonstrate for Buck what amazing orgasms I achieved atop his son. But I realized with heavy delight one Friday that we actually could do something a little bit close.

"Jack," I proposed, my expression flushed and gleeful. "Let's drug your father tonight."

I hadn't predicted hesitation on Jack's behalf, but he wasn't so sure; he asked a long series of prudent questions and didn't agree until I'd sufficiently explained every aspect of it—"You're sure he won't feel sick the next day? Won't he know something happened?" I felt as though Jack was a dubious employee at some stickler government agency and I was applying for a building permit but hadn't met the zoning requirements. Every detail had to be disclosed before he'd sign off.

He was eventually convinced, and perhaps a small bit frightened, when I relayed how often I'd gone about the process with Ford. "At worst your dad will have a headache or sleep in late tomorrow," I promised. "I do this to my husband all the time."

Jack laughed with worried eyes, unsure if I'd made a joke. When he realized I hadn't, he brought a fingernail to his teeth and chewed for a while. "You've never done that to me?" he hesitantly asked, thinking back on whether or not he'd ever abruptly fallen asleep in my company.

"It's a way of getting a break from people I don't enjoy, Jack. I'd have no reason to do it to you." This was what I hoped the evening would convey to Jack most of all: it was us vs. them. Buck and Ford were on the other side of the equation.

That evening, we agreed I'd indulge Buck's invitation to stay for dinner. Once we were all seated and the wine was poured, I made a request for hot sauce. "I'm feeling spicy tonight," I said to Buck, who lit up at the connotation with palpable hope.

"Jack," Buck ordered, chewing, "can you go grab the hot sauce?"

My stomach sank. I hadn't planned on it being a challenge to get access to Buck's wineglass, but he hadn't left my side since he'd gotten home. When we'd sat down at the table, Buck had scooted his chair so close to mine that I could smell the vinegary mix of merlot and marinated beef on his breath.

But Jack surprised me, his voice a perfect hue of casual teenage defiance. "You go get it," he replied, his eyes not leaving his plate. "She's your girlfriend."

Buck's satisfaction on hearing this intimate term and possessive pronoun applied to me completely outweighed any sense of umbrage at Jack's not obeying. Smiling, he rose from his chair and headed to the kitchen. This was exactly what we'd wanted to happen, though I couldn't help feeling a small bite of irritation at how clever Jack's response had been. It hinted toward an ability to mislead that I didn't particularly want him to have. But the callow lack of modesty in his too-pleased smile as I whispered over to him, "Nice job," erased my discomfort entirely: Jack was merely pleased that he'd pleased me. He'd done it for the greater good.

Taking the small envelope out of my pocket and emptying it into Buck's wineglass, I sloshed it around a few times until the powder fully dissolved. The anticipation of having Jack inside me with Buck's unconscious body there as a witness made me impatient; when Buck returned, I immediately extended my glass for a toast. "To feeling the heat," I said. Buck's glass clinked with my own.

"I'll say." He winked.

Since it was the start of the weekend, and having received optimistic clues from me, Buck was in party mode. He burned through the glass and poured another in a matter of minutes. It was hard for Jack and me not to laugh as Buck began to nod off, his head falling fully supine against his sternum while the two of us pretended to continue having a normal conversation. "It's a warm winter, even by Florida's standards," I remarked. "Global warming? What do you think, Jack?"

Jack giggled. "Scary stuff." I took a swig of wine directly from the bottle and passed it to Jack, who also drank.

"Scary stuff indeed. Buck, what do you think?" We both turned to view the fallen crown of his head. "What's that? I'm sorry, I can't hear you."

It wasn't long before we were giddy, partially buzzed but also delighted at Buck's incapacitation. "Do we leave him at the table?" Jack asked.

"Let's drag him to bed. He won't second-guess waking up there." Jack stood and walked over to his father, giving him a few firm testing pokes on the forehead before grabbing Buck's hair and using it to pull his head upright. He looked into his father's gaped-open mouth, pulled up one of Buck's eyelids and peered into the hollow shine of a vacant pupil.

"He seems totally dead." Jack gave me an apprehensive smile that was only half-joking. "We didn't accidentally kill him, did we?"

I walked over to join Jack in peering down the wine-stained tunnel of Buck's throat. "I didn't give him enough to kill him. Should I have?"

Jack stared at me for a moment, wide-eyed, while I tried to appear earnest, but soon enough I'd broken into hysterical laughter and Jack followed. We began a comical procession of lugging Buck to the bedroom; occasionally his head would bonk up against the wall of the hallway and one of us would say, "Oops!" Then we'd laugh so hard we'd have to put him down for a bit until we regained composure.

When we finally pulled Buck up onto his bed, I began unbuttoning Jack's pants. Jack started to stand but I pulled him back down with me to the mattress. "Don't you want to go to my room?" Jack asked.

"Let's do it in front of him. He's out, believe me." Spying a glass of water on the nightstand, I grabbed the cup and poured a small amount of water onto Buck's forehead. There was the quiet slapping sound of droplets hitting against skin, then a few whispered laughs from Jack. "See? He won't wake up no matter what we do." I dropped my bra over Buck's eyes, followed by my panties—if it had been his father's face that was bothering Jack, now it was covered up. But this felt like a form of aversion therapy that Jack needed to undergo. He was clearly still stressed about his father having found us, about Buck's having masturbated inside of me, and here was a way to prove that neither of those things mattered: that Buck, in fact, was helpless.

Jack didn't seem to understand the empowering angle of the setup. He had an erection but his eyes kept scanning the bedroom, eventually returning to the body lying next to us. "I . . . I don't think I can do this," he finally said.

"Close your eyes," I said. Taking him deep into my mouth, I began sucking with a zeal and precision reserved for when I needed to get my way. Soon he was moaning, gingerly thrusting against my tongue. I turned around and placed him inside me, climbing over Buck's body so that my arms and legs were on either side of Buck's torso as Jack pounded through to climax, the mattress rocking. Buck's slippered feet hanging off the bed's edge moved from right to left in a steady flutter.

When we were finished I asked Jack to get me a pen and a piece of paper. While he was gone, I took off Buck's slippers, pants, and boxers, leaving him completely naked from the waist down save for his socks.

"What are you doing?" Jack asked when he returned. His voice was tinged with fear; he was staring at his father's penis.

"I can get credit for tonight without ever having to touch him." I wrote a note, unsigned, that read, *You were great—thanks* and left it on Buck's nightstand. I had the urge to reach inside my panties, grab a fingerful of Jack's spunk and trace it across Buck's lips, but I didn't want Jack to see me; he wouldn't understand why I was doing it.

I found it odd that Jack didn't call me either day that weekend. Usually there'd be at least one offer, even if the window of time was so short that he knew I'd reject it. ("Just come over," Jack would sometimes plead. "He's having a beer in the neighbor's backyard. It's enough time for something. I could put my thumb inside you. You could lick my shoulder blades.") When Monday came Jack entered right with the bell and seemed distracted the whole period, staring at either the ceiling or the floor but never anywhere in between. It was enough to raise my anxiety to the extent that when Jack approached my desk after class and stated he had to talk, I got an immediate diarrheal cramp and felt tears beginning to sting my eyes. "What's wrong?" I asked. "Your dad woke up okay, didn't he?"

Jack's forehead crinkled slightly. "Yeah. I um, wondered what we're going to do for Valentine's Day."

It had always been my most loathed of the holidays since sex with Ford was inescapable. But perhaps Jack's interest foretold a conversion on my behalf; I might now get to experience it as so many others did—a day of carnal gluttony instead of torture. I sat down at the desk and reached into the top drawer, pulling out a bowl of candy and offering him some.

"Blow Pop?" He shook his head but I took one and began un-wrapping, imagining the lollipop tracing against the blond fuzz of Jack's abdomen like a sticky wand. Stretching my lips across the sucker, I twisted it between them in a hyperbolic way as a visual aid and removed it with a dramatic *pop*. "Valentine's, sure. What did you have in mind?"

The actual holiday fell on a Tuesday, meaning Buck's schedule afforded Jack and me only an hour to complete a quick act of sixty-nine and a game of Nintendo Mario Kart, but Jack insisted on a weekend excursion. I hardly remember how Ford and I observed the occasion, mainly because I'd drugged myself after getting back from Jack's house; Ford had switched shifts that evening to arrive home earlier, and we'd gone somewhere bland to eat, then had the planned act of cornball sexual variety Ford always insisted on for Valentine's—he liked to have sex on the living room sofa while fac-ing the entryway mirror, our warming skin making small squeaks of friction against the couch's leather. I nearly vomited as I watched the ceiling fan spin above me in my dizzied state; it was only the next morning that I noticed the roses and diamond pendant he'd given me on the counter. He was asleep when I left for work so I called from school to thank him on my lunch break. "I'm glad you like the necklace," he answered. "Last night I couldn't tell if you did or not. Did you get a little buzzed?"

Indeed. By the time I'd dismounted the couch, the room had

been whirling so fast that I'd had to crawl to the bedroom. Ford had already gone to take his usual postcoital shower; I suppose he hadn't noticed the extent of my temporary handicap. Did it ever register with Ford that I often seemed to be drifting in and out of consciousness during sex? Was this denial or apathy on his part? "I guess so," I answered. "But that's what one does for a celebration."

The following Saturday I told Ford I had to attend an all-day continuing education workshop so Jack and I could drive to a roller-skating rink on the other side of the bay. Something about the colored lights turned our faces into those of strangers, allowing us to momentarily transform into two different people. It was delightful to round a corner, whip back my hair, and through it see not Jack but a boy very similar to him whose entire body was fair game for my roving hands. No onlooker appeared to sense anything out of the ordinary—whether I seemed younger or Jack seemed older enough to normalize the difference between us, I'm not sure. I still didn't feel it was safe enough to push our luck and join the throngs of teenagers sloppily making out in the arcade room. But when we had a tandem fall and hit the polished wooden floor in an intertwined pile, Jack got the beginnings of an erection as we struggled to stand back up on moving wheels and our torsos kept hitting into one another. I led him out of the ring and we dry-humped behind a coin-operated prize machine until it lit up in a manic flurry of color and sound that almost gave us a heart attack—a young child had approached from the opposite side and put in a quarter. We stayed for a minute and watched her play, feeling the bittersweet pain of heat draining from our genitals. She operated a metallic claw inside the machine and tried to close it over a stuffed animal, and when it missed by only centimeters, it seemed a fitting metaphor for our orgasms that had just slipped away. To recover we bought Slurpees and cotton candy that dyed our mouths blue, and I felt a near-pharmaceutical rush at the weightless feeling in my chest as we sped across the floor for a few final songs, seemingly falling and speeding up at the same time.

Afterward in the car, Jack gave me a red envelope; the card inside was covered with glitter-outlined roses and affirmed our love to be forever. "This is incredibly sweet," I told him, though after our fun day I couldn't help but be slightly perturbed that he'd do something so stupid. "But you know I can't keep it, don't you?"

His first expression was one of angry surprise, but finally, he nodded. "We could do something ceremonial with it . . . burn it together," I offered. "Or tear it up and scatter the pieces over the ocean."

He said nothing, so I started the car. It wasn't until we got to the highway that he conceded his thoughts. "That just seems depressing," he said. I didn't respond, forcing him to dwell on it—I needed him to see that he'd behaved inappropriately. Finally, tinkering with his seat belt buckle, he tried to channel his disappointment into a romantic proclamation of selflessness. "I just wanted to give it to you," he said. "You know? What happens with it now doesn't matter, I guess." I thought he was going to say more, but those were his last words of the evening.

From then on, in fact, he began to talk less in general. It almost seemed like he was trying to express his thoughts physically instead, but that in doing so he encountered equal frustration. Our sessions had gone from being short and multiple to being long and continuous; by the time he came Jack now looked tellingly exerted, so much so that he had to jump in the shower when Buck came home so his wet hair wouldn't seem suspicious.

It was during one such marathon session in March when it happened, just before spring break was scheduled to start. Thinking back on it, I remember the lighting in Jack's room as having been different that day—somehow localized and ominous, like the umbral flicker thrown from an open fire. Jack's hands were cupping my ass cheeks as he pushed inside me; I was pinned against the wall, both of us standing up. Buck's immediate view would've been Jack's buttocks, clenching and unclenching, his scrotum swinging between his legs, my elbows braced against the wall and my head and throat tilted backward in the clutches of receiving. I was the one who first turned my face, thinking I'd heard a noise.

"Shhh," I said to Jack. I could feel him tense up inside me as he stopped and listened.

"Shit," he whispered, pulling out of me and beginning to dress. I began to get dressed too, though not with the same frenzy. I knew I'd seen Buck's figure moving away from the open door frame, and my mind was racing at a disoriented pace: I had to come up with a plan; seduction alone wouldn't be able to bury what he'd just seen. Perhaps his pride was the best course of appeal? If he went to the police and this was made public, all his neighbors and coworkers would know that he and his son had been sharing a lover. It was an angle I could take: he didn't want the shame of it, didn't want to put Jack through the embarrassment.

Jack's eyes met mine as a low wailing sound began to come

from down the hallway—it would intensify, then fall completely silent and start up again. Was Buck crying? I picked up my pace and finished dressing, hoping his sadness might be an opportunity to go comfort him, even if I was the cause. Maybe I could say that Jack forced me to do it—he'd gotten into my purse, looked up my husband's number on my cell phone, and had threatened to call Ford and tell him about my affair with Buck unless I slept with him. Even if Buck didn't fully believe it, perhaps it would be a plausible enough story for him to play along with. In the distance, Buck's warbled moan was growing louder and more frantic. How long had he stood watching at the doorway before I'd sensed him there and turned around?

"Stay here," I said to Jack. "Let me try to talk to him first." Jack nodded but gave me a look that bordered on disgust—his eyes held a fluent jealousy, and I knew he was imagining that if Buck's catching me with my pants unbuttoned had meant a bribe of sex, who knew what his catching us in the middle of the act might require. "Keep your cool," I warned him. "The important thing is that he doesn't call the cops."

Buck stood hunched over at the end of the hallway, his shoulder occasionally coming to life with a spasm. "Buck," I called gently, walking toward him with slow steps. Despite my best efforts, my voice was trembling—I had no idea what sort of animal Buck became when unhinged. Was he about to get violent? Perhaps it would be a good thing if he began hitting me; he'd lose a huge amount of credibility if I'd been beaten up when the cops arrived. Jack and I could stick to the story that I'd just been there to tutor a student in need; the rest was a jealous delusion on Buck's part. But the accusations alone could cause me to lose my job, and Ford, in a misguided attempt to prove my innocence, would probably do something over-the-top like have a forensic team sweep Jack's bedroom. No, the police couldn't get involved under any circumstances. I had to win Buck over at all costs.

As I drew closer, I realized that Buck was bent forward in a near-comical manner. His torso drooped toward the ground as though a child had just pointed a toy gun at him and he was pretending to be mortally wounded. Occasionally he'd attempt to take a step, but his stance was so off-kilter that his body merely lurched in place; he was performing the slow, erratic motions of a zombified waltz. I stood for a moment, clearing my throat, confused. It was only as I moved around to the side of him that I began to see the discoloration spread across his neck, heard the restrictive choking sound of his lungs failing to get air. Buck was bent over holding his chest. "Oh my god," I muttered. He contorted himself as best he could so that his face was looking over and up toward mine—its color alone nearly caused me to scream. His cheeks had taken on a reddish-purple hue. It looked like he was being hung with an invisible noose.

I took a silent step backward, then laced my fingers together and stood to watch. With a wheeze, he impotently tried to call Jack's name, his contorted lips silently mashing out the word again and again before he finally stopped trying. Though his face had seized up, one eye remained open and focused. His stare was filled with the hatred of clarity—he had now let go of all illusions about me. Yet unless his voice returned, I was the sole person he could appeal to. I glanced down the hallway, training my stare on Jack's open door. If he peeked out his head and saw his father's distressed posture, what could I say to Jack that would convince him to stay in his room just a bit longer?

I needed time alone, without the shrill adolescent panic that would overtake Jack, to decide if Buck would honor the system of quid pro quo. If I dialed 911, could he really repay such a favor by turning me in to the police? Seemed impossible to me, yet delusions of morality could make people justify all sorts of actions. Regardless of my heroic efforts, Buck might feel that turning me in was the right thing to do. I could hear him now: *The law is the law and my hands are tied.*

Looking down, I saw the judgment in Buck's eye had been replaced with a bulging desperation. Straining, he managed to make a thin, nasal grunt in my direction; the sound caused me to recall the unfortunate memory of Buck dully thrusting between my legs. I looked back down the hall to Jack's door. If only there were a way to be certain he would stay in his room until it was over—I'd simply have to make sure that he did. If I saw him coming out, I could run to him, pull him back inside his bedroom and say that Buck was very upset; *Your father needs some time alone to think.* Then, later, we would discover the body together. Jack couldn't be allowed to interrupt this natural chain of events. Ultimately saving his father's life just wasn't worth the risk—Buck's stumpy hands were no place at all for my fate to rest.

I froze in place as Buck's mouth grew wider and wider, seeking air, and a last flash of recognition passed through Buck's eye in a way that nearly made me feel cursed. He was aware that I was choosing to let him die. Realizing he had no hope of convincing me otherwise, I watched every ounce of life he had left channel into a stare of malignant damning that radiated toward me with a tangible heat. One side of his lip raised back to reveal a small portion of tooth, as though he was preparing to give me a vicarious bite.

I had the urge to wave my fingers in a small good-bye, but ultimately that felt too catty—I didn't need to gloat. Buck's open eye rolled back into his head and he fell to his knees without a sound—there were truly no words for the plushness of the Patrick household's carpeting—then his head and the rest of his body surrendered completely to the ground. Buck Patrick had just suffered a heart attack.

I bent down to confirm that he was no longer breathing. His rolled-back eye was frozen open and bulging; I could see a sliver of my reflection in its glazing sheen. I found myself wishing there was a way to stuff his tongue back inside his mouth, simply to avoid the sheer vulgarity of having to look at it: its purple mass had fully extended out from between his lips, as though it was trying to slither away from his dying body. With a manicured toe, I poked at the flesh of his cheeks and got no response; just to be sure I placed my foot gently against Buck's neck to feel for a pulse. There was none. A flush of excited energy ran through me, as if I'd won the lottery— everything was going to be okay.

Removed from the thumb of Buck's accusing stare, I finally had a chance to think. Why hadn't we heard him come in? I tiptoed down the hall to the living room to peek out the drawn blinds, still not wanting Jack to venture forth from his room just yet. I felt a rare surge of nonsexual affection for him as I thought about how he'd likely stay quietly put for hours more if no one went in to fetch him—I could picture him now, seated on his bed imagining the variety of vile intimate scenarios he feared finding me and his father engaged in if he left the safety of his room. Particularly after the last time, Jack didn't want to trade the calm security of the unknown for a definitive and cruel reality.

Buck's car was parked directly in the center of the driveway; mine was in the garage. It was almost as if he'd purposefully blocked me inside. Had Buck known about Jack and me? Had he been planning a confrontation? This seemed doubtful—cardiac arrest would be a dramatic response to something he'd half-expected to catch. No, Buck had been fully surprised, more surprised than he could handle. I had to assume he'd simply come home early and meant to go right back out—maybe he'd come in to see if Jack wanted to go grab a bite to eat with him. "This is complicated," I said out loud.

I knew Jack's personal cell phone was in his backpack; if need be I could wrestle him to the ground for it. His secret phone was beneath his bed in a box and would be impossible for him to get at with me fighting him. I took Buck's cell phone out of its holder on his belt, then walked to the kitchen and grabbed the home phone off its base; I hid them both in a drawer in Buck's bathroom before heading back to Jack's room.

Jack was sitting anxiously on the bed. In the haste of having been caught, he'd put his athletic shorts on backward; I noticed the way the seam created an awkward ripple atop his genitals.

"I have some upsetting news," I began, "but everything is going to be okay." I made a mental note that this phrasing might also be a good segue when the unfortunate time came and I had to break up with Jack: acknowledge the negative, yes, but don't fail to highlight how life would continue.

Jack's forehead wrinkled with confusion. "Did my dad leave? Is he angry?"

"No, he's not angry. He's in the hallway." Outside, a car drove by with its stereo jovially blaring; its vibrations shook the windows in Jack's bedroom. I couldn't help but feel like Buck's death had made the whole world seem a bit younger. Jack's eyes widened and looked toward his open door.

"Does he want to talk to me?" Jack whispered. I took my shirt back off; it seemed like the best course of action.

"Put your hands on my breasts," I instructed. "I have to tell you something traumatic and you need to be reminded of all the good that's here in the world for you to enjoy." Wordlessly, Jack clutched his palms onto my breasts and swallowed.

"I'll stop beating around the bush." I sighed. "Your father had a heart attack."

Realization crossed his face like a time-lapsed shadow. He ran out of the room but I stayed behind for a moment to collect his two cell phones, secret them in my purse, and prepare myself for the possibility of a heated debate. I flipped through his personal phone for at least a minute, trying to find the photo he'd taken of me and delete it, but it wasn't anywhere obvious and there wasn't time to waste. It was the only solid evidence that linked the two of us, and Jack certainly wouldn't offer it up to authorities. This was a triumph I was intent on maintaining—on Jack's dresser, for example, there was a plate bearing a hardened scrap of pizza crust, a relic that held the small and perfectly imperfect indentions of Jack's bite marks, his right incisor slightly askew. I had the urge to place this inside my purse as well; the prop of something his supple mouth had gnawed upon might come in handy in the days ahead if Jack chose to be upset with me and I had to fantasize about his lips. But I knew I couldn't ever have anything related to Jack in my possession, no matter how organic and disposable.

In the hallway Jack was kneeling over the body and crying silent tears. When I first laid my hand upon his shoulder, he sat down Indian-style and began rocking gradually back and forth. "We've got to call 911," he finally whimpered.

"You will." I nodded. "Later, when I'm gone."

Jack shook his head but continued to talk to me instead of attempting to go get the phone. I was, after all, the adult in the situation. "We should start CPR," he added, somewhat forcefully. But was I wrong to detect already a flat note of resignation in his protests—the knowledge that even if it were possible to revive Buck, it wouldn't be in our best interests to do so?

I sat down next to Jack and took his hands, which made him cry harder, and with volume now. "He isn't breathing, Jack." I spoke slowly and evenly, doing my best impression of a medical professional on television. "When the brain loses oxygen, cells begin to die. If they even could bring him back, he'd be a vegetable. We don't want that. Your dad wouldn't want that. We need to wait before you call the paramedics. We need to be sure."

"Be sure?" Jack cried. Mucus streamed out from his nose and began to mingle with his lips. His tears and high-pitched cries had a way of making him seem pleasantly preadolescent; in the moment I was not opposed to intercourse.

"Be sure?" Jack asked again. "No." His head began to shake. "We have to try. What if they can bring him back? What if he'll be fine if we just get someone here soon?"

Leaning my topless chest in toward him so that my breasts fell just below his chin, I gave Jack a look that told him he was being silly and wiped his face with my fingers. "Jack, he isn't fine. He's dead and that's terrible. But at least he won't have to be tube-fed on some machine for three months before they pull the plug anyway . . ." I paused, not wanting to be blatant, but I did need to close the deal. "And you and I can stay together," I whispered.

Jack's face broke apart in a convulsion of tears. I wrapped myself around him and comforted him the best I could, holding him in a crouched position just inches away from his father's corpse. Eventually the hallway began to darken as the sun set. "Let's go sit down in your room and have a talk," I told him. He allowed me to help him up, to guide him to his bed. He moved like he was sleepwalking.

I figured that if I made an advance on him now he'd push me away, but I began anyhow—he seemed so dependent and clung to me with such maternal need that it was easy to channel Jack's embrace into sexual action. I sat him on the edge of his bed and kissed up his thigh, pulled down his shorts and began sucking. I heard him start to cry again but also felt his fingers wind into my hair, grasping my skull tightly. When he came in my mouth he let out a protracted wail and covered his face with his hands. I wiped my mouth on his comforter, then wrapped the blanket around his shoulders to try to quell his shaking.

A glance at Jack's alarm clock showed that it was truly getting late. I needed to move the conversation forward; the logistics of my exit required planning. "Is your father's car an automatic? Can you drive it?" I had to ask several times before Jack finally responded.

"I've practiced a little bit with my stepbrother." His voice sounded inhospitably distant, beamed in from somewhere dark and cold through patches of static.

"Your dad's car is parked in the middle of the driveway. Do you think you could pull it out into the street so I can back out, then put it in the garage?"

"I think so," he said. After several beats of silence he amended his answer. "I don't know."

"I need you to try. Take a quick shower while I wait," I offered. "It'll help wake you up. You don't have to wash anything, just stand beneath the water." I went to start it for him, then escorted his shaking frame into the bath, supporting him as though he had a geriatric injury as he stepped inside the tub. For a moment I remained there and watched him, the way the water was hitting his face but his eyes remained open. It was disconcerting; I pulled the shower curtain closed.

Walking down the black stretch of hallway toward the corpse, I was resolved to check for any final quivers of life but in the end didn't even feel compelled to grab his shoulder and shake: Buck Patrick's death mask was unmistakable. His bottom and top lips had experienced a violent pull to opposing directions that made the shape of his mouth nearly rhomboid. I had a slight urge to look through his wallet and pilfer any cash—there would be a triumphant feel in buying something with money offered up by Buck's dead body, no matter how minuscule the amount. I imagined purchasing a candy bar and savoring it in my car, the way its sugars would combine with the knowledge that Buck had taken my secret to the grave to form a flavor of extravagant complexity.

Assured that Buck could no longer be revived, I replaced all the phones except the cell I'd given Jack, then went to check on him. Back in the shower, Jack hadn't moved at all except to drop his head; a wet brim of hair covered his downcast eyes completely. I shut off the water and opened a towel to receive him in, then dried every inch of his body with gentle care as he sat slouched on the closed toilet seat. "Here's what you'll do," I said, toweling at his feet as though he was a businessman I was giving a shoe shine to. "You'll wait another half hour or so after I leave before you call 911. There might be trouble if someone notices me pulling out one minute and an ambulance pulling in right after. When the medics arrive, tell them you were playing video games and found your dad when you took a break." Jack's cold nipples looked like tiny eyes fixed open with shock at the situation. I went out to gather some fresh clothes for him to wear, raising my voice to continue talking at him from the bedroom. "There's nothing unnatural about the death; they aren't going to question you much. You're bewildered and consumed with grief. If anything they'll be trying to comfort you." I walked back into the bathroom to deliver Jack's clothes but wanted to relay the last of the pertinent information while he was still naked and hopefully more vulnerable to suggestion than he might be with his genitals covered. "The last thing is that I have to take your secret phone with me."

I expected him to feel this was a betrayal and argue, but it hardly seemed to register; he was staring at the toilet paper dispenser with a gaze of forlorn defeat, as if he'd just taken a hefty dump but was helpless to wipe himself. Still, I wanted to offer further explanation. "You're going to have too many people watching you in the next few days, Jack. You're likely going to be in great emotional pain. It might get very tempting for you to call me, but for our sake we can't make contact again until things settle down." Suddenly Jack's frozen stare broke; he squeezed his eyes shut, then began a low scream; seconds later he was violently smacking his own forehead.

"Shhh," I said soothingly. I knew I had to distract him, give him something to fixate on. "Jack, listen. Do you know the number of my secret phone by heart?"

He nodded, grasping his hair and drawing his knees up onto the toilet against his body. This had the effect of making his testicles, which hung off the ridge of the toilet seat in solitude, seem like a normally internal appendage that had accidentally fallen out. "Good. In a few days, if you're able to walk to a pay phone without anyone following you, call me around five o'clock. Understand?"

He nodded. I sat down on the edge of the tub across from him and waited for several minutes before Jack finally stood, dressed, then began an automaton-like walk into his bedroom, where he grabbed the comforter off his bed. I followed him out to the hallway and watched Jack place it over his father's body. There was something charming about the fact that Buck's funeral shroud was a blanket covered with several months' worth of commingled seminal and vaginal fluids from his son and me. When I cleared my throat Jack finally spoke.

"I'll go move the car." We didn't turn on any lights in the house; I watched only the outline of Jack's body ambling toward the front door as I turned and went my separate way toward the garage.

When I pulled out of the driveway and passed by Jack idling inside his father's car in the street, I noted lights on in Mrs. Pachenko's house but didn't see anyone nosily peeking out through the window blinds. Although I didn't turn to look at him as we drove in opposite directions, I could somehow feel that Jack was not watching me leave.

Unfortunately it turned out that Buck wasn't the only surprise of the evening. When I pulled into the driveway Ford's police car was already home. Although I was wary about what change might've brought him back early, I was relieved that he wasn't out on patrol. I didn't want Ford to be the officer to respond to Jack's call.

"Hey, I'm in here," Ford called out from the back room. I entered the den to find all the furniture covered with plastic drop cloths; Ford himself was on a ladder, painting the ceiling a forgettable beige. "Where you been?" he asked distractedly. From his tone I knew I didn't actually need to answer him; he was about to launch into why he was home and what he was doing and would go right ahead whether I responded or stayed silent, but I felt compliant after the day's long events. "Went out for a bite to eat with some of the girls from work," I answered.

"Ladies' night," he said, a touch of grandeur in his voice. "Speaking of nights, I got switched again. New shift starting tomorrow. Ten P.M. to six A.M." There was something sickening about the slick sound of the wet brush's bristles moving back and forth across the wall, like a large predator's tongue washing its kill. "Kinda brutal but I'm trying to play the game, right? That's where they need me for now. At least we'll get to have dinner together. When you're not eating with the gals," he joked.

This news, combined with knowledge of the changes that were sure to come for Jack following Buck's death, made me feel the sliding nausea of a perfect era untying itself; it would be hard to do much of anything after school with Ford at home waiting, if Jack even continued the year out at Jefferson. The thought suddenly occurred to me that Jack would now have to go live with his mother— did that leave me with enough time to work up to a level of full engagement with another student before the summer break started? "Anyhow, they gave me tonight off to do errands and such before I begin on the vampire crew. I thought I'd finally get started on shaping this den up." He motioned to a swath of paint samples taped to the wall. "You like taupe for the shutters?"

I swallowed, worried that I might abruptly throw up on my shoes. "Yes, Ford," I did finally manage to say. "I just love it."

chapter thirteen

Jack was broken for good, though the weepy, vacant state he occupied for the first few weeks after the death did thankfully fade. He missed ten days of school; it was just after the last period let out on the second week of his absence that my cell phone sounded its alerting buzz inside my bag.

"I'm at the house," Jack said. "My dad's house. I'm here alone. Please come over."

At first the invitation sounded so perfect as to seem like a trap, but my libido overruled any suspicion; I'd been going stir-crazy in the classroom, trying to make educated guesses as to what type of underwear different boys wore by inspecting their groins when they stood up at their desks to read aloud.

I found Jack in his room lying on his bed, his fingers laced behind his head as he looked up at the ceiling. It was an anticlimactic reunion—on some level I expected him to be feeling as sexually deprived as I did, to grasp me and begin passionately kissing; if he had to cry with relief at being able to touch me again, I wouldn't have minded coital tears. Instead he barely blinked when my face came into view above his. I lay down next to him and ran my hand up his shirt, stroking his chest.

His mental perspective wasn't ideal for intercourse. "My life is over," he said, his voice cracking with dramatic inflection. "My mom said I could stay in town with our friends the Ryans and finish out the year at Jefferson, but then I have to go live with her and do high school in Crystal Springs. I'll never see you. I won't even be going to high school with any of my friends." He let a beat of silence pass, then placed his hands over his face, as though this fact horrified him most of all. "I wish I were dead."

I realized that if I was going to glean any satisfaction at all from this visit, I needed to put forward an agenda of transmuting suffering through sexual healing.

Kneeling beside him, I lifted his shirt and began to kiss upward from his stomach to his chest in slow, warm licks. "Your body doesn't wish you were dead, Jack," I told him. "Just your mind. You've got to separate the two. Live in your skin instead of your brain." With that I began furiously kissing his neck, occasionally lowering my pelvis just enough that it put light pressure onto his crotch. He was responding; I could feel an erection building though his body seemed tensed against it. "Distance won't be a problem," I lied, peeling off my shirt and unhooking my bra. I stroked his forehead and offered him a nipple in an act of mothering. When he took it he closed his eyes to suck intensely, as though some intoxicating drug might eventually come out and take his pain away. "And you'll make new friends in no time. Everything's okay."

He kept sucking my nipples, one and then the other, in a near-hypnotic trance. His brow was creased with indecision; he licked his lips and stared off in thought, like a sommelier trying to discern a vintage at a blind taste test. Suddenly a switch seemed to flip inside him and he sat up, pulling down his pants, then lifted my ass up toward him and entered me. *Thank god,* I thought—I had a flash of optimism that the worst was over. The sex was very good, his pelvis steadily driven. When he came it seemed like a natural catharsis to the entire situation, and I pulled him back down to the bed and wrapped my body around his. "That was great," I whispered, feeling a light, exuberant air pour into the room. He was breathing very quickly, his chest rising and falling with emphasis. I expected it to slow down after a moment but it didn't; although we were completely still, his body was acting like he was sprinting in place.

"We killed my dad," he finally said.

"Absolutely not!" I exclaimed. What a counterproductive and harmful thought for him to have. Pressing my lips against his head as though to beam the words directly into his skull, I tried to reassure him. "Jack," I said, "a heart attack killed your dad. It's tragic, but everything is going to be just fine."

We did in fact have a few strokes of luck come our way, namely the house. As Jack's legal guardian, his mother wanted control of the property to set up a trust for her son; Buck's siblings claimed their brother wanted money from its sale to go toward the care of Buck's ailing mother and said they'd made a verbal contract with Buck about this matter. Arbitration would take months, perhaps even a year or two, during which time the property would sit vacant and Jack and I could continue to meet whenever time allowed, though Jack often wasn't in the mood to be inside it. "We have to go somewhere else," he'd stress. "Anywhere, I don't care." It wasn't always practical to drive so far out of town, so I settled instead on blended anonymity; off one of the town's main roads there was a series of medical plazas whose driveways lead into one another like the links of a chain. After hours, their parking lots always remained peppered with cars and there was absolutely no through traffic;

not once did another car come down the road while we were in the middle of anything.

Yet the situation was far from perfect. Sometimes it was downright hellish. First there was the arrangement of illuminated signs, many of which advertised obstetrics and fertility practices. With their various lights glowing around us to form the shape of an imperfect pentagram, it seemed like an act of conception voodoo might occur: these totems of medical miracles would join forces and somehow cause my birth control to fail. The other terrible aspect was the heat and the bugs. We couldn't leave my car running and enjoy the AC in case a security guard came by on his rounds, which meant we were battling the summer's oncoming humidity against my car's leather seats. When it did get so hot inside that we felt we had no choice but to roll down the windows, every mosquito from the development's manufactured pond smelled our salty blood and came searching. On one night we cracked only the front two windows, then began to have sex in the back; by the time Jack reached orgasm there were so many of them in the car that their mass was a dark, hanging cloud—I stared for a moment, convinced their formation was about to shift and take on the shape of Buck's vengeful face, before pain brought me back to reality. Suddenly I could feel them stinging the ripest places of my sensitive flesh; our minds had been so misdirected by sex that we'd failed to realize how dire the situation was until the moment we finished. Jack then jumped out of the car completely naked—I couldn't blame him but I also could've killed him for it.

"They have security cameras," I hissed out the car door at him. "Get back in!" But instead he grabbed his clothes and put them on outside; I was left in the car with the bugs.

But the true disappointment of these meet-ups had nothing to do with location. Jack seemed to be divorcing himself from the sex and turning it into a rote act. There was a slightly tortured air to his expression throughout, as though he was doing it against his will. His thrusts became harder and harder, like he was trying to feel something but failing. In general he appeared to want to express a sentiment he couldn't quite say or perhaps even understand. "Well," he'd often start, but when I responded, "What is it?" he'd shake his head lightly. "Forgot," he'd answer, his eyes blank.

I looked forward to summer, hoping it would be restorative for him. Our last unit in English was an analysis of *To Kill a Mockingbird,* which gave me pause. I didn't want the text's elements of morality and justice to seduce Jack into walking the misguided path of honest confession. During third period, I did all that I could to steer the conversation away from relevant topics of depth. "So if we were to remake the movie nowadays," I asked on one occasion, "who would you guys cast to play Boo Radley?"

"Someone bald," answered Marissa. Every other student except Jack quickly nodded in agreement.

But even summer break brought no great reversal to his sulking. Jack had to be replaced as soon as possible, but there were obstacles. The first was my own libido. I couldn't accept the thought of a three-month dry spell until fall hit and I could find Jack's successor. The flirtatious encounters during substitute teaching that had once aroused me to the point of sustenance—a quick shoulder rub for a student who complained about stress, a celebratory hug for a recent honors society inductee—now seemed like a starvation diet after my year with Jack. The second was the nagging fear—largely paranoia, I tried to convince myself—that I needed to keep Jack fully under my spell just a bit longer, until it was certain that no aspect of his father's death would be resurrected for examination by the police. As far as I knew there'd been no suspicions at all. But what if someone *had* seen my car leaving and suddenly felt compelled to mention it? A breakup would likely feel like emotional napalm in Jack's tender state, and if he was still burning from my rejection when new questions about the night his father died came to light, the situation might indeed turn prickly.

And the fact that our escapades were more sporadic—to prepare for the late-August move to his mother's, Jack was alternating between spending a few weeks with the Ryans, then a few weeks in Crystal Springs—meant I had more patience for his stricken attitude of gloomy resignation. His father's death had matured Jack in a way that made him far less satisfying, but each time he returned from his mother's I had several weeks' worth of pent-up cravings, and this blind need allowed for a protective myopia against his dour moods: I'd take him immediately, in a ravenous attack that I considered necessary self-defense. Stopping to inquire about the comfort of his position, or to ask what he wanted, would simply have given him an opportunity to passive-aggressively brood—I could imagine him answering my inquiry with a shrug, then looking off into the distance, hoping I'd stop and embrace him and use encouraging phrases to tug at the question of what was bothering him until we began a long, dull chat that was all about Jack and his multitude of hurt feelings. I wasn't about to sanction such boredom. Instead, each time we met I'd ride him with masturbatory energy, letting him halfheartedly push beneath me with a listless stoicism until I was finished, and then I'd slide off, give him a quick kiss and leave; it was often clear that he wasn't going to orgasm no matter how long we went at it. Even so, he was better than nothing until I could secure a new beau. My very last conversation with Jack had already occurred several times in my head—taking a sympathetic posture, warmly caressing his hand and shoulder, I would gently point out that I reminded him too much of his father's terrible death—to move past it, I'd argue, he'd need to move past me, and that was why I had to insist we stop seeing one another. I even convinced myself Jack knew this was coming and had accepted it—after all, I'd never given him back his secret phone, and he'd never asked for it. Instead I continued to insist on pay phones and he kept calling me from gas stations and McDonald's parking lots. I furnished him a new roll of quarters for just this purpose every week.

Being out of school for summer combined with Ford's night shift meant intolerably long days. I accommodated Ford's schedule in some regards: I began to sleep late in order to waste as much of our afternoon time together as I could. It was impossible for me to have any sense of ease when he was home. This allowed me to spend the evening and early morning hours while he was away lost in pornographic flights of imagination about what the fall semester might bring. Ford and I fell into a routine of waking for breakfast at three or four P.M., then going to the gym, where he'd watch me work out the entire time with a proprietary satisfaction; no matter where I went in the exercise or lifting rooms, I could feel his eyes following me. He seemed to like it even more if other men were watching me as well, or if they approached me; if another guy struck up a conversation, I could always count on Ford's overly grabby hands to find my ass a second later, pinching or spanking it with a shit-eating grin as the man who had just introduced himself slinked away. Ford liked to shower at the house, but I always insisted on doing it there, in the segregated changing rooms, to protect myself from his soapy grasp. We'd return home to a horrible evening of ennui—I began making elaborate dinners each night just to pass the hours—and when Ford finally left for work each night, I had the exhausted relief of a host whose departed houseguest had over-stayed his welcome for a week.

This situation resulted in my jumping at any offer of outside social engagement, no matter how banal. I attended school board meetings, PTA functions and even Janet's birthday party. This lat-ter fete was held at a small strip-mall bar called Raccoons, in the back near a modest karaoke setup and a few arcade games. Mrs. Pachenko and Mr. Sellers and I were the only attendees. Janet began to act overserved almost immediately; perhaps she'd done some pre-partying in the parking lot.

"Why don't you have a wife?" she demanded of Mr. Sellers less than an hour in. Mrs. Pachenko seemed to grow increasingly nervous, particularly once Janet launched into a series of deroga-tory comments about the administrative staff's genital size. "It's a small dick," Janet loudly announced of AP Rosen's plumb-ing. "You can tell that just by the way he walks." In the bar's dim lights, Mrs. Pachenko had a forlorn, dumbfounded expres-sion, like a slow-witted child trying to force together two puzzle pieces that didn't fit.

"Mrs. Pachenko," I said warmly, trying to serve as a distraction from Janet's invective. "I don't believe I've ever gotten your first name."

She took a long sip of her club soda. "It's Eleanor. But I really prefer Mrs. Pachenko."

I nodded, willfully clenching my sphincter to avoid my eyes involuntarily rolling in disgust. "And what does Mr. Pachenko do?"

She shook her head slightly, informing me this was not the correct question to ask. I tried again, cheating this time.

"Where do you live?"

"Bloomingdale Green," she said. This was her first answer that reflected any sort of pride or acceptance.

"Oh." I nodded. "Nice neighborhood. Quiet."

"It could be a little more peaceful," she said. There was another round of expletive shelling from Janet, and Mrs. Pachenko stood to leave.

"Happy birthday," she announced, flashing a nervous smile. "I believe I need to get back to my son now." Then she turned and walked toward the door so quickly that she appeared to be running.

"Nice lady," Janet said to us. "Gonna help me out again next year. But boy is she wound up tight."

I became more and more fixated on getting back to school and the delights I might find waiting on the first day. I'd often spend Ford's entire shift online, looking at adolescent pornography and stealing features from separate photos to fuse together into the perfect student. The disparaged statements about how quickly the summer was flying by that other teachers made at preparatory meetings gave me strength to combat the day-to-day waiting game, and I tried injecting my dead engagements with Jack, passionless though they now were, with new perspectives of fantasy; my favorite tactic was to look at his body, never his face, and pretend that he was a boy I'd found on the side of the road, struck down by a car— that he had one last burst of life left inside of him and he wanted to use it to lose his virginity with me. This made the wounded aspects of Jack's posture, like his curled shoulders, his wincing squint I couldn't help but catch in my peripheral vision that made it look like he was fighting any good feelings with equally opposed reserves of pain, all make sense. Only by crafting these fatalistic and temporary contexts surrounding our sex was I able to convince myself that I could indeed last until the end of August, that I wouldn't have to go fishing at the mall or the supermarket for an untested, unvetted boy who could ruin me.

But the final trial of my will came just two weeks before school started. Ford wanted to take a weeklong vacation at one of the beach houses his father owned. "Can Bill and Shelley come too?" I asked. Even though I didn't like them, a couples' trip would be better than isolated alone time with Ford. But that was of course what he wanted.

His face stretched into a charmed smile of surprise. "Whoa, there, social butterfly," he teased, clearly happy that I'd asked. "Glad you've warmed up to the two of them. But no way. This one's you and me. Before school starts up and I hardly see you again till next summer." I shook my head at him to suggest he was exaggerating, but secretly I was happy he'd voiced this expectation: it meant I'd established a shared understanding that when the school year started, everything about me—my presence at home, my focus, my attention—would become extremely scarce. This sense of achievement gave me the needed courage to enter into one last hurrah of summer tedium.

Incredibly, I would go so far as to call that week one of the greatest successes of our marriage, probably due to the knowledge that a fresh onslaught of young men would soon be greeting me each morning and afternoon on the hour, save for the cognac-driven conversation on the porch the night before we returned home. In the dark, I kept feeling Ford stare at me with confusion, then look off in the distance. I knew it was a look of failed reconciliation; he was trying to understand how our life together could look so good from the outside but somehow fail to actually feel that way. I could sense him palpably restraining himself from speaking—Ford excels at never admitting he's disappointed—but a few glasses later his filter was finally breached. "I guess I thought things would be different once you started teaching," he managed to say. The dark amplified the near-mechanical sound of the cicadas' screams all around us; they seemed like an audience goading him on. "That you'd be happier," he finally added.

"I am happier," I countered. "It's just a busier, more distracted sort of happy."

I worried about what would come next but he left it at that; he stood and went inside while I remained on the porch in the warm air, hearing the ocean and wishing the eighth grader I'd soon pluck from my roster was there now to go for a naked swim. The moon's thin light upon the moving waves lent itself well to illusion; I could almost see us together out in the distant water, bobbing heads whose bodies could mingle unworried beneath the ocean's cover.

When I did finally go to bed, Ford was asleep with the firmness of denial. It was only in times like these, when he would ask a funny question but then show he was overtly ignoring the answer, that I wondered if Ford suspected more than he let on. He seemed to understand that resolution didn't need to have anything to do with truth, and to choose a sense of harmony over insight every time.

I lay down as far away from his reach as possible and had a dream about the first day of class. I entered through the classroom door wearing only a silk bathrobe that I shed as the bell rang. Every desk was taken by a young man and they all stood in unison, using their numbers to lift me into the air, their collective centipede fingers crawling across every inch of my flesh.

When I woke with a gasp it was morning. Ford's head sat mere inches from mine. It took a moment for me to realize his hands were resting atop my hard nipples, as though my chest was a control panel he'd been manning. He gave me a smile that didn't fade as confusion and a slight terror overtook my face. "Some dream you were having," he said. "You feeling horny, babe?"

chapter fourteen

The timid affect and classroom behavior of Jack's eventual replacement so belied his hidden perversities that I missed him entirely at first and had a failed attempt with a new boy named Connor, whom I misread from the first day forward. I began each class simply by smiling—perhaps my nervous hope showed through—then scanned the room for any eye contact that was returned to me with a promising streak of restraint. Connor initially seemed to be perfect: he was quiet, studious but not exceptionally smart, and didn't appear to have a great deal of friends nor an interest in gaining any.

The Monday of the second week in, having had the entire weekend to pine and fantasize, I asked him to stay after class for a moment. I'd managed to keep my portable classroom despite AP Rosen's repeated offers to take an opening in the main building; I claimed I'd become fond of its deficiencies—"It almost feels like a one-room schoolhouse," I told him. "When I was a little girl I always played that I was a teacher back in the pioneer times." He absolutely loved this white lie. Apparently a great-great-grandmother of his actually did preside over a one-room school; he told me a long story about it while I thought about humming "The Star-Spangled Banner" with the tip of a student's penis in my mouth.

I hadn't once entertained the idea that it could go differently with another boy than it had with Jack. Instead it felt like last year I'd forged a permanent path that all other candidates would obediently follow. But there was also the looming weekend—Jack wanted to take a bus down from Crystal Springs and stay at his father's house Friday and Saturday under the guise of seeing friends. If I knew with certainty that our depressive sex would soon be just one option on a menu rather than my only opportunity with a young partner, the atmosphere wouldn't feel so choking and leaden. I could relax a little, care less about when the time would be right to break it off with him and more fully enjoy what remained of our dwindling sessions.

As soon as the other students were gone and Connor and I were alone, I turned from him and unbuttoned two extra buttons on my shirt so that it hung open and exposed my bra. I expected him to stare at me as I spoke inane details about his essay topic, then I could act surprised that his gaze had met my opened shirt and possibly get a confession that he was indeed looking at my bra—information I'd pretend to find so overly flattering that I might offer to show him an even better view.

But the moment I turned around, his eyes immediately averted to the left. "Your button opened," he said, pointing to the middle of his chest to demonstrate.

I glanced down, pretending to be confused. "Oh dear," I said. "So it did." I waited for his eyes to return to mine but he wouldn't turn his head back; he was not only looking away from me toward the door but also actually using his fingers to shield his eyes.

"Are you decent yet?" he asked.

"Sure." He lowered his hand but upon seeing I hadn't rebuttoned my shirt immediately covered his eyes again.

"Aren't you going to fix it?" There was something accusatory in his question; his voice held disbelief but not excitement.

"I will before my next class. But it's nice to have a break for a moment. I've always thought clothes can be a little constraining," I said. "Do you?"

Beneath the desk, his feet were busy fidgeting. "Why did you keep me after class?" he finally asked.

I exhaled a long, disappointed sigh; this one didn't seem to be any fun at all.

"Like I said, I just wanted to talk to you about your essay topic." But he had a hard time following.

"Everyone wrote on the same topic," he said, defensive. "Was my essay worse than everyone else's or something?"

I didn't answer, hoping it would mean he'd look at me in an attempt to break the silence and our eyes could communicate the unspoken, but he didn't.

"I was just interested in yours," I said. "That's all." The lunch bell rang and his paranoia flipped into high alert.

"Will I be marked tardy to lunch?" he asked. From the fear and anger in his voice, I could tell he'd never been tardy before in his entire life. The kid was far too square. I decided to cut him loose and pop a Klonopin to help nurse my wounds.

"No, don't worry. I'll write you a note." There wasn't an inch of his body that seemed calm; his tension was starting to make me anxious too. "Look, I'm writing it right now," I said, stopping to wave the paper in the air with a little hostility. "Jesus."

I walked over to his desk and bent down, giving him one last chance at a full view of my chest that he didn't opt to take. "Can I go now?" he demanded.

"Go, go on," I said. The incident gave the rest of the week a sour, empty feel. I kept butting heads with my worst fear, a prospect so extreme that I hadn't allowed myself to think it before the train wreck with Connor forced me to: the possibility that I might go the entire year without finding a replacement.

Yet just two weeks later, all tides had turned. Normally I'd have rejected any student who acted first; it was a sign of brashness and impulsivity, both traits that could easily lead to our getting caught. Furthermore, the power dynamic would be in his favor if he came on to me. But Boyd showed a more advanced level of mastery—part of his genius was that it was indeed so subtle I hardly noticed for almost a month. Yet there the offer was one day, unmistakable as he left class. With a glance, his face transformed from an expression of blank nonchalance to the smallest possible detectable grin and he locked eyes with me. It was sudden but unmistakable: his look conveyed both that he knew exactly who I was and what I wanted, but also that he held a similar secret. We locked eyes for what could only have been seconds, but it was enough; we were two deviants who had recognized one another in an identifying game of telepathy. The next day when I asked him to stay after class, he nodded with innocence, every ounce the demure boy who always sat quietly at his desk, but when the door finally shut he licked his lips and smiled: the costume came off and he was a completely different animal.

Boyd was less outwardly attractive than Jack, another reason why he didn't stand out to me at first. He had a prominent nose and ears that he hadn't yet grown into, and he frequently wore oversized shirts and sweaters that made his short limbs appear dwarfed. His smile was a metallic track of braces, but his roguish desires had the effect of making them seem like a punitive measure that he wore as a badge of pride—a punishment for his words being so vulgar, perhaps.

His forwardness allowed me to drop all introductory pretenses. The first and only thing I asked him in that initial meeting was straightforward. "Would you like to touch me?"

He'd responded by approaching and beginning to do so. His hands were so small that one could easily fit inside me up to his wrist. After our very first time alone together, he left the classroom five minutes before the end of lunch with Jack's former cell phone in hand.

I let him have sex with me twice in the classroom that first week, but we were at work on another plan. "My house is out of the question," I explained. "Are you ever home alone after school?"

Unfortunately Boyd's parents, in particular his stay-at-home mother, were far stricter and more present than Jack's. But there were still slots of possibility throughout the day: Boyd was allowed to do after-school activities as long as he was home by dinner around six. That made a rendezvous in my car dangerous; it wouldn't be dark yet, and parking lots and shopping plazas would still be full. When I decided upon the venue I wasn't trying to be sacrilegious or perverse, only careful: Jack's house really was the best option.

Objectively, Jack unknowingly benefited from this arrangement too. Sex with Jack in the same bed where I'd had Boyd just a few days ago was an enormous turn-on. The first time Jack returned home after I'd slept there with Boyd, I bounced atop him so hard I feared his pelvis might break; there was an almost hallucinatory interplay between my mental images of the two of them as we fucked. Gasping, I occasionally looked down at Jack to see

Boyd's smaller, wryer mouth and nearly exploded. "Wow," Jack said afterward. It was definitely a change that warranted comment; our sex had grown to be more an act of hostile aerobics than of pleasure.

"Wow indeed," I replied. "Absence makes the heart grow fonder."

Although Boyd had roughly zero actual sexual experience prior to our relationship, he was far more advanced in terms of perversion. His kinkier suggestions didn't bother me the way they might have with Jack, perhaps because of the theoretical naïveté with which he spoke about them—breathlessly, in excited whispers, as though fetishes were fabled legends wrought from the fabric of dragons and mermaids—or perhaps because he'd had these fantasies even as a virgin. They weren't the product of his growing tired of routine intercourse. He wanted to try everything right away; sex and its oral variants weren't enough for his curious mind. He once asked me to pee a little in his mouth, which I did; he didn't love it but grew immediately rock hard from the experiment. He also liked to blindfold me and be blindfolded and hated my insistence that we couldn't bite one another hard enough to leave a visible imprint.

I was happy enough to indulge him in anything that wouldn't produce telltale evidence. But some of his desires simply weren't possible. Boyd longed for others to watch us fucking; he often had dreams where I was giving him head in a bustling street's storefront window. Of course we couldn't open the curtains at Jack's house or record ourselves on camera, but he did enjoy having a movie on in the background during sex; he was able to pretend, he told me, hearing the voices of the actors, that they were right there in the room looking on.

It was only after beginning to sleep with Boyd that I realized my animosity toward Jack wasn't solely due to the melancholy he'd dragged into our relations; it was also spawned by the fact that I'd almost grown to feel dependent upon him—after all, he had been my only true source of sexual release—and I'd resented that. But now, even during Jack's bluest moods, some of my initial warmth for him was returning, and I was no longer so anxious to break things off. "I hate my new school," he confessed one night. "I hate only seeing you a few times a month. I want to see if I can live with the Ryans again in the spring and transfer back to Jefferson."

"But don't you think it feels a little more special this way?" I asked. "Having to bear the time apart, then being able to fuck away the built-up frustration?" I was trying to help Jack look on the bright side, but perhaps this was a misstep.

"What are you saying? That you like me not living here?"

"Of course not," I answered. "Just pointing out a benefit."

Still, I loved being able to oscillate between the two of them. It allowed for a comparison between their bodies and highlighted minuscule physical differences that I might not have noticed and savored otherwise: the freckle just to the left of Jack's sternum, the fatty ripeness of Boyd's detached earlobes. The scheduling of it all had worked itself out so that the separate compartments of my life tied together with a manageable fluidity. I arrived home on nights I saw Boyd—allegedly coming from a curricular steering committee—just in time to eat a late dinner with Ford and send him off to work. Whenever he did request a quickie before he left, it was in a very passive way that was easy to turn down. "I guess you're too tired to fool around," he'd state, and I'd yawn and nod, trying to apologize as sweetly as possible.

My classes, too, seemed to be on a sort of autopilot that let me focus my attention almost exclusively on sexual pursuits. My students this year included several transplants from a recently closed theater magnet school who were happy to act out *Romeo and Juliet* in its entirety. All the while I sat at my desk and did my best to draw a rendering of Boyd's penis in both flaccid and erect states, then ripped the illustrations into pieces when the bell rang.

Janet was far more gregarious this fall; her spring evaluations had risen from "unsatisfactory" up to "below average" and she felt her job was safe again. "Mrs. Feinlog totally has this creepy old-lady crush on you," one of my students mentioned one day. "I heard her call you a beautiful angel. It was kind of weird." Occasionally when I walked through the main building I'd hear the sharp squeak of her oversized white sneakers on the floor and she'd place a hand on my shoulder, panting as though she'd run for days from a faraway village just to give me a message.

"Wanna grab a cold one after work?" she'd ask. If I didn't have plans with Boyd I'd usually consent; it was less painful to watch Janet get intoxicated than it was to sit around the house with Ford. I'd have a bourbon on the rocks while Janet downed a pitcher of the cheapest draft and talked about a variety of issues—her circulation problems, the HOA citations she kept receiving for negligence in maintaining her lawn or how badly she wanted to strap a given student to the front of her van and drive off a cliff. I'd follow the conversation with the passing orbit of a satellite, returning every now and then from my daydreams to feel the creeping buzz of alcohol and wonder if there would ever be an occasion when I'd be able to indulge Boyd's exhibitionist urges in earnest—take him to a nude beach or the type of seedy nightclub where couples openly fornicate beneath the woman's hiked-up skirt as they lean against an alcove wall by the restrooms. I suppose these meetings only added to my growing sense of security: Janet was the most suspicious person I knew, yet she didn't seem to suspect anything about me. No one did.

That Saturday afternoon Boyd phoned when Ford just happened to be out for a run—had he been home I would never have picked up and Boyd might have forgotten to mention it at all come Monday.

"Hello?" I said, slightly bemused. Boyd had never phoned me on a weekend before; his mother was always at home breathing down his neck and wasn't big on granting him leave unless his youth group had a church function. "I should join your church and volunteer as a youth minister," I once joked; Boyd thought it was a fantastic idea. "There's a storage room upstairs where my friend hid two porno magazines in a supply closet," he'd gushed. "We could do it in there while we look at them."

"Hey," Boyd said. "Did you just call me?"

"No," I answered. It took a moment for the implication of his question to sink in, and then I felt a sharp unraveling in my chest. "Another number called your phone?"

"Yeah," he said. "Not your cell."

"Did you answer it?" In my mind I replayed my most recent weekend with Jack—hadn't it gone just fine? We'd had loads of sex; his brooding had been minimal. There had been no awkward silences, he hadn't insisted on our leaving the house and doing it in my car. On the contrary, he'd even wanted something from his father's bedroom to take back home with him—a photo? A small trophy? I couldn't remember, but it had seemed to be a good sign of his growing comfort at being in the house. Before leaving we'd eaten a dinner of sandwiches together naked on the living room carpet.

"Yeah," he said, then, fearing reproach, added, "I thought it was you calling from a different phone."

"I'll never call you from another phone, Boyd." I didn't try to mask the frustration in my voice. "That's rule number one."

"I know, I'm sorry." The radio in his room was blaring in the background, likely so his mother wouldn't hear him speaking. "I was just excited to talk to you." He said this in a contrived puppy-dog fashion. Boyd had a manipulative tool kit that Jack couldn't have imagined; Boyd had been forced to create one early on in order to deceive his overbearing mother. Had Jack decided to launch an investigation to see if I was sleeping with another student? It didn't seem like him, but I supposed it couldn't be ruled out.

Several other possibilities couldn't. The first was that Ford had found my secret cell phone, copied down its only programmed number and called. I doubted this though; if he suspected I was having an affair, his interest in all my plans would suddenly have spiked. He'd have been firing off questions about each one of my day's activities with an exaggerated tone of indifference that tried too hard to suggest nothing was out of the ordinary. Or he'd just have confronted me about the phone. The second possibility was that it was a wrong number—rare, but it did happen. The last and most twisted was that no one had called Boyd: that he'd simply wanted to talk to me, perhaps stir up some dramatic tension between us. Did he wonder if he was the phone's first owner? He'd never asked if he was the first student I'd been with. Something had always told me Boyd wasn't the type who would care.

"What did the person say? Could you tell if it was a man or a woman?"

"Nope. It was just silent after I said hello and then whoever it was hung up."

Despite this anxiety-laden news, Boyd's hushed voice was making me horny. "Is your bedroom door locked?" I whispered. "Just this once go into your closet and touch yourself. Let me hear it." I could've asked if the number was local or long-distance. I could've had Boyd give me the number and searched on the Internet, cross-checking it with the variety of pay phone numbers Jack had called me from. Instead, I leaned against the wall and fingered myself as Boyd's heavy breathing swelled into the receiver and finally ended with a vocalized groan; afterward the danger of the errant dial seemed negligible. "I'm sure it was just a wrong number," I said. "Just never ever pick up the phone unless it's my cell calling, do you understand?"

"I know, I get it." He paused. "Do you want me to do it again? I'm still hard."

That image of Boyd's glistening, unquenchable penis was like a magic wand that carried me through the rest of the weekend. When Jack called me a few days later to arrange his next visit, I was extra friendly but I didn't mention the call. It was tempting to say something dismissive about his former phone—that I'd gotten rid of it, or that I wondered if the number had since been reassigned to a new phone—but ultimately any reference at all seemed like it would be more incriminating than dismissive. Had Jack brought it up in any context, I certainly would've taken the allusion to be an outright confession.

But he didn't mention it. He'd discovered whip-its at his new school, and the following weekend he brought two whipped cream cans for us to suck the nitrous out of while we had intercourse on the kitchen countertop. When we finished, heavy headed and spinning, he reached for my panties and held them up to the light appreciatively, like they were some rare kind of insect. "I love your underwear," he said, one of the only things he said all night. What other thought could've possibly crossed my mind than that I had nothing to worry about?

chapter fifteen

That mid-October in central Florida held on to the distant heat of a diluted summer. Dusk began its onset preternaturally early, blackening the windows with menacing speed each evening. Boyd and I would begin having sex without the lights on and end in total darkness, barely able to see one another's faces. He increasingly liked to do it to violent movies—tommy guns, stabbings, the sounds of splatter punctuating our thrusts. Once it grew dark, the glow of the small television in Jack's bedroom had an eerie, otherworldly feel, almost too real, as if we weren't watching a movie at all but actual footage of a live murder.

That evening my face was flat upon the bed, my ass in the air, Boyd behind me staring at the TV screen. There was a sudden pause when Boyd stopped pushing, but then he continued, slowly, as though he'd somehow forgotten what we were doing and how to proceed; had he stopped completely I would've looked up much earlier. Who knows how long Jack had been inside the darkened room, his eyes locked with Boyd's and Boyd still fucking me, before Jack finally emitted the primal scream that made me jump off of Boyd's cock and the bed entirely.

Being naked and in his bedroom, I had the initial impulse to approach Jack and start rubbing his crotch, see if he might calm down when there was equal affection given to both of them. The combat-heavy sounds coming from the television, though, seemed to be escalating the tension; I grabbed the remote and put the movie on pause. But the act of stopping the movie seemed to bring Jack's frozen shape to life: with a guttural yell, he ran toward Boyd and threw him over, punching him. Boyd still had a full and moistened erection.

I don't believe Jack intended the full damage incurred by Boyd's skull—it was partially the angles of geometry, partially the physics of force. The back left corner of Boyd's head slammed into a sharp nightstand corner and produced a gash that began bleeding heavily in mere seconds; by the time Jack realized that Boyd was hurt, Jack's hands and clothes were covered with so much slick blood that he seemed to have just emerged from inside a large animal. Boyd cowered on the floor, both hands cradling his head as he made primitive groans. Jack backed away slowly, with all the confusion of a recent amnesiac, appearing to feel as if he were the victim of a horrible trick.

It was a while before I realized Jack was talking. Through a series of incoherent stammers, he'd begun leveling the allegation that I was not only responsible for his father's needless death, but that my motivations were selfish ones. "You didn't let him die so we could be together." Jack's hand made a broad, dragging wipe across his face, leaving a vertical smear of blood. "You're *cheating* on me!" Every few seconds, quick spurts of gore consistently sprayed outward from the back of Boyd's head in a theatrical manner; it had a special-effects feel to it, as though the blood's release was being regulated by an electronic timer. Impressively, his rigid penis hadn't softened. He kept trying to stand but instead would merely stumble, then crawl a few more inches. A full defusion of the situation and successful cleanup now seemed unlikely.

Jack's sticky hands were gripping my wrists; soon I felt them on my shoulders and neck as well.

I knew it wasn't the best moment for a discussion, but I felt it was important to defend myself from the weighty inaccuracy Jack was casting toward me, in front of Boyd no less, although Boyd wasn't in the best shape to remember the conversation or be unduly influenced by Jack's hurtful remark.

"Jack," I responded calmly. "I am sorry your father had a heart attack."

"All so nobody would find you out," Jack interrupted, his hands straining against my collarbone.

But after saying this, his grip on my shoulders softened. Something important had registered in his mind, drawing open his lips and causing his eyes to grow alert and panicked.

Seconds later, Jack began to run.

I suppose I chased him. It wasn't even until I was outside that I realized I had the knife in my hand; I must've picked it up in the kitchen on my way out.

Stopping in front of Jack's mailbox, I was winded, searching both directions for a sign of where he had bolted to. When a figure approached from my left, blending into the shadows with the passive gait of an herbivore and carrying two grocery bags, it hardly registered; my peripheral vision initially classified the motion as a shrub moving in the breeze. When I did finally notice her, we were face-to-face, her eyes squinting as she struggled to recognize me in such an unexpected context. "Celeste?" Mrs. Pachenko finally gasped, her forehead lifting into a growing tower of surprise that caused her hairline to disappear. It wasn't Jack's bloody handprints on my chest or the knife in my hand that she noticed first at all. "You're *naked,*" she finally exclaimed. Her open lips had risen above the high, pink shores of her gums, revealing a hodgepodge of unbecoming bridgework; understandably, I was loath to take my attention from the situation at hand.

"Have you seen Jack Patrick?" I asked.

Like an answer, the streetlamp directly above my head timed on. I raised my eyes up toward its bright headlight as a gathering swarm of moths whorled into a loose formation; for several moments I actually stared on in wait, convinced they were going to give me a sign: form an arrow to say which way Jack had gone, or take off en masse and lead me directly to him. When I snapped back to consciousness, other onlookers had appeared: cautious neighbors standing on porches with phones to their ears, shocked spectators pointing at me from the edges of their lawns but not venturing a single toe over the boundary of their grass. Mrs. Pachenko had dropped her grocery bags and was retreating from me slowly; I looked to the ground to see a box of unsalted soda crackers sitting upon the asphalt. Soon an elderly couple approached. The woman was carrying a sea-foam green velour zip-up housecoat in her hands.

"Dear," she said quietly, extending the garment. "Put this on." Beneath the direct light of the streetlamp, her floating white hair looked so transparent as to be made of steam.

"Were you attacked?" the old man asked. "Are you bleeding?" It was only then, looking down at the dried handprints Jack had left on my skin, that I thought of Boyd, his head wound hemorrhaging profusely just feet away inside the house. Was there any way not to report his medical need that wouldn't be judged harshly later when he was discovered? I could feign shock, I decided. I glanced down at the blood and gave it a surprised look, dropped the knife as I stepped into the housecoat, which smelled faintly of talcum powder and cat food. I had the sudden urge to lift the garment up above my knees and run as fast and as far as I could make it barefoot. But the sharp call of sirens nearing our block pressed me to the snap decision that it was better to confess Boyd's presence and imitate extensive distress.

"There's a boy in the house who's hurt," I said, perhaps too quietly. Two police cars were turning the street corner, approaching us but not seeming to slow down whatsoever. I knew I should produce a look of worry or strain, but habit prevented me from forming any facial expression that might aid in the development of fine lines.

"What?" asked the old man, covering his ears against the siren's blare. I tried to survey the face of each officer stepping out of the cars—only after being sure that neither one was Ford did my urge to sprint toward Jack's backyard begin to settle down, though the cold, expanding feeling that soon came in its place was almost as awful. An immediate realization of loss began to spread through me and quicken; as the knife was picked up and two officers branched off to run inside the house without my telling them about Boyd or instructing them on where to go, I realized perhaps the first person to call them had not been a neighbor at all but Jack. A sense of depreciation began to shudder through my ribs like a wind: had Jack gotten his story to the police before I'd told them mine? The knife was bagged, a gloved hand pressed against my back. "We're going to need you to step inside the vehicle and come with us," the officer said. He looked familiar—maybe I'd seen him before at one of Ford's work functions. I kept my head low. If they knew who I was, they weren't mentioning it yet; the entire ride to the station was silent and I tried to be thankful for these last moments of anonymity, even if they were pretended and more for the officers' sense of comfort than my own.

Part of me expected Ford to be there at the station—waiting, concerned. Ready to make everything go away, even if it was just for the night, while he heard my side of the story. But I was taken into the station and processed like anyone else, though perhaps with a special sort of prejudice; the officers insisted on taking a variety of photos of my naked body, most at angles where Jack's bloody handprints were starkly visible, but others not. Under a thin veneer of business, several male officers circulated through the medical-style room where I was told to lie down on an examination table and spread my legs while flash photographs were taken of my genitals. By the time I was dressed in orange prison scrubs and led to an interrogation room, a growing terror had seized me—was it possible that I'd spend the night in jail? It was the first moment that I had a true urge to call my husband—suddenly the opulence of our sheets, the splendor of my walk-in closet with its rows of neatly hung pajama sets, seemed proper cause to forevermore deny my darker urges. But when the detectives entered holding Jack's personal cell phone, the one whose spread-eagle photograph of me I hadn't been able to find and delete on its SIM card, I knew I didn't want Ford anywhere near the situation.

A rough-featured detective with a shaved head and craggish voice led me through the most serious of the allegations. "We know you're sleeping with these kids," he began. In between sentences he chewed a wad of gum in the left side of his mouth with a mechanical fury. "That's a given. That's not even up for debate. What I need to know from you is what you were doing running around the street naked with a knife while blood was gushing out of Boyd Manning's skull."

I was surprised at the ease with which manic tears came forth. I shook my head repeatedly before speaking, as though it was too painful to relive. "When Jack saw us together, he just went crazy." My hands slid through my hair to grip my scalp. "He attacked Boyd and all I could see was blood everywhere. Then Jack was gone. I knew I had to run for help, to get help for Boyd." For possibly the first time ever, I didn't feel the dynamic advantage of beauty in my corner as I spoke—my hair was mussed and I'm sure the crying had swollen my face; the detective was looking at me as though I was some obscene spectacle of nature. I realized he was watching me talk with a curious revulsion, the same way one might watch a cow give birth.

"You weren't running after Jack?" For several seconds, the detective's gum chewing went into overdrive, as if to simulate the energy of a speedy chase. "According to Mr. Patrick, you were in pursuit of him with a knife."

"No," I proclaimed, inflecting my voice with the outraged shock of the wrongly accused. "That's not true." The detective kept looking down at a folder in his hand, then looking back up at me. I wondered if he had printouts of the naked photos they'd taken of me when they brought me in.

"Thing is," said the detective, "I've got roughly fifteen witnesses who saw you standing frozen in the street, looking around like you were trying to find somebody. You weren't crying out for help. But you did have a knife."

"I only grabbed it in case Jack came back to attack us again," I explained. "I did go out to get help but I don't remember anything after that." I stared down at his Styrofoam coffee cup, which had a small series of bite marks along its left edge—perhaps, I tried to assure myself, he was just as nervous as I was. "I must've been in shock," I added.

"Okay," he said. "Okay." He leaned back for a moment, staring at me with a badly hidden smile upon his face. It seemed like he was trying to run down the time on a secret clock I was unaware of— that if he could keep me talking for just five more minutes, I would instantly confess. "Help me understand this then," he finally offered. "Why didn't you use either one of the two cell phones in your purse to call 911? Or the phone in Boyd's pants?" Instead of looking at me while he waited for an answer, the detective began cracking the joints of his fingers one by one. Clearly he thought he had me.

There was nothing to do but cover my ears and begin making a high-pitched scream. I continued until my throat gave out and the detective, shaking his head, reminded me my dramatics were being filmed, then I caught my breath and began to scream more. Soon there was a sharp knock on the door that presumably increased in urgency upon hearing my distress. I didn't quit screaming entirely; instead I lowered the volume to a trillish shriek and waited to see who'd enter. Had Ford finally learned I was being interrogated and arrived to take me home? I resolved to bed him vigorously and without complaint the moment we got to the house; perhaps, if my sense of gratitude had not fully dissipated upon arrival, I would even fellate him—there didn't have to be anything sexual about it. It would simply be reciprocal appreciation for his getting me out of this most uncomfortable pinch.

But it was not Ford. Instead a man wearing a suit who looked very awkward wearing a suit stood in the doorway; he had a flat-top and a straight bristly mustache, and appeared to be somewhat bowlegged. "I'm Mrs. Price's attorney," he called across my low wail. "This interview is over."

With that, I closed my mouth completely.

chapter sixteen

Though the lawyer was a concession on behalf of Ford's family—he'd represent me during the trial and also through a speedy divorce—he wasn't free: I had to make a public apology that both glorified my husband and portrayed my grief and shame over hurting such a good man. If I could manage to weep, the attorney explained, Ford's family would give me a bonus of roughly $15,000 for personal expenses during the trial to do with as I wished. "You can keep your car," he said succinctly. I was in awe of the fact that no matter how radically the muscles around his mouth moved as he enunciated, his stolid mustache didn't once squirm; it seemed not to be attached to his face so much as constantly hovering a half inch in front of it. "They'll have all your possessions in the home packaged and moved to a studio apartment that will be paid for until your trial if they deem your set bail is reasonable and decide to pay. If your bail is exorbitant, these items will be moved to a paid storage facility until your release. In exchange for these conditions, you will agree to never publicly speak ill of Ford Price, nor imply that he was responsible, either directly or indirectly, for your actions. Do you accept these terms?"

My mind was swimming at the immediate plummet of socioeconomic class I'd just sustained—having never planned on getting caught, I certainly hadn't put much thought into the adultery clause of our prenuptial agreement. But I knew I didn't have time to mourn financial affairs at present; more important was staying out of jail, away from the cloying paws of stinking adult women. "What do they mean, 'reasonable'?" I asked. "What's the most they'll pay?"

He was honest. "Henry didn't tell me." A check of his watch revealed that it was now past two o'clock in the morning.

"I didn't think the news would travel so quickly," I muttered. Was the situation with Ford now hopeless? Perhaps his hearty reserves of denial were still pliable; if it was media attention he was so concerned about, maybe after the trial we could move overseas. In my head I fashioned a fantasy where Ford wanted desperately to come save me but his family was forbidding it. Was it so implausible that Ford might be able to come to a peaceful acceptance of my more inconvenient cravings, just as I had in deciding to live with him and agreeing to play the part of wife? "Did you see Ford tonight?" I asked. "Did he ask about me?"

The attorney, who went by Dennis but whose actual first name was Maximilian, stared at me blankly. "I only spoke to Henry."

I'd never had much of a relationship with Ford's father. The first time I met him, he was polite until we had a moment alone. Then he stared at my body as though he was making a scrutinized inspection of something he'd custom-ordered. "You know," he'd said, "I've built a sixty-million-dollar company from the ground up and I still don't have a trophy wife—you've met Margery. Ford can barely wipe his own ass and he's got you on his arm." He'd shaken his head, then removed a cigar from his pocket, licked around its end in an obscene way. His enormous pink tongue had looked like some invertebrate coming out of a shell.

I directed my attention back to Dennis. Though I hardly looked my best, I wanted him to care very personally whether or not my case succeeded. Taking his hands into my own—a move he found awkward; his fingers went limp and he stared down at them, spreading his fingers willfully apart as though he was testing out a prosthetic for the very first time—I stressed that I could not go to prison. The thought of having to do the things I'd done with Ford and Buck all over again with gruff women, but this time for nothing—no payoff of getting to live in luxury or gain increased access to pubescent sons—was too sickening to bear. Instead I'd have to perform morbid sexual acts just to avoid getting beaten up, or to get beaten up less. Not to mention that the environment would serve as a pressure cooker, mercilessly aging me; I'd emerge from lockup malnourished and sickly, with brittle hair, gray skin and fully pleated crow's-feet around my eyes. For the first time in my life I wondered if I could be capable of suicide. "I'd be an unfair target," I pointed out to him. "People who look like me don't go to jail." I realized that for once I wasn't just attempting to be a bewildered younger woman looking toward an older man for guidance; I was truly frightened and needed his help.

"You are unusually attractive." His voice had a tone of robotic assessment that made me wonder if his mustache was in fact a lifelike series of tiny brown wires. "I can argue your appearance might put you at risk for increased sexual violence. You're safe tonight; you'll be alone in a holding cell until your bail hearing tomorrow morning."

"No!" I gripped his arm with great force, as though the door might burst open any moment with a hurricane-force wind sent to deliver me to my cell. I imagined lying down on the hard cot and eventually masturbating, despite my best interests, in order to feel something besides terminal fear. Guards would walk by and shine their flashlights on my moving pelvis; surrounding inmates would see it all and yell out promises to quell my urges through a series of impending rapes.

Dennis let out a long sigh and opened his briefcase. He brought out not a tape recorder or legal notepad but a bottle of what I assumed were stimulant pills; he popped two without water and moved his neck from side to side to crack it. "If you want to do this now, have at it, I guess." The Prices were paying by the hour; I suppose he was willing to be patient.

We spoke until morning, by which point Dennis's eyes seemed to have widened and set with a gelatin of wariness. Although every window inside the consultation room was firmly shut, by the time I finished telling my version of events, his hair looked blown back slightly at the roots.

"All right," he said. Two crescent moons of perspiration, admirable in their convergent symmetry, had appeared beneath the underarms of his blue button-up shirt. "We can do this." He clicked his pen as though to begin writing, but soon clicked it again, deciding against it, and set it back down on the table. "Though it probably would've been better if I hadn't heard over half of that." This was almost enough to make me laugh—all in all, I'd barely told him anything scandalous. "I recommend you get a shower in before the bail hearing," he advised. A few trace smears of Boyd's blood upon my collarbone were visible above the zipper of my orange jumpsuit; Dennis stood and pointed at them. "The kid's okay, by the way. Boyd. Needed a lot of stitches and bled like hell. He's

all right but his mom's already stirring up shit with the media."
Though I'd never even seen a picture of her, I imagined her to be a
thin, fierce woman whose affinity for cardigans and other modest
clothing took precedence over Florida's warm climate. Would she
hold a Bible beneath her arm when she spoke to the cameras?

Having been in custody all night, I had no idea of how fast my
story had spread in just sixteen hours. The bail hearing was packed
with journalists and photographers who called out my name immediately after the proceedings and flashed cameras as they barked
questions. Overall the attention felt more adoring than judgmental;
they relished the audacity and vanity of my defense. "Your Honor,"
my attorney began, "my client's looks would make her a particularly
susceptible target for sexual violence and harassment in prison. She's
too beautiful to be in the general population of jail." There was a
hushed chorus of shock from the packed room of reporters; their
whooshed inhale was the sound made just before a match thrown
on a pool of gasoline erupted in flame. The prosecution had a logi-
cal rebuttal—they argued we're not a society whose penal system
has a sliding scale based on attractiveness. But whether the judge
agreed with my attorney, took into account my previously stainless
record (for all the times I'd been pulled over, I'd never once actually
received a speeding ticket, even before marrying Ford) or just confirmed from my personal banking statements that I didn't have the
monetary resources to flee (I knew without ever testing them that
none of my credit cards would work any longer), he agreed I could
be on house arrest until the trial.

I was charged with six counts of lewd and lascivious battery against two minors—a laughably small amount given the number of times I'd been with Jack and Boyd, but apparently what the prosecution felt they could prove beyond doubt. Though the DA's office made it known to my attorney that according to Jack's version of events I should have been charged with attempted manslaughter for chasing after Jack with a knife, they only flirted with actually trying to make a case. Dennis and I met with the DA a few days after my bail hearing to discuss a possible additional indictment, and it was clear their evidence was scarce.

"This implication that my client was seeking Jack Patrick out in order to commit a violent stabbing—well." My attorney rubbed his hand across his mustache and the corners of his lips several times, as though the allegation was a piece of cake he'd just eaten that had deposited crumbs all over his mouth. "We know for a fact, and Mr. Manning's account of events supports this, that Jack attacked him in a fit of rage and possibly homicidal agitation. How much of a leap of faith is it that my client felt threatened by him as well? When he ran from the room, isn't it likely she thought he was going to go retrieve a gun from his father's bedroom? That he himself was going to get a knife and come back to attack her or lie in wait for her somewhere else? Of course my client grabbed a knife and ran. She was so terrified and frightened for her life, she didn't even feel like she had time to put clothes on first." He placed a hand onto mine and turned to me. "I bet you could cry just thinking about it, couldn't you?"

I nodded. The detectives had their heads tilted slightly askance, examining each microexpression I made for traces of guilt. "I could," I said quietly.

"Don't blame you one bit," my attorney bellowed. Then, looking back at the detectives, he repeated himself. "I don't blame her."

While my attorney continued to play up the fear I'd felt that evening, I thought about how I probably wouldn't have actually killed Jack even if I'd caught up to him. Not unless he'd made some sort of aggressive move—lunged at me, grabbed at the knife—or had been entirely unreasonable in conversation and forced me to take preventative action. I'd only wanted to make him see the benefits of storytelling. He could've gone back and tended to Boyd until I gathered my things from the house. Then, after I'd left, he could've called an ambulance and spoken an innocent-enough tale: that he and Boyd were friends who'd been play-wrestling and the head injury was an accident. I believe that Boyd would've been conscious enough to understand the tale and go along with it, or at least commit the scenario to memory before blacking out.

The detective exhaled and traced his finger along the table in large circles. "You know," he said, "Jack tells us you were banging his father, too." The other detective lifted a coffee cup to his mouth and spat a clump of chewing tobacco inside. I realized I'd begun to hold my breath with fear that he was about to continue—to relay Jack's accusation that I'd purposefully let his father die so that my shameful secret would die with him. This could open a whole new mess of legal charges, vastly complicate our defense and the public's perception, and even cause Dennis to drop the case if he felt too put off by the surprise or guessed that others were likely in store. But apparently the past few months of despondent copulation I'd had with Jack were paying off: he hadn't passed this information on. Jack himself felt too implicated in it all—he'd been too much a part of the process of having done nothing in Buck's last hour of need. He'd also continued to sleep with me after I'd made sure Buck couldn't be saved.

My attorney's head pivoted subtly from side to side, considering. "If that were true, it would seem to go toward establishing the fact that my client is a troubled young woman desperately searching for love. Not the 'ravenous pedophile' the DA has been referring to her as in media interviews." I couldn't help but give Dennis a delighted smile—having his nimble mind on my side was truly an advantage.

The second detective spat into his cup again with more force. "Or she could just be a ravenous pedophile *and* a whore," he said. The commencement of name-calling meant our burden of defense had been met—they weren't going to bring any additional spurious charges beyond the sex crimes.

"With that, gentlemen, I believe we're done for the day." My attorney stood and I followed; the second detective stared at me as we walked past. His eyes took in the details of my body with a conflicted gaze that I knew well: even having seen all the facts of the case, he still wanted me. He wanted me despite knowing what that meant about him.

chapter seventeen

The months before my trial were spent alone on house arrest in a shoddy Tampa apartment; it had wheezing air-conditioning and low-quality gray carpet that I refused to walk on barefoot. Droves of pear-shaped soccer moms set up camp on the sidewalk across the street and picketed day and night with homemade posters declaring me to be a sick child molester who deserved life in prison. I could only imagine their husbands were happy my case had given these beastly women a new hobby that got them out of the house.

Yelling and shaking signs, they became workers in a protest economy whose currency was appreciative car honks; any time they received the blaring horn-tap of a supporter, the women's beefy arms would raise up and they'd high-five one another. Of course none of them actually looked fearful about anything, least of all me. It was quite the opposite—in my trial they'd found a sense of purpose that rendered them giddy and energized. On weekend nights when their numbers were greatest they'd often deliver choral group chants into a feedback-ridden microphone, "Teachers not touchers" being one of the more popular. There were never any men among the group, though occasionally some of the mothers did see fit to bring their young children along to practice the valuable life skill of standing on the side of the road with indignation.

My house arrest stipulations allowed for court-approved prescheduled excursions to purchase food but I most often ordered in, and once it became apparent to the onlookers just where a given food order was headed, they'd incorporate the employee into their calls and protestations. "Are you over eighteen?" they'd yell to a bewildered pizza deliveryman. "You're not safe unless you are!"

After a decade of hiding my urges, I'll admit it wasn't easy to come to terms with the fact that my preference had been publicly outed. It was as though in merely following my own desire I'd been catapulted far beyond the intended lands of pleasure into a realm of punishment. By some trick of the mind, several times a day I would nearly forget what had transpired—that everyone knew, that my face was plastered across newspapers nationwide—but then with all the panic of the initial realization, recent events would flood back to me until my thoughts wandered again and the cycle repeated itself for a whiplashed sensation of déjà vu. It made me recall a particular seasick feeling of my youth: I'd once had a spirited bus driver who liked to come over the PA system whenever a sizable piece of low-processed roadkill emerged in her path, usually an armadillo, that was going to cause her to rapidly decelerate. "Huh *ho!*" she'd yell, and we'd brace our tiny arms against the seats. The force's weight was always greater than expected; it always gave me the real fear, as I slid against my will closer and closer to the green vinyl of the seat-back in front of me, that I might continue forward and hurtle into the air.

Ford had once expressed a similar sentiment to me after being hit with a Taser gun at work during a training exercise: he'd been incredulous at how unable he was to ready himself, mentally or physically, for the pain. "I know you don't have balls," he'd told me, "but imagine having them, then imagine them being struck by lightning and a hammer at the same time." Ford always was one to ask the impossible from others, both often and casually.

"So I'm seeing everybody get hit and fall onto a mat, right?" he'd continued. "One by one. Like Noah's ark except we didn't even get a partner."

He'd raised his brow at this point, as if to say, *I'll let that heady biblical reference settle into your brain for a moment while I chug down this beer.* I'd crossed my legs, widened my eyes and leaned in, nodding in faux amazement.

"Anyway," he'd continued, "watching all these tasings, I'm getting sort of tense, right? Because when they're hit guys are screaming. Really huge guys—Bill even pissed himself."

"You mentioned testicles," I'd reminded him. "Were they directing the gun at your testicles?"

"No," he'd clarified. "Course not. That's just the best description of how it felt . . . shit *hurts*."

At the time, it had struck me that this was a somewhat intelligent perception on Ford's behalf—how arousal and pain share certain breakers on the switchboard of the central nervous system—even if he couldn't quite parse the reasoning behind his word choice. All the anguish and fear surrounding the upcoming trial seemed to have settled into my nipples; they'd begun to spontaneously harden on the hour in the hopes they might be utilized as channels of release like in the past. If only I could be allowed a few minutes of Boyd teasing them with the sharp prongs of his orthodontia. As I supposed our criminal justice system knew, withholding an orgasm brought about by a second party was a hearty rattrap for pessimism indeed. It was a type of torture, only hav-

ing myself for sexual stimulation: I could predict everything I was
about to do.

According to the news, I wasn't the only one in confinement.
Jack received six months in a juvenile detention center for his attack
on Boyd. In moments of clarity, I was willing to admit to myself
that I shouldn't have taken another boy to his father's house. But
Jack also could've saved us all a great deal of agony if he'd simply
had the consideration to call before dropping by.

Though personal effects in the same drawers as my hidden
stashes of prescription pills did get boxed and delivered to me, none
of my medications or high-end facial-contouring creams made the
journey; this was no doubt an intentional fuck-you on Ford's behalf.
I often spent entire days drinking cough syrup and scouring the
television stations for boys in Jack and Boyd's age range, their images blurry and voices echoey, to join me in dreams as I nodded off
to sleep. I still hadn't spoken personally with Ford since the incident.
I couldn't deny this disappointed me for a variety of reasons. I certainly still held the hope that he might forgive me—that we could
go back to our routine like normal. Now knowing the secret life
I'd have to lead in the hours away from home, Ford could negotiate
for greater benefits—I'd be willing to meet a more robust monthly
sexual quota with him in return for letting bygones be bygones, and
I could once again have access to luxury. But if not—if we were
over forever and there was no hope of gaining him and his money
back—Ford was the one arena where my having been caught was
a victory; now he finally knew that in our own private battle, I had
bested him. Despite his needling pockets of doubt, he had more or

less believed the whole time that I was his distant and mercurial wife, not an actress whose talents were cultivated to hide a sexual aberration.

I needed to play a part for the jurors, too. In order to appear as palatable as possible to them, Dennis wanted me to look as close in age to Boyd and Jack as I could. I often stood in front of the studio apartment's dimly lit vanity mirror and practiced my courtroom expressions: doe-eyed and frequently surprised, often shocked; seldom blinking but with exaggerated motion when I did.

Additionally, I worked to produce an overwhelmed and apprehensive shakiness in response to any loud stimuli, my moist lips puckered and hopeful with nervous hesitation. I also practiced speaking in a somewhat higher and softer voice. "When they came on to me," I breathed, pursing the corners of my mouth as though it was a difficult confession, "the attention was nice. For whatever reason I felt so isolated." At this point I would nod imperceptibly in order to seem like I was admitting the truth to myself before speaking it. "It sounds pathetic," I would continue, beginning a reflective stare off into the distance, "but I think all I really was looking for in Jack and Boyd was a friend."

Dennis was meanwhile losing no time launching a battle of public opinion. When I watched him on the news, my heart would leap with a sort of near-patriotism; never before had I felt such pride in my country as I did now in considering its justice system. There he was, immaculately dressed and persuasive on my behalf, simply in return for an exchange of money! The impeccable linear geometry of his mustache made him appear unilaterally calm on camera, never moving or changing formation.

"My client is guilty of nothing more than poor judgment," he'd often repeat. "Details about the alleged sexual misconduct will come to light that paint a far different picture than what the prosecution is claiming." He knew we'd never be able to win over the soccer moms, but for those who might be open-minded enough to accept it, he began to lay the foundations of a commonsense defense: I was young and good-looking, and adolescent boys would want to sleep with me. On one talk show, he sat with the commentator while a picture from my early college modeling days appeared behind them on a large screen—I was bikini clad, lounging on the hood of a sports car, my blond hair fanned back in the wind. "If you were a teenage male," the commentator began, pointing a leering finger back at the photo, "would you call a sexual experience with her abuse?"

Dennis did a purposefully bad job of restraining a smile and cleared his throat. "I think that's a fair question to ask in terms of this case," he answered.

Though droves of shock jocks and sensational newsmagazines offered lucrative sums for phone interviews or to bring their cameras inside my apartment for a sit-down chat, my attorney worried it might interfere with his construction of my Pollyanna image. "You're very sexy," he explained, "but what I want the jury to see is that you're not necessarily aware of it." His secretary brought the clothing I'd wear to the proceedings over to my apartment for a fitting—jumper-style dresses, Mary Jane shoes with a low heel— and went over the rules for makeup.

"Pretend you're going on a date and have to walk past your conservative father to get to the door," she said. "Transparent peach blush, a hint of neutral lip gloss. The one thing we'll play up is your eyes. Very clean eyeliner, super-thin lines. The mascara is so impor-

tampa 247

tant." It's ironic to note that her own makeup looked like that of a prospective showgirl who was escorting until her big break came. "It has to be fresh. If your mascara clumps on you, at this trial, it's like, 'She's guilty.' You know what I'm saying? You can only use the lightest kiss of it. But that tiny amount will also make all the difference in the world."

Given the reason for their interest, when the trial finally rolled around I thought I would find the reporters unappetizing. But after weeks of being sequestered, it was nice to be outside and have photographers vying for me to look at them. For the most part they were persistent but not cruel—what they wanted most was for me to give them a coquettish smile, which of course I couldn't do; instead I worked on seeming uncomfortable with attention of any sort. I clung to my attorney and acted as though I had never before been aboveground: never seen a camera or even other people before, never heard my name said aloud.

I have to confess that in the courtroom that first day, even though I truly wanted to pay attention, I caught no more than five words of the opening arguments. Instead I was creating fantasies that incorporated the prison environment instead of ignoring it: they involved the new holding cell I'd be taken to that evening. The image that immediately came to mind was being woken from sleep by the approach of a horde of famished, emaciated young men—orphans, perhaps, in tattered clothing with *Oliver Twist* accents who approached the bars of my cell and began sticking every erotic appendage they had in between—in my mind I could see them lining up to form a row of erect penises in various stages of growth. Their groping hands would reach forward on arms extended out to where the shoulder's bulk strained between the metal, their tongues wriggling and searching from eager mouths, as though they viewed me as a food source. How delightful it would be to make my way down their queue, giving each a different treatment: sometimes bending down to suck as the fingers of multiple owners greedily fought to cram inside me, other times turning around to be penetrated while my neck received the frenzied licks of deer tasting salt. At one point I was able to look up and return to the courtroom proceedings when I noticed the prosecutor, a man named Delany, pointing at me with a villainous, outstretched finger: I peered over at the jury with a hurt look on my face that insisted Delany and I had once been best friends but now he'd turned into a terrible gossip. I, on the other hand, sitting silently, had taken the high road.

I soon found that my actual holding cell did not fit the specifications of my daydream. Its entrance was a solid reinforced door that had a rectangular slot for a food tray to enter. This opening was not of a preferable height nor angle for a budding youth's penis to reach inside, a design flaw that had the effect of irrationally increasing my panic: my hands protectively reached down and held my crotch as I realized how long my obligatory stint of sexual castration might last. Rather than sleeping, I sat in the dark for some time after lights-out and wondered how many months I could reasonably go without any adolescent physical contact, not even the ability to give a shoulder squeeze or a lower-back pat. Prior to arrest, my record on the outside had been perhaps six or seven weeks—though such a drought was heavily supplemented by porn—before I'd go indulge in a flirtatious conversation in the cereal aisle of the grocery store or hit the mall and at least have the visceral pleasure of being close to adolescent males. Even these tame encounters powered up a source of electricity inside me, whether or not our bodies ever touched when we spoke or walked past one another in a crowded store. More than the sexual attacks and harassment I was sure would come, I'd never be able to make it in prison for this reason alone; there'd be no oxygen for the affliction that burned inside me.

The lights in my cell suddenly came on at this epiphany. This supernatural effect was multiplied by the fact that it was the middle of the night—for a moment I thought some divine force had just agreed with me and my cell door was about to crack open, allowing me to tiptoe out and escape. The doorknob did in fact turn seconds later, but there was nothing magical about it: no orgy of foundlings in tiny white briefs grappling for sexual consolation filed in; no masterful escape plot unfolded. Instead, Ford opened the door.

chapter eighteen

I was still sitting upright in bed with my knees bent open, both hands clutched between my legs.

Ford was drunk, but not as drunk as might've been advisable. This was completely Ford's style: coming finally to make contact at this hour, in this place, to display his wide range of privilege. In fact this was the very first thing he addressed.

"I have some buddies who work the night shift," he explained. I thought about removing my hands from my genitals but realized somewhat amusedly that their position might give the impression I'd recently been sexually assaulted in the shower room, and it didn't seem wise to dismiss whatever combination of jealousy and sympathy that might produce in him.

I said nothing; what he wanted most was for me to speak.

He produced a long exhale that was noticeably sharpened by gin. I wished to avoid any scenario where he might start crying; he wasn't entirely comfortable with tears, so he felt they required long justifications. Now that he was actually in front of me again, all the previous curiosities I'd entertained—that he and I might reunite in the harmonious arrangement of my needing money and Ford's needing a stunning wife, or the romantic notion that his breakdown might fill me with a sense of victory—disappeared entirely; he was as annoying as ever and I simply wanted him gone. He appeared to be more tan than I remembered, which brought out his wrinkles; he'd doubtlessly been staying home from work to drink conciliatory liquor by the pool. Each one of his square teeth, made highly visible as he squinted in an attempt to withhold emotion, seemed like a separate deficit. They were unmistakably the teeth of a man, and the muscles warping his thin V-neck T-shirt attested to a brute strength that felt obscenely zoomorphic, more animal than human. I realized that Ford, alone with me in the cell, could do whatever he wanted—beat me up, rape me; it might even be possible, if the paid mouths of his friends were shut tightly enough and a plausible story was created, for him to kill me and get away with it.

I actually would've welcomed any nonfatal form of battery. I wouldn't be able to report that Ford had done it—his family, after all, was footing the bill for my attorney—so the implication in the courtroom would be that I'd been beat up by guards or fellow prisoners. This leverage could bring compassion in the eyes of the jury and media, and might possibly allow me to argue for a transfer into a nicer holding area, something less severe than a jail cell.

"Why?" Ford finally shouted. His fists were flexed, ready to pick a fight with the mere idea of what I'd done. Now that we were at the point of artifice finally being over, I saw no need for dishonesty.

"It's just what I like." At this point his eyes moved down to my clasped hands. He seemed to be anxiously waiting for me to remove them, like my vagina was a mouth ready to confess to all sorts of atrocities and I was merely gripping it shut in order to silence its cries.

The muscles in his forehead began to move in opposing directions; for several seconds I watched its various folds come alive like rows of earthworms, each one moving independently from the others. "You're some kind of pedophile?" he asked.

"I'm not pilfering the elementary schools," I pointed out. "They're teenagers."

"But you married me," Ford spat. In his grief it was hard to tell if he was simply worked up or if he'd prepared himself for our meeting with a more proper dose of alcohol than I'd originally thought. "It wasn't like we didn't have sex," he countered. As if the thought was too absurd to even speak, he chuckled a little, though it was dry and unsmiling; he knew that once he said it, he'd likely have to accept it as true. But the part of Ford that hoped I'd immediately proclaim the statement to be lunacy and chime forth cries of denial did finally compel him to say the words: "What we had together wasn't fake."

I suppose I could've given him what he wanted, apologized and said that it wasn't him, claimed to be sick in the head. But the boxy gold rings on his fingers were too much a reminder of the nights I'd had to sacrifice a part of myself to placate him. Now that there was no further reward for pretending, it simply felt too difficult.

"You should go home, Ford," I said, as gently as I could bear it. I felt a surge of injustice at the irony of it all: Ford was completely inattentive to the unlimited sexual potential he could leave my cell and start enjoying. How simple it would be for him to walk into a bar and find a partner of legal age whom he was attracted to, take her home and proceed to orgasm. Yet he had no sense of appreciation for this liberty. Instead he'd go home and drink and sulk. Perhaps make an ill-advised intoxicated drive to a late-night gun range. While I'd have given anything I still owned for just an eyedropper of Boyd's semen to play with, there was nothing stopping Ford from running off to taste the full spectrum of the *Kama Sutra* rainbow, but he didn't even care.

"Do you love me?" he asked. When this question failed to gain an answer, he soon began looking for a consolation prize. "Does any part of you love me? Did you ever?" I didn't mind anger, but his expression was turning to one of injury and it sickened my stomach. His pain seemed like such an internal, private thing, no different from excrement—something to be dealt with in private. But here he was, putting it before me and making me smell it.

I realized his eyes had grown wet with disbelief; he was truly seeing me for the first time but couldn't reconcile it with his memories. He seemed to need some verification that I actually was the same person he'd lived with for several years—that his authentic wife wasn't trapped somewhere, kidnapped, while I acted as her imposter. So I lay down on my cot, finally rolling away from him toward the wall as was my usual custom when we'd get in bed at the same time. With an air of normalcy, as though we were at home for one last evening together, I uttered the words I'd said so often in our bedroom. "I'm tired, Ford. Could you please turn out the light?" As I closed my eyes, the question brought on a nostalgia for my soft pillow, for my nightstand of applied creams set to begin working as I slept, repairing any damage done through daily exposure to free radicals.

I held myself taut awaiting his reaction; my buttocks involuntarily clenched, partially expecting him to attack. Instead he stood there for what seemed like hours, staring at my back as I kept my eyes fixed on the wall. "Fuck," he finally exclaimed. He then began a loud bang on the metal door that echoed indefinitely and had the effect of making it seem like we were inside a submarine. Moments later the door buzzed open and everything grew quiet.

It was the last time I ever saw Ford. The light inside my cell stayed on all night.

chapter nineteen

Whenever the prosecution rattled off a list of the physical acts that comprised "lewd and lascivious battery," the judge's face held a look of delighted interest suggesting he wasn't the least bit bored by the details of my trial. In general, his constant expression was one of content inquiry, his eyebrows raised expectantly like a tourist sent to the future who was trying but failing to comprehend what he might see next.

He certainly wasn't prepared for the spectacle of Janet Feinlog.

She was my defense's sole character witness; in addition to hardly knowing me, all the other teachers at the school, in fear for their jobs, would never have agreed to come say anything nice about me on record. Perhaps Janet wouldn't have either, had she still been employed at Jefferson. Shortly before the Christmas following my arrest, Janet had had an expletive-laced meltdown in front of her class and thrown her chair against the wall. Nearly half the students captured video of the incident on their cell phones: by the end of the day, the recording was well on its way to going viral on every social media website imaginable.

The entire court seemed to come to a standstill as she waddled to the podium in a black sweat suit that appeared to have dried toothpaste around the collar. Once she got seated inside the witness-box, she grabbed the complimentary glass of water and began chugging as though she'd just finished a marathon. But after her thirst was quenched, she was more than ready to go.

She didn't wait for a question from my attorney, instead choosing to take an "open mic" approach that lost her some points with the judge. "Celeste is a good woman," she barked, pulling the microphone closer to her mouth. "Teenage boys' minds are in the gutter." After several warnings to only answer the questions asked, she apologized in a conciliatory manner that warmed my heart: it was clear she wanted to be an effective witness on my behalf.

"Mrs. Feinlog," Dennis began, "have you ever known a teenage boy to make a sexual advance on a teacher?"

"Does a bear shit in the woods?" Janet scoffed. "I taught junior high for nearly twenty-five years. Their brain is a gerbil and their libido is Sasquatch. You really think the gerbil is going to win?"

On cross, the prosecution chose to focus more on Janet's recent career change. "You were fired from Jefferson last fall, isn't that correct, Mrs. Feinlog? For low job performance and inappropriate classroom behavior?"

Janet chose to perjure herself just a little. "It was mutual," Janet remarked. "I didn't want to work there anymore." Then she rubbed her nose with the back of her palm several times and squinted at the prosecutor as though his head was rapidly shrinking and she could hardly make out his face anymore.

During the prosecution's presentation, Jack and Boyd had been asked nothing beyond simple questions that established if the events had taken place—they didn't need to prove why or assign blame; if it had happened I'd broken the law and was guilty. Jack had kept his head low, refusing to look anywhere near me, while

Boyd openly grinned and repeatedly tried to catch my eye. Rather than cross-examine them then, Dennis decided to call them back as witnesses for our defense—he hoped this might give the jury more of an impression that the boys were still on my side. This was certainly true with Boyd; he was a smiling, gift-wrapped witness who wore his pride at having slept with me on his sleeve. From the moment we'd begun having sex, Boyd's greatest wish was for the world to somehow know all that he and I had done together, and now that it did, he couldn't have been more ecstatic. When Boyd came back up to testify, his newfound confidence made his steps nearly buoyant; I half expected him to pause on the way up to the witness-box and do a backflip.

The prosecution objected to the relevance of nearly every question my attorney asked—the details, in their mind, didn't matter as long as the crime had occurred. Most were sustained, but occasionally some slipped through. It was still a payoff to ask them and have the seeds of doubt planted in the minds of the jury: Was he sorry that it had happened? His smile said it all. Had he enjoyed our time together? Before an objection could even be made, he'd already begun nodding enthusiastically. "You began the sexual advances toward Mrs. Price, didn't you, Boyd?" my attorney asked. This was a risk but a calculated one: I knew how much he'd want the credit and the attention; given the chance to claim initiation, he'd certainly accept. It was overruled but the jury knew he would've answered yes had he been allowed.

Bringing Jack to the stand was a much greater gamble. But since we'd brought Boyd back up, if we didn't call Jack it would seem like we were scared of what he might say. Which, in fact, we were.

Though there was nothing my attorney would ask him that would be a platform for his going off on a tangent, if he grew upset enough, he might yell something out of turn in anger or frustration that would look very bad to the jury. Dennis was confident he could spin any outbursts; in short, if Jack grew upset, Dennis would imply the anger stemmed from my cheating on him with Boyd. Still, when Jack took the stand a second time, I'd never been more nervous in my life. I knew that one deeply credible explosion on his behalf could easily send me to prison for years.

Looking at him was no small chore. Far more than Boyd, he'd aged greatly during the year that had passed since my arrest. I supposed his stint in juvie certainly hadn't helped. His voice had dropped and was coarse with grief; even though he was still shy of sixteen, trauma had expedited the development of adulthood's physical design upon his body. Although I'd always known he'd quickly age beyond attraction, I suppose a part of me had hoped that somewhere—in Jack's eyes, perhaps, or in a fleeting expression—I could see that our relationship had been forever preserved, a sign that laying my body upon Jack's had been like stopping the moving hand of a clock on at least one part of him. But the eager and credulous boy of eighth grade whom I still thought of with desire didn't seem to be buried inside him at all. The fluorescent lights of the courtroom magnified his newly pronounced stubble; the ill-fitting suit he wore, likely one of Buck's that his father had optimistically held on to in case he ever lost his spare tire, didn't help either. Each moment of his testimony, I had to look away and think of the future and the hope of other boys in other places. His adult features felt like an insult of erasure, a failed experiment on my behalf that would never cease to finish failing.

"Jack," my attorney began in an authoritative tone, "we all know the things you did with Mrs. Price." Jack shifted in his seat and looked down at his lap, his lower lip wavering. "I just need you to tell us a few things honestly. Did she force you to kiss her?"

Jack exhaled too close to the microphone, causing the sound of a loud gust of wind to echo forth. "No." I knew Jack well enough to guess what was spinning in his thoughts. Admitting that I hadn't forced him was surely making Jack contemplate his own guilt in the entire situation—at not pushing me aside and calling 911 the night his father died, at losing all his old friends and his former home and way of life, at being sent to juvie after attacking Boyd. Jack started to cry.

My attorney approached the stand and laid a fatherly hand upon its wooden railing. His voice softened as though he and Jack were speaking completely in private, the only two people who would ever hear the words. "And did she force you to make love?"

"Objection," said the prosecutor. "'Making love' is not an acceptable euphemism for statutory rape."

"I'll rephrase," my attorney offered. "You had sex with Mrs. Price. Was it consensual? Did you want to do it?"

"Yes," Jack answered. "I wanted it." His voice was breaking; it sounded like a confession to something much greater.

"Thank you, Jack. I'm sorry you had to come here and do this." My attorney returned to the table and sat. "No further questions, Your Honor."

Despite being told he could step down, Jack stayed for a moment, crying, then looked over at me. It wasn't at all the look of hatred I'd expected. Instead it was a look of mutual knowledge, Jack conveying to me his new understanding that the world could be a terrible place. His eyes said that no one at all was looking out for him or able to fix this essential flaw in life's fabric; my eyes stared back and told him that he was right.

But the jurors and my attorney, and even the prosecution, apparently, saw something far different within the span of that gaze. "Dynamite!" Dennis proclaimed after court was adjourned for the day. "That look he gave you after testifying? It was like he wanted to crawl off the stand and into your lap! Plus the tears. The tears could not have been better. Hell, *I* felt ashamed for making him feel guilty about his own impulses. What that jury saw was a red-blooded American teenage boy asked to repent for nailing a hot blonde. I think our chances are good."

We still had psychological experts ready to testify that I had a mood disorder and low impulse control, but Jack had proven himself to be a gift that kept on giving. Worried that jurors might sympathize with the boys for being attracted to me, and sympathize with me for having given in, the next morning the DA offered me a plea deal of four years' probation that I accepted. I couldn't go within one thousand yards of a school, couldn't be unsupervised with anyone under the age of eighteen, and had to attend group meetings for convicted female sexual offenders. But I was free.

On the day of my release, my attorney wrapped me in a congratulatory hug that suggested we'd proven triumphant in a noble moral struggle. "We did it," he announced proudly, then he gave me an exaggerated pat on the back; his eye flinched with what may have been a passing thought of discomfort, but only once. "Now keep your hands to yourself out there, hear me?"

A year after my release, I got permission to move away to a sleepy beach town and was reassigned to a probation officer who wears flip-flops. She commonly uses the phrase "your best estimate is fine" during our Q & A at my monthly check-ins. It's low-key.

Currently, I work at a cabana bar for a seventy-year-old man named Dave who is overly fond of Viagra jokes. "I've had five heart attacks," he'll say, opening the flap of his Hawaiian shirt to reveal an impressive collection of sternum scars amidst his reddish-tan, papery skin, "and I probably wouldn't survive a sixth. But dying might be worth getting it up for you." I just roll my eyes and call him a pervert. His antics are easy to put up with because he pays cash under the table; so far, I've never had to tell anyone here, save my probation officer, my real name. I rent a grotesque trailer on the swampy edge of town so I don't have neighbors I have to divulge my sex-offender status to; the nearest resident to me is a Citgo gas station three miles down the road. This town is nothing more than a place to regroup, and it's temporary; for now the most important aspects of my self-care—restarting the oxygen-infusion and LED-light facials, adhering to a micronutrient diet for optimal skin elasticity—eat up nearly all of my earnings. Someday soon when my patience has rebounded, I'll find another wealthy man to date, but after the ordeal of the trial, it's nice, just for the present, to not have to do anything that repulses me other than live in squalor.

Most of my time is spent on the beach by the resort hotels or at an open waterfront bar where I sit in wait for disgruntled teenagers fed up at being in a hotel room with their family—sometimes they come out at dusk for a solitary walk. I look for the telltale pallor that implies they're on vacation; I'm not willing to take any risks on local boys. Instead I give them a name like Mindy or Jenna and tell them I'm on vacation too, state that I'm in college and ask questions that assume they are as well. A few lie and pretend they actually are but most laugh and confess they're only fourteen, then feel flattered when my interest doesn't wane. We find the pool-supply sheds of their hotels or one-person fast-food restrooms, dark corners of the beach where two bodies on a towel won't draw attention. When they insist on a phone number I give them a fake; if they're adamant about meeting up the next day, I tell them to meet me at a snow cone hut on the opposite end of the beach and never appear.

For now, my youth and looks make this easy. I try not to think about the cold years ahead, when time will slowly poach my youth and my body will begin its untoward changes. I'll have to pare down to certain types: the motherless boys, or those so sexually ravenous they don't mind my used condition. Eventually I'll have to find a better-paying job in an urban area with runaways hungry for cash whom I can buy for an evening. But that won't be for many more years; there's lots of fun to be had between then and now.

I'm certainly mindful not to press my luck too far. On slow weeks, I'm training myself to be more content with memories. I have a near-photographic recall of my good times with Jack and Boyd and still think of them often, exactly the way they were when they entered my classroom. Sometimes the thought that they're now nearly eighteen wraps around my images of their younger selves like a snake, and my stomach reels as I imagine them fully grown. If a vacationing Boyd were to stumble into my bar one night, I would have a visceral reaction of nausea—it would be no less horrifying than seeing a three-hundred-year-old corpse reanimated. The two of them are still my favored fantasy, if only by aggregation—after all, I had them each so many times—but occasionally the subconscious knowledge that they are basically adult men now is so bothersome as to make masturbation difficult. Some nights, in order to orgasm, I have to reimagine history and tell myself that neither of them made it past the eve of my arrest alive: that Jack suffered a fatal wound at my hands in the woods, and Boyd, bleeding alone from the skull in Jack's bedroom, succumbed to shock and died.

acknowledgments

I have enormous gratitude for my agent Jim Rutman, whose encouragement and support nurtured this book from its inception. Your warm humor, avuncular counsel, and savvy feedback have been indispensable assets on this journey, and your unflinching bravery and restrained poker face when exposed to my office décor and fast-food habits are likewise noteworthy of admiration. Thank you for excelling in humanity on all accounts. A hearty thanks also to Dwight Curtis, Kirsten Hartz, Anna Webber, and everyone involved in helping this manuscript find its way.

I'm likewise indebted to my genius editor Lee Boudreaux, who could not possibly be smarter; the brilliant wisdom of your comments was a continually energizing wind, and the nuclear glow of your enthusiasm brightened each day of this great adventure. A boisterous, thundering thanks goes to Karen Maine, Andrea Molitor, Michael McKenzie, all the phenomenal people at Ecco/HarperCollins, and Kathleen Schmidt. Equal thanks go across the pond to Lee Brackstone for his immediate enthusiasm, vision, and belief, as well as the keen notes and fabulous insight that helped shape the book's final version.

Thank you to the relatives, friends, and peers who surround and support me—I am so lucky to be encircled by a fantastic group of fellow writers, academics, artists, and eccentrics who make a rich creative life possible. Thank you to my family.

For all your unconditional love and support, thank you to my husband, Shawn. You could not be more essential to me, in every way. And thank you to Sparrow, who was my literal copilot for much of the editing of this book. Welcome, my love. You are already my everything.